Lamorna Publications
Yew Tree Studio, Marshwood, Dorset DT6 5QF
www.lamornapublications.co.uk

First published in 2011

ISBN: 978-0-9559832-3-8

Set in 11pt Times New Roman

Contents

List of Illustrations and Photographs

Romany Road

Life on Wheels

by

Beshlie

Illustrations by the author

Lamorna Publications

Macrame lace and
white voile – lace jumpset.
velvet and spanish hat

Lace, Velvet, and a Spanish Hat

This book is dedicated to every Romany, Gypsy and Traveller, who has pulled-on with hooves and iron-bonds or with motor-drawn living trailers, with the hope that, to be allowed to stop on green turf beneath an English blue sky, will never be denied to them. This manuscript and the illustrations were written and drawn whilst living in waggons and trailers on the many traditional stopping places, commons, roadsides, and famous horse fairs and events, including the Derby Week at Epsom Downs.

This book is also dedicated to the memory of Boggy Price.

Return of the Romanies

In memory of Boggy Price

Bright and proud the barrel-tops
Sped along with green and rocking sails
In the Christmas weather, but cheerfully,
The Prices took again the road to Wales.

They sang a song of freedom, the iron-bonds:
Slipping hooves dug into the icy roads,
Traces tight, the drivers wet and walking,
Horses straining with their heavy loads.

Tilt-frames creaked and groaned,
Mountain winds smote each canvas sheet,
Smoke curling from the Queenie stoves, as
Men and horses battled with the sleet.

Returning to the country of their birth
After a lifetime on foreign trails,
In the Christmas weather, but joyfully,
The Prices took again the Road to Wales.

Beshlie

Footnote.

The Prices are a very large family of Welsh Romanies who keep themselves to themselves. Many keep alive the deep Romany language and wonderful names; Crimea, Craddock, Freedom, Danger, Pretty-Boy, Merry, Silver, Frisco, Deer and Crystal. One can tell a Price encampment from afar by the type of vehicles and trailers, plus the situation, which can be in wild places where others fear to go.

The "Queenie" stove is a cast-iron stove, originally made for sailing-ships and produced in several sizes. They heated the waggons, cooked food and boiled water . Made in rococo style and as well known as Queen Victoria. The "Queen" stove became "The Queenie" and part of history.

Foreword

Dominic Reeve

In this book Beshlie, possibly one of the most talented yet least appreciated artists of her generation, has produced a remarkably detailed account of the Romany life-style, both past and present, and of her experiences within it.

Derby Week at Epsom features prominently in this book. The first time *we* 'pulled-on' for Derby Week was 1965, and we continued to do so almost every year until the end of the 1980s. This book with its delightful sketches (now of almost historical interest!) is a very personal view of the scene, from the Travellers' perspective. It is acutely observed with affection and pleasure in detail, both in persons and in fashions. For, of course, the Travellers' world is greatly ruled by fashions of its own making, to some extent in clothes, but to a much greater extent in the particular make of trailer-caravan and motor vehicle that are chosen.

Part of the interest in this book is that it covers a period of twenty years in which the possessions of the Travellers, especially their trailers, gradually progressed toward a display of *rococo* ornamentation, externally and internally, probably peaking in the late 1970s in an almost unbelievable display of 'flash.'

Beshlie is a fine artist, illustrator, multi-talented inventor and craftswoman, her unremitting variety of productions continuing to amaze those who know her. She is also to be admired for her ability to sum up instantly the characters of all who come within her sphere. She would indeed be an expert in the Romany art of *dukkering* (fortune-telling) should the circumstances arise. As the last model of Augustus John, her unusual features were recorded for posterity, calling to mind the portraits of Lady Ottoline Morrell. Their like will not be seen again. As her lifelong companion and partner I have never ceased to be astonished by her activities. And so I commend this her longest book to date.

Dominic Reeve – 2011.

Introduction

A Few Facts

Until 1956 there were common rights on Epsom downs. Until then Romanies stopped there freely, under "immemorial rights." Not everyone took kindly to the money charged during Derby Week, the week of the famous races. There was free parking for the public. One year the Board of Conservators hired Securicor to assist in the collecting. These uniformed Private Police were said to have issued over fifty summonses, only half of which could be served, every other Traveller being called Smith. Nineteen appeared in court, each fined £3. The cost of the operation has been put at between seven and eight hundred pounds.

In 1937, Romanies were barred from stopping in 'The Bushes' near the race track and were allowed into a field by a local well wisher. There exists a photograph of Romanies and Travellers with horses and waggons encamping in this field off the Downs road, during this ban.

In Section 124 of the Highways Act 1959, one can find the following: "if, without lawful authority, a gypsy pitches a booth, stall or stand, or encamps on a highway, he shall be guilty of an offence." From 1936, no stopping on common land or verges was legal.

The 1899 Commons Act, aided and abetted by the Caravan Sites and Control of Development Act 1966, Section 23, is really the most important legislation against Romanies and Travellers. In this, planning permission from a County Borough and a licence from the District Council are required before any land, even with the owner's permission, can be used to site trailers or caravans which are being lived in. It is surprising how many non-itinerant people are unaware of this. In 1965 the Ministry of Housing published a study of England and Wales, called Gypsies and Other Travellers, and this included a census. The 1961 census put the number of itinerants in Britain and Ireland at seventeen thousand five hundred. Undoubtedly thousands did not contribute to this, any form of count being rightly regarded with suspicion.

1966 saw the publication of a Ministry of Housing circular, *Gypsies*. I quote, "…. only local authorities, County Borough Councils are in a position to act" (they need not wait for legalisation). It advises that each County Council should take the initiative in assessing the need in its own area and deciding, in consultation with District Councils, as to how the need can best be met.

In 1964 one District Council estimated a cost of over £7000 a year just to evict and keep Travellers from stopping in their area. Horse-drawn Travellers were banned from pulling-on Epsom Downs in 1946. No wonder that the stainless steel vendor pulled on with a waggon up on the back of his lorry!

This book was written, and the illustration drawn, during the 1960's and 70's, but for various reasons has not been published until 2011.

The difficulties faced by Travellers is well illustrated by the following:

A Travelling Woman's Tale

"We was stopped at Gallows Cross, where me Grandfather sold me his watch on his deathbed. The *Gavvers** came and moved us on. We then pulled-on right behind some tree-fabs.* They was so close you could've picked up a stone and hit one with it.

"We hadn't been there more than a' hour when the *Gavvers** came and moved us on. We went to Sedgehill Common. Sam had disremembered* it was trenched off. We filled in the trench and pulled-on. I had only just got the *yog** going with some dry whitey fuzz* when the *Gavvers** came. 'Get off,' they said. 'No,' said Sam. 'We'll soon have you off,' they said and kicked the *yog** into some dry fuzz* bushes, setting it all on fire. We had to shift then as Ben's trailer was all in the fuzz.* I lost one of my snaps* and had no time to look fer it. We never had enough *pani** to doubt* the *yog.**

"On the way to Poacher's Pond at the stop and go lights*, a *rackli** in a bubbly-car* came into the back of the trailer. 'Oh,' she says, 'I didn't know you was going to stop!' I told her she'd done hundreds of pounds of damage, you know the price Astrals* is now, and all she says is, 'Sorry.' We was all very upset.

"We get's to Poacher's Pond, you know where all the retectives* came to us, after the Great Train Robbery; it's all tumps* and full of earywigs* and battymices.* There was a *gauji** woman there waiting for a council house. She never washed down the trailer in five days; a dirty woman. It was a molocoly* place.

"Sam met his brother out calling*, don't you know. 'Where are you stopped?' asks Sam, and Boggy says, 'On a lovely place right by the motorway; you can stop there till you'm grey headed.' So when

Sam and Ben comes home, we packs down and shifts.

"When we got by the motorway, there was seven lots* there, so we had a day out, and Sam bought Sam-boy one of they bowarrows* and me a knocking basket.* I bought Sam a lollipop* for his new Bedford 'Joey,'* and Carrie a dress with two rows of laps.* It was a good day out.

"My sister Dolly came to visit, you know, her that married one of the Webbs, then we went to visit her, but she's taken to being a *gauji*.* She put down newspapers on her seats; it made us discomfortable.* 'It's not smoking that gives you cancer,' I said, 'it's all that tinned food.' I see'd her fridge was full. She gave me a black look. 'Well, I haven't been moved on four times in one day,' she said. There wasn't much I could say to that.

"When we got back, the council had been to say that if we are not all off by tomorrow, we'll be towed off. 'You just don't know where to go, do you?'"

*Interpretation (true *Romani* words in italics)

Astral	make of trailer
battymices	bats
Bedford 'Joey'	Bedford J.O.
bowarrows	bow and arrow
bubbly-car	mini
calling	knocking on doors
discomfortable	uncomfortable
dismremembered	did not remember
doubt	douse
earywigs	earwigs
fuzz	gorse
gavvers	police
gaujo	non-Romany
knocking-basket	basket used for calling
laps	frills
lollipop	small red ball fixed to wing
lots	living trailers
molocoly	melancholy
pani	water
rackli	girl
retectives	detectives
snaps	gold earrings
stop and go lights	traffic lights
tree-fabs	pre-fabs
tumps	hummocks
yog	fire

Chapter 1

Derby Week: Setting the Scene

Written on the Downs

The Grandstand.

T he Derby! What magic the words hold. Gypsies, Romanies or as they now almost universally like to be called, Travellers, scattered all over the British Isles, have slowly made their way south.

Extra money has been put aside for the Great Spend. No *gaujo* (house-dweller) father taking his family on holiday ever has such commitments as the Romany father. Everyone must have a new outfit for Show-Out Sunday, and for each of the following days, plus evening wear. Food and fuel must be bought for the time the turnout is being towed *en route* and when encamped. Money cannot be earned during this time.

All the children down to the smallest baby – who will be a centre of attention, not having previously been seen by countless Aunts and Cousins – must look as smart as possible. Any new living trailer-caravan which has been ordered from the coach-builders must be ready for Epsom. By their possessions, a family's capability and standing are judged.

Travellers are not ashamed of imitating. A certain lack of originality has helped to preserve and keep their traditions alive and to make them a separate race with a world of their own. Any academic trying to deny this may as well try and turn a frog into a prince – the stuff of fairy tales!

I look now at fashions in possessions which have developed at amazing speed. When a brother comes home with a new forward-control Ford or a new Bedford lorry, others in the family then trade-in *their* motors for the same; they cannot be said to lack the ability. There are many signs indicating that these are Travellers' vehicles, if you know what to look for. To arrive at Epsom with an out-dated turnout (motor and trailer) can only be depressing for those upon whom fortune seems not to have smiled.

Various years on the Downs have shown such 'fashions,' which to the casual observer are but 'caravans,' each one of which is a known make, proudly crafted by coach-builders of great reputation. These trailers are known as 'Travellers' Specials,' whose age can be assessed by some change in exterior ornamentation, or interior design. An open door can reveal this all-absorbing information by the mere colour of the Formica lining, the style of blinds, or the shape of the windows. I observe now that the trend has gradually swung from the robustly built, boat-shaped, heavy gauge aluminium trailers requiring a three ton towing vehicle, to the present day small seventeen and nineteen feet tandem-axle trailers, such as the one I am sitting in now.

Trailers and towing vehicles just cannot be separated from the people who drive and live in them. On the walls of some settled-down Travellers' homes are photos of the living trailer-caravans they once owned. The vehicles are the workhorses of our times, the means by which those in the itinerant way of life live. I often reflect sadly upon the seeming lack of appreciation, even by the non-biased and tolerant, of this most important factor.

With so many *gaujes* out of work, the stigma of Social Security removed, perhaps more people will realise the frightening aspect of the day-to-day, hand-to-mouth existence, which Travellers have faced for generations, without any Welfare help. In order to survive they have had to make the division between 'Them' (non-Travellers) and 'Us' (Romanies).

Although the space allotted to Travellers, or Traders as officials diplomatically call them at Epsom, is large enough, it is wise to arrive in good time, on the Friday if possible, leaving Saturday to wash the turnout and set up the china ornaments etc, ready for Show-Out Sunday on the morrow.

I can see the Army personnel zooming about in short wheel-base Landrovers. They usually erect a huge tent or tents, in which they carry on their secret day and night lives, to do with security no doubt, keeping a low profile outside. It would appear they are impervious to the 'night racing' of vehicles by young reckless Traveller youths who each year spoil the holiday for the other trailer-dwellers by roaring in and out among the trailers and livestock, even close to tethered mares and foals. Often this aggravation continues all through the night. The police say they can do nothing. My opinion is, they know that only Travellers are in danger, and who cares about them?

In the old days, young men showed off by racing their ponies and cobs. This still goes on at horse fairs such as Appleby and Stow, under the guise of the horses being shown their paces by sellers. *Gypsy Life* by Sir Alfred Munnings shows this in a beautifully painted and detailed scene. I like it especially for the hats in high fashion at the time, worn by the Romany women. His *Campfire and Caravan*, in a rural setting, shows great attention to precise detail, the mark of a great painter. Would that all paintings of Romany life were as truthful. It is so lovely not to have to cringe upon seeing non-Romany faces peering out from stage-gypsy costumes, figures in strange incorrect poses, and muddled encampments of those playing at gypsy life – or so imagined; for no actual reality has been closely observed.

Even Cambridge Fair is not exempt from mad car drivers. Many shrewd Travellers now find private stops outside the town, rather than endure it. If, at Epsom, the youths kept to the Downs it would be bearable, but the fun-thing seems to be playing an American game of 'Hunt,' the hunted hiding among the trailers. Some new vehicles have been damaged beyond repair. This game of 'Hare and Hounds' goes onto the public roads and through the town. To be on the end of a row of trailers is not advisable. A lone *gaujo* caravan has come and stopped at the end of one of the rows. I give it one night.

The television engineers have arrived and begun the marathon task of erecting huge scaffolding towers for their cameras. Later we'll hear the tedious testing of the public address systems. The Scouts, the Red Cross, the beer tents, the bookies, will all soon join us across the increasingly dusty track. Cheapjack stalls, hot-dog sellers, ice cream vendors along with well known and unknown touts, all stake a claim to a piece of turf.

When the private motorists arrive, often at an ungodly hour in the morning, extravagantly hatted, well groomed occupants spill out from expensive cars among the *hoi polloi*, where they attempt a certain nonchalance, as if they were used to walking every day among the more comfortably attired, through mud and last night's rubbish, fashionably dressed. Optimists come in flimsy dresses and straw hats, those expecting British weather in thick woollies, overcoats, waterproof hats and faded gamps. Surely nowhere else could you find such a great diversity of people? On Derby Day, strange characters pass at one a minute. It is not a bad thing for those affluently cocooned from such sights to see and train their glasses on a fellow human who needs to scavenge in a litter-bin and devour someone's leavings, if only once a year.

In pursuit of such a large, and possibly wicked, captive audience come various religious groups, hanging-on, as we all do, to something; in their case to their fellowship and the comforting belief that *He* walks among them. They stand in isolated groups, shoulders bowed, in circles, like white men of old expecting the attack of American Indians, singing their hymns, the music lost amid the cacophony. A private individual, a sandwich-board man, proclaims to the over-joyous among us that THE END IS NEAR. I remember him from previous Derby Days; he never seems to harbour a flicker of doubt that he has got the prophecy wrong!

Hundreds bring their dogs, on leads or loose, children run wild. Elderly ladies proffer money to bookies from bags of small coins and take tickets with gloved hands. People are seated on the ground amid the milling throng. By the end of the first race of the day the Downs are a-glow with coloured rubbish. It will be blamed on 'The Gypsies' of course, because it blows across in the night and settles among the trailers, underneath and among our outside tables and chairs; caught under tent-ropes and dog-boxes are wrappers of food we never eat.

Apart from those left to baby-sit or keep watch in the trailers, we all walk across to watch the main race – The Derby Stakes. On Wednesday the third of June, eighteen ninety six, the one and a half miles was won by Persimmon, owned by H.R.H. the Prince of Wales. The three year old won five thousand, four hundred and fifty pounds. The betting was five to one. The fateful Derby of nineteen thirteen in racing history was the most exciting yet tragic race ever run at Epsom race course. In a somewhat controversial win, before the days of the photo-finish, Aboyeur was brought down by the suffragette from Northumberland, Emily Wilding Davison B.A. at the famous Tattenham Corner.

The Derby has always been a race where not only fortunes are made and lost, but where jockeys' reputations, however great elsewhere, suffer when the most coveted prize eludes them. Consider for a moment the jockey Jem Coater who was among the most revered of the racing world in the days of Queen Victoria. He made about twenty eight attempts. John Osborne won after trying on thirty eight mounts. Twenty five times round the course went Doug Smith, but no victory for him. Sir Gordon Richards won once after twenty eight tries, and as is common knowledge, he was Champion Jockey at the time. Being then forty-nine years old it was also a race against the sportsman's old enemy, time. I quote Sir Gordon because in nineteen forty seven he had a total of two hundred and sixty nine winners, which made him a world record holder, yet winning the Derby eluded him until nineteen fifty three, when he rode Sir Victor Sassoon's Pinza. Once again the famous race course and its association with the Royal Family, was woven into the story of this outstanding jockey. Only four days before this fateful Derby, the young Queen Elizabeth was engaged in the Coronation Ceremony. Her Majesty was also going to give him a knighthood, and the chestnut colt Aureole was to run in the Queen's colours. Rather a pity that he could not have ridden the royal horse to victory, in his great day of triumph. Aureole came in second, but then Sir Gordon was not up.

In nineteen seventy one, we bet on Mill Reef, but in seventy two we saw a bitter controversy and an astonishing Derby finish, when Broker, with the Australian Bill Williamson up, came down at Kempton Park about ten days before Williamson was due to ride the favourite,

Roberto at Epsom. He was about the same age as Sir Gordon was at his win. The Australian was not badly injured and rested before his great chance. It had been announced that Lester Piggott would ride Manitoulin, stable companion of Roberto. Then Roberto's owner arrived from the USA, and, being doubtful of Williamson's fitness, wanted Piggott to ride Roberto. The deposed jockey was compensated, but no monetary value can be put on the prestige of a Derby win.

As Piggott had already won five times, and doctors pronounced Williamson fit, the last minute switch shocked the racing world, and it was dubbed "un-British and unsporting." At the start the betting was Roberto three to one and Rheingold twenty two to one. The stakes were sixty three thousand, seven hundred and fifty five pounds. At the finish a photo was called for, and the mood of the crowd, even the winners, at the name of Roberto going up on the board, was one of dismay. No enthusiastic reception was given in the unsaddling enclosure; many felt that Roberto would have won with his original jockey up. In a following race, Bill Williamson romped home on Captive Dream, Piggott finishing third. On the same afternoon, the Australian tasted victory again on Capistrano and Piggott was again beaten. It was not one of the best Derbies from the racing fraternity's point of view, as the skill shown by Piggott was eclipsed by the crowd withholding the acclaim they would have shown under other circumstances. I find it interesting when a large crowd of greatly assorted types acts as one. Following his wins in the other races at Epsom, a few weeks later Williamson won the Irish Sweeps Derby, on Steel Pilse, beating Roberto. That year I bet on Rheingold and Meadow Mint with Willie Carson up. In nineteen seventy four we both had a good win on White Knight. Dominic supplied the bet, and so we shared the winnings, as I had picked the horse. I bought a set of flowered iron cooking pots with my half of the fifty pounds.

After the crescendo of excitement terminating with the end of Derby Stakes Race day, evening parties in hired halls or around the fires, events take a dive. While on the subject of fires, please never make the mistake and cause Romanies offence by referring to them as "camp-fires." Campfires are the fires of Boy Scouts, Girl Guides and campers. Romany fires, called *yogs*, are built in a different way. They are not a few twigs set in a ring of stones. They are mostly cooking fires and large branches and logs are burnt. *Yogs* are a serious practical thing, not adults playing games.

The Travellers from Devonshire, being well known for their late night parties, get every last ounce out of their holiday. They are nice neighbours if you want to join in, but not if you cannot stand the pace.

6

There is a feeling of anti-climax. The litter from such vast crowds, with thousands munching their way through masses of wrapped food, and throwing away the papers, has to be seen to be believed. An army of men with spiked sticks and sacks trudge in ragged lines across the Downs, then the wind changes direction and much blows back again. A great deal is un-spearable, often the case where trailers are. You may well never deposit rubbish yourself, but return to the trailer to find a sea of it blown from other trailers and overturned dustbins. It also blows from near-by bus-stops, lay-bys and from foxes tearing bin bags left by house gardens.

Although most Derby Weeks see fine weather, rain can turn the well-tyred grass into a sea of mud, thoughtless drivers then edging closer and closer to the trailers to avoid the worst mud. This sends up a spray that seeps behind the decorative strips and beading, taking weeks finally to come out – sometimes it never does. Each subsequent rainfall brings down further rivulets of mud from these strips. The first thing that I did after arriving at the next stopping place was to wash down the roof and outside walls. Then clean the inside, which means polishing all the surfaces. In the old days no good quality waggon ever left the maker's yard without a lightweight ladder to reach the roof and chimney. Usually one member of each family will have a pair of steps. The grime on a roof after a race meeting is amazing; a kind of brown soot adhering with a sticky consistency, some of which is from trailer chimneys, the fires using so-called 'smokeless fuel.'

One or two trailers may depart this afternoon, after lines of coaches and buses have snaked their way among the cars onto the road. It is not good for the engine of a towing vehicle to be in a traffic jam, constantly stopping and starting. Once Travellers decide to go, they can depart with surprising speed. The display china is wrapped in cloths and laid on seats packed with cushions, or put into drawers which lock. Once one or two depart the restlessness infects others. Those who have come out of official council sites often have the wildest children taking advantage of the open spaces. They hang on till the last, finding the empty trodden grass and lack of neighbours preferable to life inside the seven feet wire fences and concrete plots deemed by the authorities to be suitable for 'gypsies.'

The Year of the Cream Suits, Dresses, and off-beat non-primary Colours

There is never a dull moment for the observer and I find it hard to get a moment to record the year's fashions. Having started, however, I mean to go on, for I feel that, as so often happens, if no-one thinks to record things at the time, they are lost forever, like the historic winners of the first ever race at Ascot on the common, said to have been the idea of Queen Ann, one day in seventeen hundred and two.

Certainly no-one shows any interest in Travellers apart from speaking of the one solution to the 'Gypsy Problem,' by banishing them from all their traditional stopping places in favour of ugly compounds. Years hence, in retrospect, this solution may be deplored. Half a million was spent on modernising coal-board houses for the poor, which later had to be demolished because no-one wanted to live in them. A councillor said, "We can't push people around and make them live where they do not want." Are Romanies not people too?

The Derby is over for another year, memories linger of the excitement of arriving in good time. Watching the trailers arrive is one of the most looked forward to pastimes of the week. There are few things that can match the thrill of rounding the corner, going under the bridge, turning left along the front of the Rubbing House and then pulling onto the Downs with a brand 'spanking' new trailer and towing vehicle, knowing that envious eyes will swivel in your direction – a pleasantly harmless sensation shared by those born to the gypsy way of life. Travellers order their new trailers in good time for a grand entry at Epsom. I have often witnessed the makers of coach-built trailers arrive with their 'show trailers,' the equivalent of a model boat at a boat show. On the strength of these samples they will take orders. Other members of the firm will arrive towing previously ordered models, the proud new owners changing homes there and then.

Anro 1976

Chapter 2

Scene at the Derby: Show-out Sunday

Surrey Travellers assembled
ready for the races on Derby day.

Queen Victoria was taken to see the Derby Stakes in 1831. As a little girl, she could not fail to have been amused and entertained by the amazing panorama of human activities unfolding before her on the green undulating Race Course at Epsom Down.

It has been said, that if one stands still in Piccadilly Circus, eventually all the world passes by. On Derby Day it appears that all the world has decided to have a 'day out' at the same race course. Drawn from all classes of society, colourful characters push and jostle in a good humoured milling throng, the green sward below, and the blue sky above.

As much part and parcel of that colourful scene, yet even more colourful than the jockeys in their silks, the jugglers, acrobats or fairground showmen, are the Gypsies: the Romany people or the Travellers. Not for them a mere day out, or even a sporting week of daily visits by the dedicated racing fraternity, but a continuation of their way-of-life woven into the canvas of one of Britain's great racing and social events. The eyes of the young Queen-to-be would have looked down from the Grandstand onto a mass of horse-drawn waggons of all ages and degrees of splendour, canvas-topped carts and humble bender tents, grazing horses and ponies, for in those days, the Romanies were allowed to camp in The Dip at the very heart of the proceedings and in full view of the Royal Box.

A veritable barrage of field-glasses must have roamed with curiosity upon these mysterious, strange and sometimes feared, 'dark and handsome' people. But little would the observers have learned by such means. It is worth noting, that even today, early arrivals frequently take a walk, sometimes with honest curiosity, and sometimes with studied nonchalance, in and among our encampment. Strange manners are sometimes displayed, as, without permission, or even a glance or friendly nod, noses are flattened against living-trailer windows, so that interiors and owners may be spied upon. I recall one year when a family decided it would suit them perfectly to park their car in the space where our neighbours' car was normally parked, by their trailer home. They had gone out to buy food. The family laid out their picnic on the convenient Axminster carpet put down, as we all do, outside the trailer. For a while no one spoke; we were all too flabbergasted. They did not stay for long!

In the 1830's Epsom Downs would have been a sea of horse-drawn vehicles. Nose-bags and vehicle brakes would have been put on. The would-be owners sitting and standing on the gigs, traps, trolleys, hackney-cabs, elegant waggons and private carriages, shining or shabby. A great number of farm-waggons would have come bringing the farm hands and their wives. The happy throng would make their way home down the bumpy tracks clutching a 'fairing,' a cheap figurine which is a collector's item today, or some trifle won at a fairground booth.

While the Travellers' waggon horses could be loosed or tethered on the far sides of the Downs, the horses of the visiting public, although many of them tired and fidgety with the heat, would have stood in the confined spaces by the track. Those in two-wheelers would be taking extra weight as friends were invited to climb up to get a better view. Even now open-top buses line up in valued positions giving the passengers a splendid grandstand view. Of course many would have unhooked the traces; "Let me graze yer 'orse, Sir," a tradition which lingers on in some western films.

I don't deny the truth of the saying "One man's meat is another man's poison," but in this instance "one man's pleasure is another man's work." For hundreds it is a full day of hard work. Leaving aside the professional showmen and fairground operators, who like the Travellers arrive in their living-waggons and take up residence on their

11

normal 'pitch,' some spending the nights in a tent across the road in the lee of a group of trees conveniently close to the swings, roundabouts and fairground booths. There are hundreds of stallholders who set up their stalls just for Show-Out Sunday.

Showmen's waggons are larger than those of Travellers

A Showman prepares his Children's Ride

Here it is possible to purchase almost anything. Contrary to what customers might suppose, shopkeepers know that it is actually better for business to have two shops selling similar goods in the same street. So, if the stall trading began by small pockets being dotted about, through restrictions concerned as ever with neatness and order, these are now gathered together towards the near side of the Downs. Given fair weather, which is seldom disappointing, a roaring trade is done. Show-Out Sunday is the first of many subsequent social occasions during which the Travellers delight in showing off their personal attire, the

Romany Fashion Parade: in fact a world within a world, the significance of which is lost on the general public.

Just as the Brighton Promenade was originally a place for display, where Victorian and Edwardian fashions were shown off by extraverts, so the grass or clinker and ash paths become a promenade for men, women and children, for even the children of the Travelling families are extremely clothes-conscious. By the end of the day expensive shoes with utterly impractical high heels are ruined and children's white socks and shoes are stained by grass and ash, but as an outfit includes feet no one would dream of wearing non-matching shoes or practical low heels.

In the enclosures across the track, the 'quality', the 'nobs', or the rich people arrive, in expensive cars, of course, and in new and fashionable clothes. It is of small matter to them if footwear is ruined, although they do not have to walk on cinders and ash. On the wrong side of the track, a great diversity of apparel is seen. While the majority have put on their best attire, there are, however, those for whom a day out has nothing at all to do with showing off, and who are not in the slightest concerned with what other people may think, though they are the minority.

Travellers do not carry a badge: it is by instinct and an understanding observation they recognise one another at large gatherings when there are too many for all to know each other personally. First and foremost it is the face, by which you can sometimes recognise a family. The face is always the most revealing part of the human anatomy; it registers the hardness of the life, and the insecurities connected with the problems of a race, who, for generations, have been given the impression that they are on their own, sometimes it seems in an alien land, with every man's hand against them, with every day a fight for survival. No Race Relations Act or minority group campaigners for them! Other Traveller traits are alertness, anxiety, and cunning – I'll not use the word clever, as it might be confused with book-learning, as opposed to *life*-learning or self-taught knowledge, which, to me is altogether more admirable, since many a successful Traveller can neither read nor write, a state that is considered a terrible handicap for other people. For Travellers it has long been a mere inconvenience, a nuisance, which has not stopped a man earning a slice of cake, or as the old saying goes, "getting the baby a new frock."

To be *à la mode* is considered very important, as it is by outward show of possessions, which include a wife's and children's clothes, that a man is judged. This is because there are traits common to all Romanies and recognised by them, like a physical race-feature, which cannot be denied. Of course there are exceptions, as rare as the Welshman who cannot sing. One of these traits is the love of possessions. I noticed it is often *gauji* (non Traveller) women who have never wanted for anything, and who themselves have plenty of expensive possessions, who scorn this 'materialism.' Having known both plenty and poverty, see-sawing up and down all my life, I can fully understand and sympathise with this pride and satisfaction in possessions. To return to this trait, knowing this to be the case, a man who has a poor horse or an old lorry, shabby waggon or rough trailer-caravan, is not given the benefit of the doubt, should he proclaim *preference* for these. Self-made millionaires do not have any time for losers, for those who have, according to them, failed to meet life's challenge. In the Travellers' world there are equal opportunities for all, and far less excuse for failure. Sadly, there have been men who have reached the pinnacle of Romany aspirations, who have been much admired, but through gambling or drink have lost it all.

I hope that you are beginning to appreciate the great importance of Show-Out and the Derby in the Romany social calendar. Their presence on the Downs has of course been noted and remarked upon by people, Press and Royals alike. Our Royal Family are among the few 'outside' things which Travellers bother about, and there are not too many of them! Conversations run along more important roads such as family matters, gossip, trailers, and vehicles. Stopping-places cannot be too seriously discussed, apart from those 'taken' beforehand, such as a private field paid for in advance, since, like the Romanies themselves, a well-known stopping place can be here today and gone tomorrow.

Since the Romanies first crossed the sea to Britain they have been besieged by academics, referred to in past Gypsy history, as "scholars," by famous artists, by great and lesser writers, and by those who by character or talent to get themselves noticed by Romanies, have been given the title of *Romany Rawnie* (Gypsy Lady) or *Romany Rai* (Gypsy Gentleman). It is the Romany part which is the operative compliment, *Rawnie* being reserved for a non-Traveller woman of lady-like ways, and *Rai*, a title of equal worth, being given to such legendary figures as Augustus John, and after John's death to Dominic. If you were to ask Travellers who 'Dominic' is, they would not know who you were talking about, but ask about the '*Romany Rai*' and you would receive a different response.

Hippies and drop-outs seeking an alternative way of life have made many a Traveller happy by paying vast sums for often rotten old waggons. Many, indeed, appear to have incomes to live on and wealthy parents to buy them waggons and horses. After a few summers and winters, however, the stark reality of the lifestyle, even without the constant need to make a living, which is at the forefront of the Romany's mind, proves too much for them. There are occasional landowners who have managed to get a council to turn a blind eye to Planning Permission, and who allow many hippies to stay on their land for long periods, in old motor vans, buses, trailers and the odd waggon: really a settled existence! There are a few 'oddities' and 'loners' who, hanging on in quiet corners with horses and waggons, do make a living by farm work or crafts. Then there are the 'misfits,' accepted by locals and police as harmless. One encounters them perhaps several times over the years, each time a little older but content; loners by choice. Travellers have, in fact, no right at all by, Law, to travel the roads and stop on the road-side. I am always pleased to see loners and tramps, in accord with my own idea, that we should all be allowed to live wherever and in whatever we choose, without conveniences, or as one Traveller charmingly put it where "there are no civilities," so long as it does not ruin someone else's Eldorado!

Leaving the harmless loners, there are 'oddments' attracted to the Travellers, some of whom have left their backgrounds and follow a trade which is useful and profitable in all respects. In order to be a maker or painter of waggons, these craftsmen have settled down and built up a good reputation. Few things earn the respect of Romanies more than success. Travellers still commission new waggons to be built (popularly known as 'Gypsy Caravans'). Those who have horse-drawn waggons need expert painters who can 'line-out' and apply gold leaf. There are people with Romany blood who are skilled in this and who are much in demand. It adds to the value of a waggon for it to have been painted by a well known name. The work of Jim Berry, a Yorkshire Traveller, is greatly renowned. He died but his handiwork lives on.

There have been (I hope I can write in the past tense) those seeking notoriety, those with political leanings, or both, as well as religious cranks, and genuine religious representatives – British and foreign – who have seen Travellers as a source of possible riches, in every sense of the word. One such, rumoured to be Left-wing, arrived one year at Epsom Races, with a Traveller who, it was said, had not travelled for twenty years. Reports were given to the Press that a 'Gypsy King' had arrived. Travellers found this hugely amusing, as it was the first they had heard of a King. What followed was not so amusing. The Press were told that the Travellers were upset at the new entry fee being charged; and that we were going to pull our trailers across the Race Course, inside the rails, and so prevent the racing! Everyone was amazed to learn that they would be doing this. It was very depressing to realise that the general public had been told this. They were not to know that the beautiful and valuable living-trailer caravans, with precious possessions proudly displayed during Derby week, would be utterly unsuitable for such a task. No way would the Travellers put their costly homes at risk, for the sake of a few pounds. Compared to other fairs, Epsom is quite cheap, being at that time, only five pounds. At Doncaster we pay twenty five pounds for trailer and vehicle; and some families have more than one. At Cambridge it is thirty two pounds for the trailer and one pound for the vehicle. Charges are all an accepted part of the scene, quite lost in the overall far larger expense of the entire occasion, to each head of family. Romanies are philosophical regarding expenses.

Notoriety seekers are never too concerned with the truth. Not being in the travelling way-of-life, they are unlikely actually to know it. In general, the political leaning of Travellers is towards the Right, any Left-wingers or far Leftists are on a losing wicket. It seems very rare, in fact almost impossible, for the real opinions or voices of Travellers to be heard; or for them to be consulted before such erroneous views, as those published at that Epsom Week, are read by the all and sundry, not only in local newspapers, but national papers as well. As so often, Travellers are shown in a poor light. I immediately wrote to the Queen, via Prince Philip, and explained the *true* situation. I was not disappointed with the reply, which I read to those Travellers who knew that I had written to deny that which others had claimed in our name.

There was another occasion when this same agitator was said to have organised a demonstration on behalf of Travellers, who again, were not consulted. They were horrified to see a newspaper photograph of some disgusting, rough-looking trailers due for the scrap heap, parked outside Buckingham Palace. I now forget just what the demonstration was supposed to be about – non-events fade in the real world. Luckily, by then the Royal Family had been told that this person was certainly no official spokesman for the main body of the Travellers, who deplore such atypical photographs, and pathetic tactics. Hopefully those responsible have returned to obscurity.

One word on those who have attempted, and still attempt, to *organise* Travellers; they are like thistle-down before an electric fan. Travellers do not *want* to be organised. It is all against their very nature. Even the Travellers' societies, formed in their name, soon disintegrate and form splinter-groups.

It can be quite confusing to the outsider, and to press photographers and reporters, hoping each Derby week will spawn a good story; rarely have I not taken a cutting from a paper during this period, for my collection. But wandering through the trailers, reporters find that people have a tendency to vanish. All or most of the above people attracted to Romanies and the Traveller-scene visit Epsom, and Show-Out Sunday is a good day for visitors of all kinds. Travellers parade up and down the area of the stalls or watch a few late-comers leave the main road and wind up on to the Downs. Few things are more interesting than to see a trailer or a convoy of trailers on the road. Interest in them, in detail of make, age, and type never flags. And this is what is so misunderstood by other people.

Sightseers

A crowd, even if drawn faithfully, that looks like cartoon characters, in by-gone fashions, walks towards the Travellers trailers on Derby Day morning. The couple on the right are <u>not</u> travellers.

They come in all shapes and sizes to " see the Gypsies" and peer into trailer windows!

Sightseers

The public also visit the Downs on Sunday, of course, and the sun reflects on the hundreds of windscreens in the car parks. The great wheels of the fun fair steadily turn to music geared to entice customers. People meet people they have not seen since last Epsom. There is much to see and hear. Sometimes there are 'chopper' rides and Travellers dare each other to go up to view it all from the air. "If the Good Lord meant us to fly we'd have had wings," pronounced one elderly Romany grandmother.

The original Gypsy Law Society, formed in 1888, was for 'Scholars and Gentlemen' rather than for Romanies. It was, and presumably is, more interested on *their*, rather than *our*, side of the hedge. In ethnic societies, language is of paramount interest; this is difficult since the Romany tongue is not a written language, and therefore all interpretations have to be taken on trust.

Many a writer has fallen foul of the Travellers' sense of humour by including in his book, in all innocence, very rude words. An argument for writers of non-fiction to keep to their better known subject matter is well illustrated by the nonsense frequently written on the subject of the Romany life. A few months travelling with Gypsies, sitting at their firesides with a notebook, does not produce an expert on the subject. The resultant writings sound hilarious to the Travellers: would that there were more books by Travellers themselves, setting the record straight.

There are of course the 'Do-Gooders,' those desperately anxious to improve living conditions of Travellers, and greatly concerned with education, or lack of it, among the *chavies* (children). Those retired from the legal profession have been able to give assistance in individual cases. Some, despite good intentions, have made matters rather worse. Naturally, as in every society, those members who can be cajoled into coming forward as 'examples,' are not from the higher ranks, the most intelligent, or the most erudite, or even able to express themselves at all. They are flattered to be asked and that anyone of note from among the non-Romany ranks should actually seem to care, be concerned, or take unpaid trouble on their behalf. When cases appear on television (watched in all trailers) the more upmarket Romanies can hardly keep their seats.

To my mind, born of long experience, the only education needed to enrich the adequate home education, is reading and writing. The former is useful for road signs when a well known route is altered. The telephone has been of great assistance to Travellers*. When one is ill in hospital, daily visits are made. 'Phone calls to far off relatives are made. News spreads across the country like wild-fire. An event which occurred on a Sussex encampment on Sunday is known to Travellers in Devon by Monday. It might have taken a few days longer before the call-box, but the fact is, news always did spread fast. Dominic can never go out without meeting another traveller; sometimes passing those he has been stopping with a few weeks earlier, now in another county several hundred miles away, such is the strange world of co-incidence.

*Since this was written the wand of the *mobile* 'phone has waved its magic: everyone now has one.

18

Chapter Three

The Social Calendar

Depending on their social standing and inclination, but hardly ever depending on their geographical location, Travellers attend various fixed events. These are equal to the events in the social calendar of a member of high society, who might regard Henley Regatta, Ascot Race Meeting and the Centre Court at Wimbledon as compulsory dates. The social name for an event, that is the non-Traveller name, for example the St Leger Stakes at Doncaster, or York Races are referred to simply as Doncaster or York. York was the scene of the great match race in 1854, when the Derby winner, The Flying Dutchman, triumphed over the horse he challenged, Voltigeur, another Derby winner. Issue from the former's daughter and the latter's son, in turn became famous as the winner of the 1875 Derby.

Except for a few habitual gamblers, the actual races are but a sideline, the track rarely visited. If this is so, you may ask, then why go to the race meeting? Well, it is known that Travellers owned and used horse-drawn vehicles long after the general public gave up using horse-drawn trams, post-chaises, or keeping a stable for carriage horses. The Travellers' interest in horses will never die. In the past, race courses were places where people from all walks of life could gather to display their goods and skills of many crafts. Wheelwrights took the latest samples of their work, coach-builders showed the latest inventions in improved springs, fittings and other refinements together with their most recent samples, the owner of a coachworks proudly driving his showy (or refined as the case may be) turnout among the admiring and hopefully very interested crowd. Tradesmen were among the best customers, since their goods were often judged by the smartness of their vehicles. A smart new lettered van or cart could well reflect a wealthy tradesman able to buy the best and so pass this quality on to his customers. This tradition is sometimes to be seen in elaborately painted and lined-out motor-lorries (the old word for which is 'lurry'). On the motorways and main roads treble-lining-out and flourishes with scrolls adorn some lorries, all adding to their cost. I have a certificate that states that my name was chosen to decorate one of the legendary Eddie Stobart fleet of transport lorries. In contrast, by the way, my name was also given, to a species of Viola bred by the then Keeper of the British Viola Society, Richard Cawthorne. I find these extremes amusing!

Lamorna Publications

Specialist Interest Books

Wildlife   Romani Life   Art   Theology

Yew Tree Studio   Marshwood   Bridport   Dorset   DT6 5QF   UK
Tel: 01297 678566   **www.lamornapublications.co.uk**   E-mail: frleonard@btinternet.com
Proprietor: *Rev R Leonard Hollands obOSB MRICS MASI MFPWS MRSPH Dip Theol*

With Compliments

Thank you for your order and payment.
We hope you will enjoy the book!

Leonard †

The moonlight yellow Beshlie viola

This tradition of the coach-builder taking his latest example to public gatherings such as races is still carried on by the few remaining coach-builders of the Traveller style living-trailer-caravans. Their arrival is a much looked-forward-to event. The rival firms line up their trailers, sometimes bringing members of their family. These builders are much admired and their fine designs are forever entwined in Romany history. It came as no surprise to me that an 'armchair gypsy,' when asked, could not name even one of them. Those outside the life fail to see the importance of trailers and vehicles, the contemporary equivalent of the horses and waggons they find so romantic and accept as part of Romany life. During the day the Show-trailer doors are open to viewers and serious buyers, and the windows to the wistful. Quite often these samples are sold within hours of arriving, with the understanding they will remain on display. There is not a little prestige value in being pointed out as the owner of one of the Show-trailers, linked, of course, to the vast sum printed on the price card. Any deal is subject to the seller accepting the buyer's present trailer in time-honoured part-exchange. This arrangement is called 'chopping in,' and is the normal way of obtaining a trailer. The money handed over would be in cash. There is no Hire Purchase in an itinerant life.

Harness-makers have always found the Race Course one of the best shop windows. Different styles of vehicles have different styles of harness. The heavy farm harness has the wrong fittings for a Romany waggon. Many a novice buying a farm horse and harness will have discovered this. The collar for a heavy horse will not go over his neck until it is turned upside down so the widest part can go over the wide forehead. Ideally, all collars should, be made to fit. The next best thing is a collar that opens and can be adjusted. I recall a Welsh cob that had an extremely arched 'rainbow' neck. We could not find a collar that fitted for several months. Re-lining them with red cloth was no easy task, I found. Harness is still taken to the Races and Fairs, usually second hand although now rarely by the maker. The reputation of the double buckle 'silver' of the red or yellow Morocco waggon harness grew to such an extent that few in the world of Travellers have not heard of it. The additions of this colourful leather in decorative shapes hanging from fillet straps on saddle-pad, collar, browband, blinkers and nose-band etc, was of, course, in keeping with Travellers' taste for the ornate. Today second hand sets fetch an amount sufficient to have purchased a waggon horse when we had our first Morocco set.

I do not want to give the impression that Travellers are not interested in racing; some own racehorses. The settled down Traveller's 'dream home,' which is a smaller version of a Dallas style ranch, is considered incomplete without a few loose-boxes with well-bred palominos or coloured ponies peering out at the white stone horse-heads on the front gate posts and the black and gold ornamental wrought iron gates. Perhaps their favourite form of racing is trotting. After York Races a move is made to 'The Trots.' At Mussleborough, another social event, attended mainly by Northern Travellers, trotting is the order of the day, the practice of which wakes one at dawn. Small lightweight two wheeled 'Daisy-Cutters' are used. Every so often word is spread of a dawn trot, often a Match Race. In racing parlance a Match Race is one with only two contenders. This was the early form of racing from which all racing stems. Not run on any old ground, a straight stretch of public road is selected. The contestants arrive in their horse-boxes, and the ponies are soon harnessed and ready for a few warm-up runs.

The start and finish being agreed, nothing further is needed but the starting signal. After one or two exciting races during which there does not seem to be any of the elaborate protective gear professionals need for horse and man, the meeting disperses in an orderly manner, and with luck, no one is the wiser. Very occasionally a car or van comes along, but seeing the crowd and ponies, in true British fashion, does not question the legality of the event. It would not occur to most people that in this day and age anyone would actually dare to use a road to race a pony! Roads are for vehicles; you are not supposed to enjoy or use them for archaic purposes. This is the age where there is so little freedom; you are probably supposed to get planning permission for a bird-table!

At one such 'Trot' I witnessed a furious lady driver, apoplectic at such freedom. She immediately sent for the police. They made very slow progress down the rows of parked vehicles and were able to watch most of the racing, before hastening our departure, prior to a few contestants having had a chance to participate. I can imagine her self-righteous smirk. The Police seemed to enjoy it, however.

There are certain fairs all over the country, simply known as Horse Fairs. These fairs have, to some extent, survived the kill-joy closure of many such, which are now but sad memories. Those who wish to sell or buy waggon-horses, ponies and foals make a point of going. At the time of writing Appleby New Fair, which takes place in Cumbria (Westmorland), is the most famous. Apart from these, where it is still possible to arrive and live in one's home, the various Race Courses afford the facilities needed for a large gathering of Romanies. It is the fixed date, or relatively so, that is a very useful feature, for example the first Wednesday in June. It would cost a fortune on 'phone calls to ensure an attendance elsewhere, even if the County Councils were as accommodating as they are with Pop Festivals, and allowed an event. So it follows that the racing calendar and Travellers' meetings are juxtaposed. In 1973 two hundred and seventy eight trailers were in the enclosure and a hundred and forty-seven unlawfully on the Downs, the Epsom Downs Clerk told the Conservators. While such a gathering exists in one place with a surety of being able to remain for a certain time, the opportunity is taken for other specific social events. This is the nearest that Travellers come to being involved in any kind of organised event. Usually some well-respected man of social standing decides to be the host. He hires a dance hall and band, arranges for caterers, and if at Christmas when drink and driving don't go to together, a fleet of cars or coaches. Tickets or invitations are given to respected families in their area. In the past there have been gatecrashers. Once, easily two dozen young men arrived through a third floor window, only a few feet from me. After such daring, those next to the window feigned the maxim of the first of the three wise monkeys, I among them.

Since these functions are very expensive, and since the room or rooms are filled to bursting as a result of over optimistic ticket selling, any extra persons are unwanted, so it is not unusual to find hired doormen or 'heavies' who scrutinise each invitation, retaining the evidence. Alas this cuts down my scrapbook collection. It is worth noting that not *one* single non-traveller writer of books on this subject, who claims close friendships, nor do-gooders or hangers-on, have ever been present at any of these Travellers functions. So where are they?

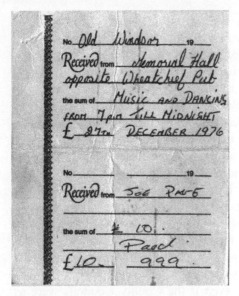

Typical Invitation

If what they claim is true, why have they never been invited; surely a reflection of Romanies' true feelings? Dances are made or marred by the band. Young musicians soon grasp the fact that slow or romantic dances leave the floor free for a few older couples with almost no variety of steps, a shuffle-shuffle-turn being endlessly repeated. A contemporary tune with plenty of beat soon has the floor filled to overflowing to such an extent that no one who *can* dance has the space – men and women dancing with, but not touching their partners. Women dance in pairs or threes. Sometimes a small or large circle of women dance together. The main aim is to *dance* regardless of who you are with or whether you are alone. This is totally different to my style of dancing; women dancing together seems as sad as wallflowers. Needless to say, lack of space does not deter any show-offs from exhibiting rock-style learnt as children, by the simple method of shooting out arms and legs oblivious to anyone being nearby, so that a space is soon cleared! Since movement of feet by other dancers is restricted, most of the 'dancing' is done with the body only.

Actions seen on television are faithfully followed. Travellers have a wonderful sense of rhythm. Movement to and fro, back and forth, being restricted, they dance on the spot wiggling bottoms, not always a pretty sight! Husbands may occasionally be seen to be pulled on to the floor to dance with their wives. Courting couples dance, and brothers and sisters may, but mostly *women* dance. Lack of any organisation or ability to think ahead has spoiled many a dance or party. Brought up in a different world, with a horror of being a wallflower and where it was unthinkable to dance with another woman, I never enjoy being invited to follow the rest of the ladies from where we have been sitting (the men up at the bar) especially as they stay on the floor while the band plays several dances in succession. In the already baker's-oven heat, all windows tightly shut, I am deprived of being able to dance, which I love, even dancing in the contemporary style and not holding one's

Travellin'
Dance

partner. It would be difficult to dance energetically if the woman or women opposite are merely shuffling; it would be seen as showing off. I am miserable inside whilst keeping up the appearance of intense enjoyment.

The traditional Romany step-dancing, in which the arms are held, Irish style, straight to the sides while various rhythms are tapped by the heel and toe, is fast dying out. A few well-known dancers remain, but younger copyists do not have the skill. Nothing remotely traditional is ever danced at parties or dances, or, as they are sometimes called, Travellers' Balls. This name may stem from a well-attended Showman's Ball at Cambridge. I have been privileged to watch many a wonderful and memorable performance in the past, when some well-known dancer has got going on a bit of plank. One such was little Nan-Nan, an expert never to be forgotten. The dancing, for there is no musical instrument, is accompanied by mouth music. Lorry tailgates are sometimes taken off and used. It is always heart warming when some well dressed (in the manner of a merchant banker), well-to-do, heavily built, cigar-smoking traveller puts down his glass and goes back to his grass-roots, so to speak, in the performance of a step-dance, his hand made crocodile boots twinkling with a lightness and dexterity, belying his vast silk shirt encased paunch. Such public performances are greatly appreciated by all present.

Step-dancing is done by men, which leaves women in a quandary, as to how to express their natural desire and inborn flair, or rather it would, if anyone had time to think about it. Pop music dancing may satisfy the inner yearning but unless taken to its professional length as done by dance teams on television, it is not as satisfying to watch. Some observers might find it as incongruous as a tribe of desert nomads suddenly dancing a waltz. This is, of course, irrational; all peoples have to change with the times. I find it rather shocking in a purely visual sense to see nuns in short skirts and women dressed as vicars. Tourists in America may be taken aback to see Native American Indians driving about in flashy pick-ups. Watching a tribal dance on television recently, I thought that black-rimmed glasses took away the ethnic splendour of some of the 'Braves.' So much of life is fantasy images. A black eye patch on the last of the Mohicans would be peculiar but, I feel, just about acceptable, whereas a pair of granny glasses would not. I could be wrong.

"Nan-nan" Step-dancing.

Some Travellers' Balls have waitress service, and we remain at the tables, more or less, some tables being moved together at intervals, so that friends can talk more easily, for it is *talk* that goes on non-stop. Bottles and glasses mount up with incredible speed and begin to collect under the tables until too numerous to be systematically cleared. Tables are knocked over and soon the floor is littered with broken glass, spilled drink and food and the parquet floor has been ruined! But it is a life-style in which everything comes to grief sooner or later, mostly sooner. No great importance is attached to this, an attitude which is hard for those who do not share it to understand. It can have its tearful or funny moments. I can recall waiting through hours of unsuitable (for me) music and an over-filled dance floor, until at long last a danceable tune and space occurred, as many people who had got up together were exhausted and had left the floor together. We went on the floor and I took the first happy steps only to feel myself gliding and sliding more than I wished. Looking down I saw the area covered with large lumps of pink blancmange. Hemmed in by dancers who were chatting to us, it would have been rude to move away. Dancing on blancmange is not my idea of a good time.

Sometimes 'turns' are hired, often well-known 'Show-Biz' personalities. When their humour or songs are not to the listeners' taste, the noises 'off' get steadily more loud until puzzled MCs have to take the microphone and ask for "a sporting chance." I well remember the first unfavourable moments of a small rotund lady billed as the Mighty Atom. The entertainers, and indeed the band, can have no idea that it is not just another one night stand, or if they are booked at that particular hall that it is not just one more evening like any other. It is very amusing to see it gradually dawn upon them that they are playing to a strange or different kind of people. I would dearly like to hear their puzzled comments backstage. Some are deflated and after each number hasten away. Some fix their gaze above the sea of faces below; others rise to the occasion, as did the Mighty Atom. Gathering her multifarious frilled crinoline about her, she walked to the edge of the stage and beckoned a standing man, demanding that he lift her down, which he did. The music had stopped; this unusual fraternising twixt a Traveller and artiste immediately had the whole room's attention, and the space in front of the stage became smaller. Lifting herself to her full height of four feet, tossing her short blonde hair and gazing unswervingly ahead through her round glasses, she marched in a determined manner to those seated in the chairs in front of her and told them just what she thought of them. I could not hear the actual words, but actions speak louder and everyone got the message. As she marched back, the Traveller gallantly stepped forward and replaced her on the stage: not without some effort as she was as wide as she was tall and her costume of crinoline almost smothered his torso. This broke the silence with laughter, by which time, as a true performer, she had swung into her act as if nothing had happened.

Immediately everyone in the room was on her side. She had unwittingly struck at the very core of their feelings. Before she was only a *gauji* funny-woman, and as such was shown no respect. Singing

27

a song that was not Traveller's style, she had been a target for mockery. Now she was one of them, trying to make a living knocking on a door. When that door revealed rude inmates, she had not scurried back down the path, but had put her head in the lion's mouth. I do hope she discovered who the audience were and realised how great had been her triumph. Along with the disappearance of the step-dance during evenings of such sophisticated entertainments, has gone the old Romany song. Should a folksong collector request a traditional song, a singer may promise, "I'll sing you a real *old fashioned* Romany song" and launch into 'Danny Boy', or even my 'My Yiddisha Momma.' Popular music hall and First World War songs are all mixed up in a hotchpotch of melodies. Without written history and only word of mouth to keep old songs going, and with no press or TV, a kind of education until recent years, it has not been possible for the source date or origin of a song to be known to Travellers.

Just as thousands of people buy Greetings Cards for the verse or the printed sentiments within, so do Travellers favour and remember songs, which similarly express their feelings. This is, of course, the reason for the survival of all popular songs. So while the folksong purist may flinch, a 'good song' may be of any age, the criterion is the *content*, and the tune of course. Almost all Travellers like Country and Western music, me included. Cowboy songs, pseudo or otherwise, Hill-Billy or electric finger-picking, most Traveller girls have cassettes of these songs which, whilst parents are out, are played on powerful Hi-Fi sets, full volume, non-stop. They imitate the singers, Tammie Winette's 'Stand By Your Man' being a favourite. Their ambition is to be able to perform like the singers at Travellers' parties. Another favourite often sung is 'Please Don't Take My Man.' (Recently, in the Reality TV show *X Factor*, a Traveller girl, Cher Lloyd,from Malvern, reached the Finals.) The smooth effortless voice of Jim Reeves could well be a model for Traveller men who have style, timing and volume, and a polish which a professional singer might envy; all without training or being able to read a note of music. A virtuoso piece is the exacting 'Auctioneer's Song,' which ought not to be attempted when words are slurred by drink! Good singers have to be given a great deal of encouragement and persuasion to get up and sing. A play of modesty ensues during which they protest a lack of the required talent, but after prodding and, "Gooo-on, give us a song," with a great show of reluctance they oblige. There is silent hesitation should a band ask, "What key?" then the singer will start off and the band follow. Song after song is then rendered while family and friends applaud. Rival singers and their families wait a chance to take the 'mike.' On such occasions it is nice to see the musicians pleasantly surprised that a singer, who did not know what key he was singing in, could be so good – and they have been known to applaud with the audience.

Recently at York Races, a small boy of eight was put upon a stool by the landlord, and he sang faultlessly most evenings in the same pub. Not only that, but many of the songs were *real* old-fashioned Romany songs. Could anyone ask for more? Many children sing, some of them precocious show-offs who have been made aware of their talent and spoilt in consequence. All dance, and until recently, the first half of every ball was a seething mass of children on the floor and around the tables, roaming to and fro, running up and down, the area cluttered with prams. Now it is the age of the baby-sitter and evenings can be more of a pleasure for those who, once, could not get away from their constant supervision of three, four or five children, and everyone has a chance of a 'good time' – a *good time* being the purpose of all parties and dances. As the hour gets later and later, some feel this has not been achieved …… but there is always another day and another party.

At weddings and birthday parties, both an excellent excuse for hopes of a good time, drink is often free, included in the invitations of the latter, up to a certain hour. This is very reasonable since such vast quantities are consumed by those who do not intend to drive themselves home. As soon as waitress service stops, men find an excuse, like going to fetch drinks, to go to the bar and not return. It is very much a men together, women together society. Those who have dealings with Romanies, such as social workers, might do well to remember this. It is not the done thing for a woman to go up to a group of men, or even a man on his own. The men at the bar forego the pleasure of dancing with their wives. It is not done to ask another man's wife to dance, unless both men are very close friends, such as two sisters married to two brothers and all travelling together. A young man may ask for a dance with a woman of the age of a grandmother, referred to as Auntie, Aunt Mary, or whatever, a term of respect – and, of course, courting couples dance together.

At the bar men are at home and talk can be free as any evening in a pub. The room is now a sea of women; still a few are seated jabbering away to distant friends they have been able to spot now the men have gone. Others looking tired and worn, eye their men none too kindly. Older children lie sleeping and the band packs up and is replaced by a record player. Loud singing at one end of the bar signifies someone has had too much to drink. Considering the amount most men can 'put away' it is surprising how well they manage. Some have been known to drive with their dear ones' lives in their hands; others rely on their wives to drive. Travellers take to driving like ducks to water, some as children, none having any difficulty with the mechanics of driving and they pass the Driving Test without much effort.

A man may wend a crooked path to his wife. "We're going now," she says as she puts on her mink coat which has been carelessly flung on the back of a chair, and many times knocked to the floor. "You're not *going*?" call shocked voices from friends, all being loathe to admit that the party's over. The husband has started for the door, but jovial friends grab him and he has a drink in his glass again. This is an oft repeated pattern; down sits his wife again, having said goodbye to her sisters and friends. If a woman of some character, she will follow her man and stand by him. It is not done to be seen to make a man leave his friends; it is shaming. He is head of the house and he says when they shall leave. Parties in pubs go on long after closing time; any attempt to end the evening is nearly always a cause of trouble. Landlords are known for 'liking' or 'not liking' the Travellers who will often take over a bar, spending far more than the locals. It's up to the host whether he'd sooner have a lot of profit over a short while or a little over a longer while. Troublemakers are often barred. If it is considered justified, trade will continue there, if not, no Travellers will drink there again and the pub is left alone by all of them.

The Rubbing House

Chapter Four

Origins, Tents and Waggons – the Turnout

Before the Turn Pike Roads Act (1730-1780) Britain relied greatly upon water transport, using natural waterways until the spate of man-made canals in the late Eighteenth Century. Roads were appallingly bad, rough tracks of mire with mountainous ridges to the ruts at each crossing. Roads in towns were hardly better. Men known as crossing-sweepers tried to keep the roads passable at junctions. Building a raised platform for pedestrians, called the sidewalk, helped the problem in American towns: Clogs and wooden-soled shoes may have helped in Britain. Imagine the state of the horses after each journey. A coach needed a team of six horses which were changed at intervals or stages along the journey, hence the name stagecoach. At one time people thought that the gaily-painted 'Gypsy caravans' had come from across the sea with the Gypsies. On better roads across the channel, travelling Showmen, owners of wild beast collections, and Circus proprietors had already made a beginning with horse-drawn wooden cages and attached grooms' rooms, as in some horse-boxes today, but no examples have survived. Over here, the Gypsies travelled with tents.

These tents are still in use today, and are known as bender or rod tents, the rods being bent round. There is a full or half-bender tent; this is a style peculiar to Travellers – semi-circular, or with two tunnel-shaped benders facing each other, the fire in the centre, the smoke going up a funnel shaped chimney. The smaller half-bender has the fire at the front and is more of a summer or fair-weather tent, while the longer bender is better for the winter. Although anything upwards of five feet in height, there is not much room to move about round the fire. The smoke often spirals in perverse, choking circles before going upwards. The fire has to be kept fed with dry wood. Bender rods of hazel, ash or willow could be cut at each stopping place, but good rods develop hardness from being smoked, and there may not be the right kind or length at the next stopping place. Many people carried some rods. They were transported by donkey, pony, or pony and cart, along with the covers of blankets and canvas. The covers were anchored to wooden pegs; ropes were not used. Such a tent is described by Borrow in *Lavengro*.

We lived with one at one time, cooking on the *yog* (fire) in front of a half bender and sleeping in a waggon.

Living with a Bender or Rod-tent

Note the arm basket or kipsie. The cane scallops around the rim protect flowers whilst allowing them to be seen.

No wonder mystery surrounds the Romany race, arriving here in a flurry of myths; they were, perhaps, themselves the first to start the slow-to-die fiction of having descended from the Pharaohs. It is generally accepted that they were, in fact, from India, after a mass wandering across Europe, which was noted in many countries in the Fourteenth and Fifteenth Centuries. Several factors suggest their Indian origins. Even today many Sanskrit words are still in the Romany language. Throwbacks to those first 'pure-blood' strangers have an undeniably Indian look and a skin tone difficult to describe, with jet-black glittering eyes. They are referred to as having 'black-blood' and are remarked on with pride. Of course the blood has been watered down since, but many families seem to be able to reproduce off-spring true to type for many generations, so much so, that to have an ancestor belonging to these respected family names is noteworthy and remarked upon in 'one-upmanship.'

News of the 'Scotland invasion,' tinged with fear and suspicion by the natives, preceded the large band on horseback and afoot. This fear, felt by people themselves wild and lawless (according to history), says much about the strangers. It is quite conceivable that this fear would have induced the Crofters to give the more readily to hasten the departure of the fearsome callers.

From the very beginning, Travellers could have been left in little doubt as to their unfriendly reception. A need for, and subsequent skill at, deception and the denial of one's race, was born when laws were passed by the Elizabethan parliament, to the effect that to be an 'Egyptian' was an 'offence' for which 'death was just punishment.' Whoever instigated this strong measure must have thought that the 'Egyptians' would return from whence they came, and that would be the end of the problem.

It is worth noting that there are still bands of wanderers in Scotland and Ireland who have been given the title of Tinkers, 'minks.' British Romanies draw the line between them as strongly as between Travellers and Showmen. It is only non-Travellers who lump them together, as they do all Indian races or all black races. I am constantly astonished when casting directors cast two black men as brothers, when it is obvious that they come from very different ethnic roots; face features, body shape, skin colouring all totally different. I pity the poor actors having to keep up the pretence, knowing the truth. Irish Travellers (many now settled here), Scottish Travellers and Welsh Travellers all have different ways and appearances. When in any of these three parts of the British Isles, it is very noticeable how much more like the original Gypsies the Welsh Travellers are. It is the deep Welsh Romany language that remains the most pure, free from slang and thieves' cant. Perhaps it is on the Welsh coast that the first Gypsies landed. In early days, among a people short and dark and among a population of indigenous itinerants, the presence of dark people moving about would not have caused comment. Only when journeying upwards to Scotland would the contrast with the fair-skinned, red-haired, Scots have been noticeable. But I must not start any more myths. It is bad enough that a flaxen-haired, fair-skinned, blue-eyed Romany child is often thought by non-Travellers to have been stolen.

So we had a band or bands of 'Egyptians,' later known as Gypsies, moving across the British Isles, trying to keep a low profile, earning a living by various skills and crafts, out-witting the local population, and visiting fairs where rich pickings were to be had . Round about the mid Nineteenth Century the wooden horse-drawn Showman's waggon would have been seen at these fairs, by which time, in my opinion, the most forward of the Romanies would have recognised the advantage of putting hazel rods on a cart in bender tent fashion and leaving this erected permanently. Some people have discarded this idea supposing that the outside fire, which dies to a heap of warmth-giving smouldering wood and ash close by the sleeping tent-dwellers, or closed in with them in winter, could not be used to heat a cart. But this is not the case. Once, when I was a child, I visited some Travellers who my grandparents knew; they had stopped on a near-by common. There was a family in a wooden waggon and the old grandmother in an accommodation cart, a two-wheeled cart with the shafts propped on a shaft prop. The cart was covered by rods over which old carpets and bits of blanket were fixed. I well remember being puzzled when the old woman poked her head out, removed her black pipe and called, "Ain't yer never bringing me a bit-of-fire missy?" Her daughter shouted some reply and began to scoop up the hot fire ash and embers into an iron pot. As this was lifted up into the cart, the grandmother said to me, "I never goes to bed without me bit-of-fire." I have used wrapped hot stones as hot water bottles and have since been in a waggon at Southampton Water in 1963 where the only heating was by the same method, used by a Sussex Traveller: only a variation on the copper warming pan. The iron pots with fire ash were put on the wooden floor, on a bit of tin for protection.

In the Old Curiosity Shop, Charles Dickens describes a Showman, or in their case, Showlady's, waggon – "A smart little house upon wheels pulled by two horses" (about 1840). In the super book *The Romany Rai* (1857), set in 1825, a Gypsy tells *Lavengro*, "We hates folks as live in caravans." This could have been referring to showmen or to the new style of Gypsy caravan-dweller who would cause jealousy among the less fortunate Gypsy tent-dwellers. With the coming of better roads came better vehicle design and the great days of the Stagecoach. Showmen, always conscious of the value of novelty, would have realised the crowd-drawing prestige over rivals in possessing one of the new 'Caravans.' Unfortunately, these were not made in hardwood and many of the early examples soon disintegrated. Whereas previously, front-boards with showy lettering and paintings needed to be erected, depicting the delights within the booths, now a large area on the waggon sides could be used, either alone or incorporated in the front. How Travellers' eyes must have boggled at the carved scrolls and rococo embellishments. Because of this practice, Showmen's waggons had no windows in the nearside. This advertisement would then be on view to the public when *en route*. Also, if the Showmen were drawn up in a circle, some privacy was available in the inner space at public gatherings. I think it is worth spending a little more time on the early waggons, as the motor-drawn trailer-caravans evolved from those early beginnings. Many of the traditional features were retained – the one begat the other.

34

Who built these increasingly elaborate waggons? Few remember their names today, yet despite there being no written contemporary history, the fame of many fine craftsman can be unearthed. In all parts of the country, wheelwrights and carpenters, who were, of course, building non-traveller horse-drawn vehicles in town and country, began to make Showmen's and Romany waggons.

Dealing with Travellers was then, as now, a different experience from dealing with farmers or tradesmen. They do not respect anyone they can 'get the better of.' I have observed in my dealings with craftsmen, how many have an air of independence, as though their skill gives them great confidence. Travellers enjoy a battle of wits – the basis of many a true tale. There have been trailer-makers who have never got on with Travellers. Some, in deed, have had to give up dealing with them, whilst others have relished the time-honoured style of dealing, and in consequence, have become famous and respected. So it may well have been in the beginning, with waggons.

Then as now, Travellers rarely get a name right. This is hardly surprising, since seeing it written is meaningless to Travellers who cannot read. So the 'Dunkin' waggon was in fact made by the revered Sam Dunton, or his son Alfred, or his grandson Albert. A 'Sam Brooks' trailer is in fact made by a Mr Sambrooks. Dunton and Sons of King's Road, Reading, favoured a style of waggon which became universally known as the 'Reading waggon' and is one of the six types of 'Gypsy Caravan,' as these waggons were called by non-Romanies. One of the classic external features was the beautiful arched axle-case, carved out in butterfly-chamfers: a ruse to lighten the load, weight always being a consideration, whilst being in every way decorative. In fact, in the wooden sailing ships and Romany waggons the two ideals of practicality and beauty were for once in perfect harmony; not often the case in design, the one frequently being sacrificed for the other.

Reading Waggon – *set within a vine of Traveller's Joy*

Although builders specialised in certain types of Romany waggon, should a traveller take one of another make to a coachbuilder, he would copy it. So there were Reading Waggons made by George Orton of Burton-on-Trent who, as George Orton and Sons and Spooner, made the equally famous Burton Waggon or Showman's; not at all confusing to the expert who was, and is, able to spot the characteristic features. This was not intentional deception, as a coachbuilder would sign his work. Walter Watts and Son of Bridgewater turned out good 'Burton' waggons; Freddy Thomas and Henry Thomas of Chertsey built stout waggons for both Travellers and Showmen in an area with a thriving population. William Wheeler of Guildford made Tradesmen's vans and tidy waggons for Travellers. One of the most famous builders of living-waggons for Showmen was Frederick Savage, one-time mayor of King's Lynn. He specialised in the larger type which had two or even three rooms and catered for the comfort of the owner by a fire-stove in two rooms and a kitchen range in the third! Many a horse must have become a victim of broken-wind, from pulling these excessive weights. There are stories still told among Circus Families of teams of horses hitched onto the waggon-horses traces, straining to get these waggons out of muddy fields. (Of all adverse conditions, snow, ice, rain, hail, blizzard, wind or fog, I think the most dreaded by itinerants, is *mud*.) Once, I nearly bought such a waggon from a lady Confectionary Stall Owner, who rejoiced in the nickname of 'The Gobstopper Queen.' This huge Showman's had fittings for a motor-lorry, a 'V' shaped iron drawbar. Savage was also a noted maker of all fairground equipment, furniture and fittings. His foundry was known to Showmen the country over.

Some building firms did not just consist of one or two carpenters. A team was needed of carpenter, wheelwright, blacksmith, carver, and sign-writer/gilder/liner-out, plus many apprentices. The larger the firm the more of these craftsmen they could employ. You may notice the absence of a designer. Although books were kept of various horse-drawn vehicle types to show to tradesmen and private customers, with many books containing thousands of drawings of every conceivable fitting, especially Saddlers' books. The makers of Travellers' waggons were proud, like the builders of farm barns, to work 'by eye.' Carving was done as the work progressed. There was a time when a firm would specialise in the carving alone. Their pieces were ordered by a builder according to what he was working on. Some ornate waggons had masses of carved pieces, all of course adding to the richness and weight. When Romanies visited a coachbuilder to place an order, they would see several waggons standing in the yard under construction or repair, and, as always, they were very interested in what someone else had ordered. This could give them the opportunity, as happens now with coach built trailers, to improve or give additions to their order, on the spot. Many a contemporary Traveller has been put in an ill humour when collecting his trailer with 'Special features,' to find another almost identical in the workshop. Some specify that no one be allowed to see in – not always easy in a busy yard. By these means, and seeing waggons gathered at Fairs and Races, fashions were born and copied, each trying to out-do the other in elaborate carving and painted embellishments. As a Traveller once remarked to me as I was painting a flying bird on the door of a scrap-man's lorry, "I spect you does it off'n yer eye." The waggons were built to scale and these measurements mostly kept to. It's rather a pity that some illustrators of 'Gypsy Caravans' do not realise that they *are* built to scale, that only certain types have all wheels running *under*, and that the shafts do *not* fit onto the footboard or porch-step, but onto the cradle or lock, and that only French waggons and Brush-Waggons (belonging to Broom-Squires) have doors at the *back*!

It's impossible to mention all the makers who took to building waggons, trolleys and carts for Travellers. Many specialised in this kind of client and rapport, and sometimes respect, grew between them. A builder might have to haggle and insist on a deposit, but he was sure of one thing, he would be paid in ready-money, cash-on-the-nail, no waiting for months for a cheque. A waggon built by George Cox in 1925, possibly a Ledge, for which he was famous, was discovered by a gentleman who took the maker to see his handiwork of so long ago. Mr Cox, who was seventy-two at the time (1966), immediately set about restoring it after which he pronounced it, "Good for another hundred years." Such waggons took him half a year to build and were given ten coats of paint and a top coat of varnish. Originally it would have cost £170. The last waggon he made in 1938 cost £2,620. One in 1981 sold for £7,000.

No! It's no good; I cannot move-on without mentioning two more very famous makers. The Tong family comprised: Tom Tong, son Joe, grandson Tom, great-grandson Tom and great-great-grandson Andrew! The original Tom could trace his Craftsmen forebears to 1823. In their Wheelwrights' shop at Kersley in Lancashire, the fine Tong waggons were built from timber seasoned on the premises and sawn from the great hardwood trees. No doubt they had a pit-saw with one man on one end of the huge saw working in the pit below ground. The Tong reputation spread, in particular the artistic son's decorations. Burton, Reading, Ledge and Bow Top waggons were built by the Tong family before the horse-drawn traffic side of the business closed. Some of the most beautiful and elaborate waggons were this family's handiwork.

Bow Top Waggon

Converted Baker's Van

Reading Waggon

*Showman's
Waggon*

The name of the die-hard waggon builders, the brothers Wright, still holds magic when mentioned in connection with Romany waggons. Father Bill, sons Herbert and Albert, all knew how to treat Travellers, acting as hosts for those who journeyed many miles for a Wright-waggon repair. From 1865 when Bill Wright started, until about 1986, they built for Travellers. Unlike a lot of their contemporaries, after the First World War, they did not turn to motor traffic. The Wright Brothers built the elaborate Potters' carts called Pot-Waggons. Travellers hawked pottery-ware from these two, or four wheeled, lightweight, richly embellished 'shops.' Hoops and canvas sheet fitted halfway along the bed, this 'tilt' converted it to an extra sleeping-room. A refinement was a bed-box with hoops, which, when covered with canvas, was in fact a barrel shaped four-poster bed. As well as being placed on the Pot-Cart, this could be placed on the ground. This was known as the York accommodation, or the 'Accommodation Cart,' an up to the minute variation of the very first horse-drawn sleeping cart. Later, the openwork or spindle sides were built of less draughty matchboard. A later development was the Yorkshire Bow, or Yorkshire Open Lot. This was so successful that they can still be found on the roads today. Man, as Nature, sometimes manages to create a perfect design.

Another Trade caravan – I use the word caravan as this and the Pot-Cart were all 'Romany caravans' – was the Brush-Waggon, specifically built for Travellers hawking brooms and brushes. Whereas the early Pot-Carts showed enticing glimpses of pottery through the spindle sides, the Brush-Waggons showed the wares stored in racks along the sides. These caravans were proper homes in which the family lived and moved and went every day through villages and to outlying farms selling useful brooms, brushes, light-weight wicker chairs, baskets and bird-cages. In order to be able to reach the wares stored inside, this waggon had an unusual design; the door was placed at the back and had fixed steps. Other than that, it had all the characteristics of a Romany waggon. There is a Gypsy caravan illustrated in the well-known book *Wind in the Willows* in the edition illustrated by Arthur Rackham. The door is *not* in the front and therefore must have been in the back, but it was not by any means a Brush-Waggon.

It is not difficult to work out that, when the Brush-Waggon had the horse in the shafts, it would not have afforded easy access had the door been in the front. Those owning this type of waggon were known as 'Broom-Squires.' For many rural people they were the only source of domestic paraphernalia. This would have included rush mats, used as kneeling mats for scrubbing floors. Some lightweight but bulky articles were carried on the roof, which, like some early waggons, had no skylights. To keep these articles in place, a rail ran round the edge of the roof. A similar small spindle-rail, once used round stoves and shelves in ships and Narrow-boats, is still fitted in some Traveller's trailer-caravans. I have put in a few myself – a bolt goes from under the shelf or ledge up into each stanchion along the rail, which is chromed. Regarding the sides of the Brush-Waggon, on every available space, spindle-racks and even glass-fronted cases were built, in which brushes and smaller items were displayed. The lower racks above the back wheel were arched, and this gave the Brush-Waggon, together with the door in the back, a slight resemblance to French waggons. A ladder was carried for reaching up to the roof racks and top spindle-racks. An added refinement was a rounding sheet of wet-proofed material that was thrown over the whole at night or in bad weather, leaving a slit for the door. Sheets, usually of white, un-proofed, cotton duck – which I have used to restore old waggon roofs – well bedded down with linseed oil and paint, were often used to cover, almost completely except for the window, new or newly painted waggons. This was to protect them from our old enemy the sun, which shrinks wood when the waggon is stationary. We always covered the wheels on the sun-side to prevent the iron-bonds becoming loose as the villies shrank. These sun-sheets can still be seen on Showmen's and Circus trailers. Some Travellers have mud-sheets made, which are hung across the front of the trailers, for protection on the road. So it is interesting to note that such old traditions carry on into the twentieth century. The Brush-Waggon is the rarest type of waggon and was thought to be extinct, but I recently heard of a re-discovered one in the hands of a waggon-builder and painter at Selbourne.

The more hilly country of the North gave birth of the lightweight Bow Top. The front and back is of rib and matchboard, with decorative carving and chamfered ribs, the shape rounded like a barrel, so it is also known as the Round-Barrel Waggon. The roof, following this rounded profile, is of canvas, green or blue, bearing a fleeting resemblance to the 'Prairie Schooner Ships' of the early American settlers. Here it is generally accepted as a romantic type of waggon, and features much in artistic compositions of Gypsy encampments. We once owned a Bill Wright Bow Top of about 1905, which I had to restore! I remember getting a blacksmith to make two new S-irons for the front; these supported the ledge that was built out over the wheels like a Ledge-Waggon. To my mind it is one of the most successful waggon designs. On the practical side, you can keep further into the kerb with no roof gutter to damage on overhanging trees. The latter is, incidentally, why all waggon chimneys are on the offside - artists of Gypsy subjects please note! When you enter any waggon, the fire-stove is on the left hand side. By careful observation you can avoid dreadful mistakes. One of the most disrespectful efforts on Hippy horse-drawn vehicles, is a *cranked* chimney, protruding anywhere and then going upward *outside* the width of the vehicle; as pathetically awful as putting a figurehead on the stern of a sailing ship!

The correct position of the fire stove in trailers continued until some thoughtless builder actually put the stove on the near side. This reduced window space on the 'side to London,' and resulted in sooty particles falling on visitors. Travellers like their trailers drawn up so that the door is not facing a hedge or wall. For a house-dweller it would be like the front drive going up to the *back* or kitchen door.

The Open Lot can be called the Yorkshire Bow, which causes confusion to those studying the subject. It is, as I said before, an elaboration of the four-wheeled Potter's Cart, with a back similar to the Bow Top, ditto the roof. The front had a crown-board (this is the piece across the top of the door) which, with the lower door-panel, lent itself to carving of special significance to the owner and carver. There were side-panels and two carved pillars, a dipped front-board but no foot-board. The driver rode high up with a comfortable view. With such an excellently light waggon, it was hardly necessary to get down on hills. I remember how we and other Travellers trotted up hills (horses left to choose their own pace will choose to do this, preferring a quick nap to a slow pull), with smoke coming out of the chimney in puffs and the birdcage swinging, despite the extra ties. Sheets of canvas, little curtains, closed off the front in cold weather. The inside of the roofs of canvas-covered waggons were made bright and gay by flowered cloth, then thick material, or ideally felt, was laid on top, under the canvas, which was kept tight by twelve bows starting at the ledge. Later, boards were added along the ledge for a depth of a foot or so. An iron plate with a hole in it allowed the iron chimney through and kept sparks from the canvas. The most noteworthy feature of the Open Lot is that it can be a conversion, sometimes made up on the bed of a trolley, and sometimes from a four-wheel tradesman's vehicle, which also made a useful hawking, rag or scrap cart. We had one in the days when Dominic drove the waggon and I followed in the cart, allowing for more possessions and two horses for emergencies.

On the hills around Dorset we would often see a square version which became known as the Dorset Open Lot, not to my mind as elegant as the Bow, with much less in the way of added carving, but again built out over the wheels of the trolley, dray or cart, since the beds of these were not wide enough for the six foot sleeping beds across the back, from side to side, where, without exception, all waggon beds should be.

As the coachbuilders turned to the motor-drawn Showmen's living-trailers and Pullman cars, Travellers were forced to repair their own waggons; this led to one or two taking up the trade as full-time waggon builders, static of course. As I know, carpentry is difficult on the road, so building a waggon, wheels and top would not be possible. I recall an occasion when we encamped on a wide green cut-off down a very quiet lane, full of Wiltshire summer flowers. I was working on a Dorset Square Bow to which I had added a new sheet (canvas tilt-cover) having primed the front and back wood which had been taken off (this pins down the edges of the sheet). I was halfway through applying an undercoat to these woods, which, with a top coat, waterproofs them before nailing them back on, the woods standing up against the hedge. An old Landrover appeared round the bend and stopped in the track to the field gateway alongside the waggon.

Restoration of a Dorset Square Bow

A stockily built man in a cap and dealer's smock extricated his large black boots and came towards me, scowling and waving his arm. I went to meet him, smiled and said, 'Good morning,' which can infuriate those who neglect such courtesies. I asked after the health of an elderly Farmer we were on nodding terms with, who lived further down the lane and whom we had not seen for two years. Somewhat put out by this knowledge of someone in his area, he realised that I may not be as bad as the waggon and grazing horse had led him to believe. He said he was the brother of the man who owned the field behind us, who did not like Gypsies. Seeing us he had stopped on his brother's behalf. Showing him the painted wood, I explained that it was not possible to move with the paint still wet without spoiling them and the canvas. One thing led to another until we were at the back of the waggon and I pointed out the back window shutters I had made with the louvre-boards set at an angle. The idea is that the rain cannot get in but air can, so that the sash-cord windows put in Showmen's waggons and Reading waggons, among others, could be opened when the shutters were across, but that this was lost on hinged-opening windows. At this stage a bantam hen emerged from the ditch at our feet, followed by her brood. My visitor asked if I had any for sale. Fearing that he was after farmyard bantams which are usually out-crossed and oversized, I said I only had Old English Game pure bred or a trio of Golden Sebrights. At the mention of this beautiful breed his eyes lit up. He said that he and his wife had some Silver, Amhurst and Golden pheasants. Being the daughter of a Keeper she had reared English pheasants at home and was now very anxious to obtain some fancy bantams.

The result of this initially unpromising meeting was a good sale of bantams, a future sale of quail, which I was expecting due to previous barter with a bird-keeper, and a promise that I could have a pair of old carriage-lamps and a pair of gig-lamps. "What about your brother," I asked. "I'll deal with him," he replied, so I returned to my task more relaxed than before. Potentially, every passing vehicle is a possible threat. Far from freedom, it is a life of anxiety and tension. The fact that the Council, and not a Landowner, owns verges and off-cuts has little to do with the law as practised by those immediately concerned.

Any major restoration of a waggon is ideally best left to the time when one is in a place long enough to do it. During the years of harassment and moving-on, for those like us who move all the year round and are not on a summer jaunt, it is no use waiting for this ideal time; as soon as a waggon came our way in a deal, if it needed doing-up, I immediately began to do it. It might be as well to remember that, at that time, they were not museum pieces: one did not search for wood of the right tree, and they had often been worked on before by all kinds of hands. Only those not living in a waggon during the repairs had the luxury of stripping them down to the bare bed as it were. This is not to say that I ever repaired with either hardboard or plywood. I was careful

44

not to spoil further a good waggon; I have too much respect for the old craftsmen. I greatly regret that I had no place where I could leave any waggon or vehicle under cover. They would be worth a great deal today.

The quail deal led to my long line of fancy pheasants. The offspring of these started the stock of fancy fowl on a smallholding, where they are still reared. Whenever we were in that area, Farmer 'Bigboots'' brother allowed us to stop by his gateway in the green lane....until the farm was auctioned and yet one more pleasant stop became a memory.

The evolution of Travellers' living waggons was hampered by a little considered but important fact – horsepower. Showmen have always used powerful vehicles as, to them, getting heavy equipment to pre-arranged sites on time is the objective; whereas for the Traveller no such need existed. Although the trap, trolley and light cart were the forerunner of the private car, useful for going calling or shopping, only a very limited mileage could be done every day. It was not possible to be near to a good calling area every day. Showmen had some idea of the lengths of their stay, whereas Travellers were moved-on at a moment's notice, sometimes when the women folk were out hawking and unaware of the fact!

Ready to Go

Since this chapter was written two very good books have been published on the subject of traditional Romany waggons. *The English Gypsy Caravan* by C H Ward-Jackson and Denis E Harvey (1986), and *Romany Relics* by John Barker and Peter Ingram (2010). In the latter, full colour photographs show all the classic horse drawn waggons and vehicles. All the famous coach-builders are represented. We were presented with a copy – just as well since all copies rapidly sold. At £75 it was worth every penny. I cannot praise the book highly enough.

A fine example of a Bow Top waggon, built by Hirst Brothers in 1918, and restored by Peter Ingram - seated on the steps

The elegant Reading waggon

Chapter Five

The Motorised Turnout

We'll leave the Showmen on an eager road to their winter quarters, where their craftsmen can repair and re-paint their large Living-waggons, mend equipment and have a well-earned rest, and follow the hesitant beginnings of the Motorised Traveller, calling not a little, upon personal experience. At first there were no custom-built Living trailer-caravans. By now you will have realised that we have our own names for things, places and people, which is quite apart from the Romany language. Scholars may learn much *Romani*, but without being able to use the nicknames and old and new phrases they could not communicate.

So, with an often sad farewell to the faithful waggon-horse, some being put out to graze on land belonging to settled down Travellers as an 'insurance' rather like the oil-lamps always kept in old cottages with 'new electrics,' ordinary touring caravans became trailer homes, and very uncomfortable they were. They lacked any over-wintering features and, of course, all the beautiful and colourful rococo decorations which are features of the Ledge, Reading and other famous waggons. It was a visual shock to miss every inch of space being carved or painted. The well made furniture, the traditional lay-out, the cabinets for china, cupboards for clothes and the lace and velvet bed-covers, all exchanged for stark reality of the then contemporary tourer, by contrast so plain and sparse: no lovely iron fire-stove as the focal point of comfort and warmth, no colours or glitter.

There were small cupboards, mostly roof lockers, tiny wardrobes that were damp, storage for bedding under bunks, non-insulated flooring and long ugly railway-carriage seats. The wardrobes were on the wheel-housing cutting down the length. Some Travellers installed a small stove in a wardrobe, putting a chimney up through the roof. I recall how *bright colours* were favoured for the early Travellers' trailers, so much were the ornate waggons missed. Later these vivid hues became the trademark of the Welsh and Irish, as other Travellers began a period of more refined and subtle taste. Then the *Berkeley* and *Bluebird* arrived, the name of the latter being instrumental in its popularity. They were both sixteen feet long, and what amazing experience it was actually to be able to *walk* thirteen feet or so, after living in a waggon with only seven feet of walking space at most. The *Fairholme* and the *Sprite* were both sixteen feet, but there were twenty-two foot models, the size of the *Palladin*, also available in this early period, and more models were soon to follow.

In the mid-fifties things looked up, as caravan makers became aware of an entirely new market. After a few trailers with traditional and deleted features had been noticed in the Trade, such makers as *Siddel, Freeman, Lunedale, Jubilee* and *Eccles* made trailers especially for Travellers, of sixteen, eighteen and twenty-two feet. There were also trailers called the *Coventry Steel Knight* and the *Warwick Knight*, I remember, designed by an imaginative Mr Lown of Newport Pagnall. These were mainly bought by Showmen. I would dearly have loved one; they are worth a mention for their interiors, which were quite different from any previous designs, and, of course, for the ribbed polished-steel and straight-sided exterior shape, reminding one in colour of the still famous American *Silver Bullet*. I gazed wishfully at these but we could not afford one. The name of *Carlight* will be familiar to all holiday caravanners, considered to be the Rolls Royce of caravans. The design was dedicated to a structure of an 'ever-lasting' exterior of the most exacting craftsmanship, with a distinct shape and incorporating the famous 'Mollycroft' roof previously used on waggons and Pullman cars and on early American railway coaches, although in the latter case the raised roof ran from end to end. This feature took the fancy of those Travellers able to afford this splendid caravan. Inside, the woodwork was a tribute to the cabinet-maker's art. The lay-out design was naturally geared to making the touring holiday of those householders used to gracious living, an enjoyable, and not a 'roughing-it' experience. Carlight retained their distinctive design, and cocktail cabinets, and separate kitchen, while other makers fluctuated. Some years later Carlight made some trailers for Travellers with several interior alterations more suited to a different lifestyle from that of their original customers.

From the early sixties and for the next ten years, various other firms began to make trailers for Travelling People. They were put on the general market, but, as in the old days of ordering horse-drawn waggons 'to order' from a coach-builder, trailers were now ordered with specifications down to the smallest detail, on payment of a small deposit. Then, after a deal, either with a few Makers who would do this or more usually with a Traveller's trailer-dealer (many such sprang up, sometimes from the Motor-Trade and already dealing with this demanding type of customer able to pay in cash; some of the Romany blood themselves, some disliking Travellers but glad to take their money). Fortunes were made and lost by dealers whose businesses collapsed through a mountainous stock of old trailers taken in part-exchange, the 'Super-mountain Dealers.' This is known as 'chopping-in.' A few dealers made too great an allowance on an old trailer, in order to persuade Travellers to 'have a deal.' However old or out-dated a trailer might be, there was always someone worse off, ready to part-exchange their second, third or fourth-hand home for one a little better, and, hopefully, thus moving another rung up the ladder. In this hope they were sometimes a little optimistic. I have had much difficulty in explaining this core feature of the Travelling life to those academics and the art-fringe, who are comfortably off, but prefer to drive ancient vehicles in a kind of inverted snobbery. All such folk need to do, is to recognise that Travellers do not have an annual wage to rely upon. Their trailers and vehicles are their only assets.

The first days of exchanging hooves for wheels were difficult times for all: great struggles for a proud people, wrestling with such enormous changes. Old motors coughed and spluttered their way up hills, those in them tense and worried, engines steaming at the top. Puzzled owners peered into the mysterious depths of oily engines without the faintest idea of any of the mechanics. Handed-down knowledge of horses was now of no use whatsoever. Old trailer wheels sheered off, jockey-wheels rarely worked from rough treatment. You were lucky if you got two out of four trailer-legs to descend. No one bothered about the brakes or lights. The stocks of old trailers in the dealers' yards improved as the ever resilient Traveller bettered himself. As more and more were able to place orders for *new* trailers, the ones part exchanged for them were in better condition. There was a time when only the Irish, who came over here in vast numbers with anything that could just about be towed, were customers for the 'rubbish' stuff – English Travellers would not live in them – so again the yards became full of old battered out-dated 'sticking' stock. Much later Irish Travellers came to roam all over the country, some good, some bad, most of them becoming wealthy and flash, owning new trailers, but a few remaining 'rough and ready.'

The greatest consideration is for a new purchase to be in *fashion*. People accept that their car will devalue because of its age, but fail to realise that exactly the same is true of trailers. Trailer and vehicle must be in fashion, not obsolete. The 'fly' dealer learns this early. I find that most people who have written about 'the Gypsies' have no idea of the importance of the age, make or fashion of Romany possessions, which is such an important factor as to be, and to have been, the main influence in the nomadic life of which I write – with long awaited truth. How is it possible that self-styled 'experts' have failed to comprehend this? Many of the better condition but outmoded trailers are bought by Showmen and the Fairground fraternity. Showmen do not seem to be quite so dogged by the pressing need to be in fashion. This is the reversal of waggon-days when Travellers were pleased to have the smaller of the Show-waggons, Showmen's cast-offs, which gave rise to the fallacy that many such Burton (or other waggon on Chertsey 'unders,' with wheels running under and two windows on the side) was a genuine 'Gypsy Caravan,' and as such are innocently purchased by householders to put on the lawn as a summerhouse. As if regretting their daring, the new owners paint the waggon dark green or brown to 'blend in' – they mustn't let the neighbours think they are Gypsies! It is even sadder to see a Showman's exhibited at some café or Garden Centre actually labelled 'Gypsy Caravan,' revealing that little research has been done by the owners of a sometimes rare example, even though they claim to be interested in the subject.

23 ft long.
Formic interior.

The late Mr Vickers' (of Morecambe)
'Lunedale' Special.

In the world of trailers, Mr Vickers of White Lund Road, Morecombe is probably the name that evokes most respect, alas now tinged with nostalgia since his famous firm ceased production in the late 1970s. Until then his Lunedale trailer – a name that never caught on, it being better known as the 'The Vickers' – was supreme. As I have said before, all makers should have been more careful before naming each model. If a name does not prove popular, unless a nickname is substituted, as in this case, the trailer will fail also! Beginning at the modest sixteen feet long and progressing through to twenty-three feet (outside the legal towing limit by a foot, but by then most large models were twenty-three feet). Vickers' workshop produced increasingly heavier trailers with progressively more outside and inside ornamentation. The former was the consequence of the addition of sheets of stainless steel to the bowed and shaped ends, with centre waist-strips along the sides in a distinctive downward curve. Onto these, coloured strips were embedded in polished alloy, on which decorative ends were placed. There were scuff-boards fore and aft of the most elaborate designs, with bands of these strips both vertical and horizontal. Not one grab-handle but two, not one headlamp but two on each side, were the order of the day once it was known that Mr Vickers would do *anything* you wanted. He was reputed to stand with a notebook calmly adding a hundred pounds for every 'extra' a customer ordered! Travellers queued to order and waited with eager anticipation for the delivery of these amazing glittering monsters, the like of which there will never be again. I fondly hope that some museum will have bought examples with an eye to their becoming vintage trailers; and I hope they will not be labelled 'Showmen's'! Fearing to offend Romanies some makers referred to them as Showman's Trailers, adding to the confusion, and the notice-boards at Epsom read 'Showmen,' meaning Romanies! From the first modest little Lunedale of the late fifties with leaded windows, to the grapes and leaves cut-glass windows of the late seventies models, this form had great influence on the lives of the Travelling People and will go down in their history, by truthful writers.

Contrary to what people think, Travellers work hard. The turnout, which reflects a man's ability, has always been of extreme importance. To those non-Travellers who have taken to the roads for a few years, seeing it as an alternative to the rat-race, and thought themselves suitably dressed in ragged trousers or long skirts and woolly jumpers with a newly acquired waggon, it must have been a shock to learn that however rough a Romany Traveller may be, it is never his intention to remain so. It is the aim of all of them to better themselves. I recall an American religious missionary speaking to me. "Do I look too smart?" he asked. "I don't want you to think I put myself above you." I assured him that his suit and tie were a better advocate for him than the out of place pseudo-Indian dresses and shirts of the other religious group present at the fair. I added that both groups were wasting their time calling on Travellers.

When one member of a family says he has ordered a Vickers, the rest of the men feel obliged to achieve this goal and, spurred on by their wives as there is often rivalry between sisters, the men work even harder. Should a family pull-on with more than one Vickers, those already there in older models feel deflated. Women flock to see inside a new trailer almost before the newcomers can unhitch. The interiors of these palaces on wheels have to be seen to be believed. Not for them the straight walls of a *gaujo* trailer; everything has to be curved and bowed. Every edge of every drawer and cupboard is covered in Formica, as are all the surfaces, including the ceiling, even the inside of the cupboard doors. It all began with Formica-covered kitchen work-surfaces until one Traveller asked for the kitchen walls to be covered as well. Someone went one better and had the whole trailer done, after which *all* trailers were 'all Formica.' In the beginning, the only obtainable Formica design was an uninspired fiddly design of a non-colour used in the kitchens of tourers. Better and more colourful designs followed. Sometimes more than one design was used in a trailer, but this looked as if the Coachbuilder had run out of one design. The favoured design was Milano-marble, white and clean looking with marble veins.

Beshlie and Trailer Interior

Silver, china and glass ornaments were displayed in glass cabinets, bow-fronted, like the drawer fronts. All glass and china cabinets had strip lights and were backed with mirrors sending many images into other mirrors all through the trailer. Mirrors on the mantle-shelf and full length mirrors on the wardrobe doors were spoon-edged and fastened with beautiful flowers of mirror glass petals, sometimes in contrasting colours. These flowers had a centre of diamond faceted glass which hid the mirror screws. I once had a trailer which had every locker and glass front cut with grapes and vine leaves, a design popular on the crown boards of horse-drawn waggons. Flower baskets, another popular design, were in the centre of the wardrobe mirrors. The cost of the mirrors alone was two thousand pounds. It would be many times more today. Equal to, and it's debatable whether better than, a Vickers, was another splendid trailer built at the Lakeland Caravan Centre, Penrith, called the Westmorland Star. The 'Star' bit was memorable but the Westmorland was a mouthful for Travellers, so it was rather charmingly christened 'West Morning Star,' and this name stuck. This more evocative name assured the trailer years of success. These two super trailers became status symbols. The Westmorland Star started at twenty feet with a few of the last twin-axle models going up to twenty-five feet, ignoring the legal towing limit!

Both these firms went out of production, possibly due to inflation and impossible rising costs. It was a struggle to buy them in the seventies. The powerful motor-lorry needed to tow them was also a consideration; they were really heavy trailers. The heavier the trailer the lower it sinks into soft ground, putting a great strain on the vehicle pulling such a dead weight with no firm purchase. Running wheels onto boards on arrival is not the Travellers' way, although they are likely to dig a trench on the upside of a hill in order to level a trailer, causing some damage to turf on Epsom Racecourse. On take-off there is a strain on the sunken wheel emerging from the trench. A pity that makers never seem to bear in mind the fact that Travellers' trailers do not lead a genteel life on tarmac and hard surfaces. While the later twin-axle models had the advantage of steadier towing and were better puncture-wise, campsites abroad are on hard standing, so designers did not consider the problems that arise when Travellers have to back into, or out of, awkward places and small spaces. Whereas the single-axle trailer can be lifted up manually by the drawbar and turned round on the spot by two men, or one man using the jockey wheel, the same is not the case with four wheels. Tales are told of tyres coming off, or, as is often made necessary by uneven ground, moving the trailer sideways in order to hitch-on at a level patch, etc. A jockey wheel will only screw up so far, which can be awkward if, through uneven ground, the vehicle ball-hitch is then above the trailer draw bar. Having a longer wheel-housing, the extra two wheels also take up more room inside the trailer, decreasing valuable cupboard space.

'Vickers' and 'West Morning Star' interior mirrors echoed the contrasting colour schemes by not only being cut and etched, but by having mirror glass of a bright colour, or contrasting colour, let-in as a decorative frame. The chosen colour would often be carried on in cut-glass flower vases and baskets, and cut-glass mushroom-shaped light shades on lamps which had crystal drops much like a chandelier. Glimpsing some Prussian blue vases in a window would mean that the second, or contrasting, colours would also be blue. The leather buttonback seating with rounded backs might also be blue with blind tassels and fringes to match. The most popular seating was that called the horseshoe seat. This was at the front end, with curved backrests along the sides. It pulled out at night to form the master bed. There were drawers underneath for bedding. It is interesting to note that in one of the contemporary foreign trailers, the Weippert (known as the more easily pronounced 'Whippet'), which enjoyed a place in Travellers' fashions, there is a similar but plainer version. The West German Makers proclaimed of their creation, "*In allen drei Spezial-Modellen steht im grosszuegigen Wohnbereich eine bequeme Rundcouch mit einem Couchtisch vor einem grossen Panoramafenster.*"* Weippert also incorporated in these holiday caravans several features which appeal to Travellers: richly embossed lace curtains, and framed and panelled woodwork reminiscent of some waggons. The glass-fronted china cabinets had coloured, opaque glass, but it could be replaced. They had sliding doors to a permanent bedroom, a decorative bed-head, etc – quite unlike any UK holiday tourer.

The Weippert exterior, while following the then current fashion for plain and more refined designs, had coloured plastic stripes. These trailers lacked the graceful peaked roof that gave extra headroom inside. 'Whippets' had a novelty value, and were rather expensive. When the 'Vickers' and the 'West Morning Star' living-trailers reached their greatest weight and price, rising living costs began to affect Travellers and the heavy lorries gave way to lighter vehicles which were unable to tow such heavy trailers. It will not have escaped your notice that the lives of the Romanies are completely bound up with their vehicles and living-trailers. Failing to grasp this important point, someone once asked me why I spoke so much about the lorries!

Gradually, for a variety of reasons, Ford Transit or Bedford vans began to supersede the larger lorries. Goods and outside possessions can be carried under cover in a van. A couple of less expensive and lighter weight trailers then entered the market, the 'Aaro,' seventeen feet and twenty-two feet models, and the 'Astral' at twenty-two feet. These more economic trailers gained great popularity. One year at Epsom it was all 'Aaros' and 'Astrals.' The Astral Company at Stoneferry, Hull, almost scooped the market with the brilliantly named 'Lavengro' – only the second company to name a product in *Romani*. In 1978 Aaro brought out a twin-axle model with a good and memorable name, 'The Travella.'

---

*All three of these Special Models have a built-in wraparound sofa and coffee table in the living area. There are attractive and generous panoramic windows.

This had a straight line of stainless steel across the front and double grab-handles, and was seventeen or twenty three feet in length. In 1979, however, the manufacturer embellished the design of the stainless steel front forming a kind of bow-front effect with the added splendour of a full width chromium plated grab handle. It also had steel on the sides to the height of the splashboard front, wider trim bands above, and let-in square front lights. Naturally these improving extras made the earlier model 'out-dated' with consequent loss in value.

By improving and altering the exteriors each year, makers ensured new orders. Just as a number plate gives away a car's age, so these details date one's trailer and, of course, devalue the earlier versions. Trailers, like vehicles, have a 'book' price and devalue at an alarming rate. When people say accusingly, "Travellers don't have to pay rates," they do not think of the loss of value each year of their possessions, whereas property values rise. Astrals began with a green band model with single wheels, 'The Ranger,' and after that the aptly named 'Lavengro,' whose interior I liked, the furniture having scrollwork embellishments. I sometimes wondered if Astral used the ideas I once sent to Mr Kirk after I had seen their first efforts, which were not Travellers' style. I sent an improved layout and drawing of an exterior with scroll decoration. Then 'The Varda' arrived, which in *Romani* means waggon. Astral have now stopped making Travellers' style trailers.

Both Aaro and Astral introduced an end-bedroom, where a double bed, wardrobe and dressing table filled this small end-room. It was not only a novelty, but practical, as it saved the woman having to fold up and stow the bedding, then make up the bed again at night. If someone was ill, they could stay in bed with some privacy. The bed was much like a horse-drawn waggon bed, only larger and lower, with a fashion for satin ruched and frilled bedspreads, and flounced and frilled matching pillows. All this was on view through a seven foot wide side window and from the lounge when the doors were slid back: being able to have this display endeared this make of caravan to Travellers. This was the forerunner of the Island-Bed, which, back to the end the window, stood away from the walls. There was a bedside cupboard each side with a lamp with silk shade. Cushion-sellers at Fairs who cater for Travellers, whose cushions can be very costly, found an equally lucrative market for pillowcases and bed-cushions, slipover covers, and day covers for pillowcases.

During long wintertime stops, Travellers place orders for cushions. These are encased in zipped plastic covers. If this sounds strange, I had better explain that these cushions are not at all like the scatter-cushions on settees in houses, but velvet, rich brocade or duchess satin, all ruched and frilled, and cost about forty pounds each. Six are required for two trailer seats. Travellers know how to sit on a trailer seat, the cushions being propped in the corners above windowsill height, so that they can easily be seen, but just as easily slip down and be ruined. A non-Traveller may not be aware of this and happily might lean back, or even sit upon a cushion which cannot be ironed. At Epsom Races we all keep an eye open for the 'Cushion-Lady.' She also sells elaborate 'over-pillowcases' which match the bed covers and are slipped over the pillows which can then be put on the bedcover. One can also buy lace-edged bed sheets. These purchases are made in front of an admiring circle of customers, whole families coming away with armfuls of new bedding.

The Cushion Sales Lady

I can remember when clothes were washed in a cauldron of bubbling soapy-water over the outside fire, stirred and lifted with a stick. Washing was lucky to get one rinse, the water having to be carried from afar. Today the satin sets must go to a cleaners, all other articles being taken to the 'Bagwash' as it is still called. Several women will go together in one car. One will mind several washing machines while the lucky others take a look around the shops. I have always washed our clothes myself, although it is not easy. It is the drying which is more difficult, especially when everything has just been pegged out and we suddenly have to move. In Travellers' trailers there are no sinks or washbasins, it is considered unhygienic. Stainless-steel washbasins on steel stands are kept outside. 'Bagwash' laundry is brought back to hang up and dry – towels, sheets, teacloths. "Haven't you been busy!" remarked one Social Worker innocently to me recently.

Returning to trailers, another newcomer was the 'Portmaster,' seventeen and twenty-two feet models, made at St Andrew's Loch, Hull. Along the same lines as the 'Aaro,' it continued the preference for the exterior white with stainless-steel trim. With twin axles and over eight feet wide, it contained the usual requirements such as a *full-sized* cooker, costing two hundred and eighty pounds, run on Calor Gas, a refrigerator, all-Formica kitchen, laminated interior elsewhere in wood-grain finish, and a large solid fuel fire-stove with an airing cupboard above. These big fires, of tremendous weight, were made to heat six or seven radiators in a house. Travellers all feel the cold and like to be warm. Many such a stove has set fire to a trailer, and almost every second-hand one has the firebricks cracked. Stoves are stoked to capacity. The fuel is often the 'three-penny bit' or the 'eggs' variety, and the heat is overpowering. There are vents above the fire but makers have no idea just how hot the room will get. The air vents in the floor under the cooking stoves provide unwanted draughts in cold windy weather, however. We once owned *two* 'Portmasters' at the same time; it was the first time I had a studio, but it was a short lived experience, as Dominic had to make double journeys, as I cannot drive, and fuel prices even then were rising. I kept the later model with the rounded stainless-steel drawbar cover and the all-across grab-handles and left the other one with our favourite dealer to be sold on commission. A flaw in 'Portmasters' was that none of the mattresses could be turned. One side was sprung and upholstered but the reverse was wood! Whose crazy idea was that I wonder? One trailer we had, I forget the make, was even more idiotic. The end seat, that makes up into a double-bed, usually incorporates several back cushions, but this one had *fixed* backs so needed *extra* cushions. These were stored during the day in, of all places, both wardrobes!!! Where was one supposed to hang clothes?

Lots of deals are now concluded over the 'phone. The customer is told by the dealer of his present stock and what he is expecting in, giving details such as the all-important date of manufacture (which cannot be concealed because of the giveaway extras, and the number on the drawbar), and the condition, normally immaculate. The customer then chooses a trailer as thus described. This, of course, is if the part-exchange is being negotiated for a second-hand trailer leaving the yard. Although allowances for a customer's old trailer against a *new* model are also made over the telephone, and orders placed. The dealer usually *delivers* new trailers personally, collecting the old one.......and a roll of bank-notes! A dealer's word is his bond and neither party would renege, or as Travellers say 'run word' on a deal. We recently heard of a large house and grounds, the property of a wealthy settled-down Traveller, exchanged with another Traveller for a smaller property and a trailer, without either seeing the other's property. It was nice to hear of this old-fashioned '*chop*' of modern newly built houses, man-to-man with no agents involved, and no viewing!

Whereas we always sold our waggons direct to the buyer for Travellers, there is a daily constant stream of customers and enquiries at a Traveller's dealership. People know what they want and quick decisions are made, so a dealer's commission is worth every penny in order to save weeks of 'many-minded' aggravation, during which a trailer devalues even more.

The 'Portmaster,' like all other makes of Travellers' Specials as they are called, became more and more expensive and eventually went out of production. A maker who realised the dire need for a trailer featuring the obligatory requirements, if not comfort, of Travellers at a more realistic price than the 'giants,' yet not sacrificing good workmanship, produced a trailer known as 'The Jubilee.' Again two lengths were offered, nineteen and twenty-two feet, perhaps the best trailers of the cheaper range. I remember 'The Butterfly,' 'The Queen Bee' and 'The Butterfly Special,' all nice names. I once had one made to look as much like a Vickers as possible. It was the first of its kind, and having been seen and much admired at Epsom, others were ordered and 'Jubilee' moved into the luxury and 'flash' class of living-trailers. Alas, after a few years they followed several other makes and ceased production in an increasingly difficult economic climate.

In the early nineteen-sixties the 'Knowlesley Princess,' was produced, an admirable and strongly built twenty-two footer, which became quite popular but did not 'catch on' in vast numbers in the fickle Travellers' market. Another firm achieved fame by making its own version of 'The Jubilee,' the Vickers and the Eccles 'Traveller' (not to be confused with the Aaro 'Travella').

Mr Sambrooks' trailers, from Leafield, Brownhills in Staffordshire, were well made and I am sorry never to have owned one. Many pulled-on to various places where we were stopping during the height of their popularity in the late nineteen sixties and early nineteen seventies. Travellers made many visits to Mr Sambrooks, or Mr 'Sam Brooks' as they called him, and he allowed them to stay overnight after long journeys if they were placing an order with him for a trailer. At present his trailers are out of production. I hope the family, so much in sympathy with this way of life, will start production again, as there are no Travellers' Specials in every way satisfactory, at the time of writing. Of special interest to me was that Mr Sambrooks had, in his office, a blue and gold macaw which afforded us all much pleasure.

The nineteen and twenty-three feet Marshal 'Supreme,' made by a family firm, is square shaped and sturdy, possibly the only firm in production up to the eighties whose emphasis was on quality of workmanship. It was fairly popular among Travellers with restrained or refined taste. Three Traveller trailers were produced by Buccaneer, of seventeen, nineteen and twenty-two feet, and at the time of writing they are certainly the most fashionable trailers on the scene, perhaps rivalled by the 'Roma.' Since the demise of so many coachbuilders, these firms appears to have almost captured the ever-present market for something new. Catering for all tastes, some are very 'flash' with lots of decoration on the exterior, whilst some are made plain for those who wish to travel incognito and be able to pull-in on holiday-caravan sites, during the months these are licensed.

For many years past, families often buy a second, smaller trailer referred to as the 'kitchen trailer.' This is towed by the wife or eldest child, usually with a car, and serves also as an extra bedroom and sitting-room as well as being where meals are generally cooked, thus saving the main trailer from damage, it being reserved for social use only – a splendid status symbol, unused except for grand occasions, rather like a Victorian parlour, lit up from earliest dusk, showing off the finery within. Some use quite humble tourers as kitchen-trailers, while others have those made for the Caravan Club market, such as 'The Windrush,' by the Cotswold coachbuilder, who won the Best Tourer Award in 1976, 1977 and 1978. The double-glazed fifteen footer was very suitable for cooking and quite without condensation. Foreign makes, such as the 'Adria,' and others, following continental design, had double-glazing, central heating systems, twin-axles, and colonial-style interiors of panelled woodwork. The 'Grand de Luxe' model was very popular. These tourers have an advantage over the living-trailers, as they are narrow by comparison, with the eighteen feet 'Adria' being only seven feet wide, and hence much easier to tow on narrow roads, in traffic, and in particular when pulling-in through narrow gates. It is not always the width of the gate-way that has to be considered however, as a dip in the entry path can cause the wide heavy trailers to lean suddenly and without warning to one side, colliding with the gatepost – with distressing and expensive results! The old-fashioned smaller farmer is the most likely to allow Travellers to pull in for the time allowed by Law, but he is the more likely to have old-style narrow farm gates of wood or iron, whereas the newer gates of tubular alloy construction, although looking unlovely by comparison, can be double gates, each as much as twelve feet wide in consideration of the huge combine harvesters and ever larger tractors and trailers.

A Trailer or Two – and some Pretty Dresses!

With the coming of the end-bedroom trailer, trailer-life took a further turn towards luxury of living rather than luxury of possessions. Children could be put to bed earlier, not that chatter, T.V. or activity in the living-room ever stopped small Travellers from going to sleep. It is a characteristic of Travellers to be able to sleep through anything, and at any time. The extra wardrobe in the end-bedroom afforded much needed additional space. There was space under the bed to store blanket-boxes. The new style of trailer was wider, there being five feet of space from the wardrobes to the seat opposite, and fifteen feet to walk down the trailer. This created an illusion of space. The peaked roofs were also an improvement in this respect, and dressing, an arms no longer hit the ceiling when dressing. The improved round ceiling-lights are close to the lights at evening functions, a factor overlooked by those who have never had to prepare for bright lights by fluctuating gaslights inconveniently placed at the back of one's head. The bedroom, now being at one end where the 22 ft trailer kitchen had been, the new kitchens were a small rectangle of work-surfaces and cooker opposite the door. Since this door is open, except in bad weather, the trailer-wife could see and be seen, as a great deal of time was spent in this area. Being able to see out is something house-dwellers take for granted. There is only one window in a trailer that one can see out of, when standing up. Holiday-caravan makers assume the occupants want to sit down and relax, all the windows are at sitting-height. Designing windows at this height in living-trailers makes a uniform band of glass, seen when viewing the exterior, but this does not best serve the interests of those who live within.   The kitchen, where a woman will be standing, could easily have a window at eye-level.   It is as well to consider that a house kitchen overlooking a back garden does not expect strangers to pass, whereas a trailer kitchen is vulnerable to strangers frequently passing. It is more important for the trailer-wife to be able to see what strangers are doing. Keeping an eye on children at play means the trailer mother has to bob up and down, unable to look straight out. I labour the point as it is not one that is apt to come to the mind of those not in this way of life.

Comparison between trailer and house kitchens leads to another consideration. A visitor, the first of several expected, arrived, walked through the mud outside, despite my instructions as where to park to avoid the mud, and then came straight into the trailer without wiping her feet! When the rest of the visitors arrived at the steps to see filthy carpet and mats, they probably wondered what the fuss of re-parking was all about. I could not very well say that the first, *not* so intelligent, visitor had caused the hitherto clean rugs to be covered in mud. Another habit of non-Traveller visitors is leaving something in the car, which after everyone is settled with cups of tea, they decide they need. Out they go upsetting the guard dogs and, of course, they walk in the mud in front of the car-boot and back up onto the rugs. They fail to realise that shoes should be wiped on the first mat, nearest the mud, which leaves the rest clean. Also they are not familiar with trailer doors which open outwards, unlike house doors which open in. They leave the door swinging, but it has to be hooked back on a catch if it is to remain open, otherwise it can bang-to and break the glass.

Trailers are not carpeted with any old carpets, but good quality Axminster and then a runner. While only a small area, these cost as much as a small sitting-room to buy and have fitted, there being many more irregular shapes, caused by bow-fronted cupboards, than in a straightforward room.

Another visitor, having preceded us into the trailer, had taken in walnut-sized dollops of sticky mud. The visitors who followed, dazed as most people are, by the glittering interior, trod back and forth, embedding the mud into the rug and carpet. By the time they had all been seated and cast their eyes to the floor, I was wishing I could sink under it! What does a hostess do? far too late for a dustpan and brush.

Produce a bowl of soapy water? It would need *several* clean water rinses. Use the kettle ready filled for tea? I was taught it was not the done thing to embarrass guests, yet they had come to see how we lived, and we do not live like hippies or New Age Travellers who might not differentiate between the ground outside and the interior. It is not easy; it takes self-discipline, like changing shoes for boots if you want to walk off the outside rugs

These *outside* carpets, which require constant cleaning, have a life of their own. If put down on mud, they have to be folded up mud-side out for transport. If laid on gravel, when they are taken up all the stones stick to the backs. It is understandable, I hope, that, after such trouble has been taken, one is angry if after a moments thoughtlessness, one's trailer carpet can be ruined. So, after, "Would you like to park off the mud?" I then say, "Would you like to leave your coats, hats and scarves in the car?" and then, "If there is something you wish to bring in, could you bring it now, to save another journey?" People unused to our kind of trailer life need to be shepherded. If the trailer door is the stable-door type, visitors can close the top with the lace curtain shut into the hinges, and if covered with hinge-oil it is difficult to get off.

Visitors sometimes expect some kind of banister. Finding none they grasp the glass or mirror-glass top of a sideboard just inside, or worse still, put all their weight onto the chrome towel-rail which is on the inside of the lower doer, so that when this is open and hooked onto the proper catch a tea-towel can be dried. Once the screws of the rail-ends come out they cannot be put back, as the holes are then too large, larger screws are no use as they would not go through the rail-ends. Trailer doors are not constructed of solid wood as in a house, but of thin board on panels with a narrow framework of wood which is the only fixing for any screws.

All the foregoing may seem, a boring subject to those who, although from all walks of life, prefer to live in what some term 'charming disarray,' and others term 'a tip' or squalor. A surprising number of people react against their upbringing and once free, choose the exact opposite. Travellers with all their legacy of close proximity to the elements, earth, fire, water – living in conditions not foreign to primitive man, yet with a taste far above the latter – possess a strong desire to have cleanliness about them and things of quality as opposed to trash. They have no taste for colourful cheap trinkets or tatty ornaments. I can well understand that, and I can only hope that you can, as well.

Another Vickers' Lunedale

An early Winchester Trailer

And a "vintage" Bluebird Trailer

An Eccles Traveller

An Aaro Travella

Astral Lavengro

Nuvardo Sorento

Portmaster

Dominic with a Roma "Crazy-band" Trailer

Chapter Six

Goods and Chattels

Nowadays, good quality touring caravans have small lockers for Calor Gas bottles, with doors on the outside for ease of changing the cylinders and to keep the smell outside, and are fitted with awning lockers underneath. Showmen sometimes bought site-dwellers' living-trailers and converted them. I remember one year on the way to Sussex we stopped on a lay-by at the other end of which were some Showkeepers. One man was doing just such a conversion, putting the trailer body on another chassis and building lockers all round underneath. On our way back the others had gone, but he was still there with the work nearly finished. I remembered the conversions and repairs I had done on roadsides. At that time, Showkeepers were allowed to stop almost anywhere without question, as long as they had the Showmen's Guild card, gained by inheritance, whereas we were moved-on, carpentry half-finished or not.

Clearly extra space was needed if only to keep some of the outside things under cover. Tents always being part of Romany life, the square-framed or cottage-tent put in an appearance one Derby week. By the next Races there were hundreds of them! A wooden frame was joined on three sides by cross-spars which were bolted, thus enabling it to fold together like garden trellis. When opened, four spars of wood, each with a flat metal end with a hole in it, dropped over the four spikes, one in each corner post, surmounted by a frame-work of four roof-timbers, rising in the centre fitted. Over this frame heavy-duty canvas, standard green colour, was heaved with no little effort. The edges of this roof were scalloped or deckled and hung down eight inches. This hid the fastenings at the top of the walls. Later square-frames became easier to erect and were obtainable in a choice of colours. One of mine was the first to be blue with red edging to the scallops; it was the blue canvas as used on some canvas-topped waggons. Over the metal prongs at the four corners one placed finials of turned wood, about five inches high, and these held the eight guy-ropes. The centre finial had no ropes. My tent had red ropes and the bantam boxes and dog kennels were painted red and blue to match.

The best cottage tents were made at Martock in Somerset and became universal. Sizes began at six by six feet and went up to twelve by twelve feet, which could become a complete home with cooker, television, table and chairs, solid-fuel stove, all on a carpeted wooden floor, which was made in sections. Travellers spent more time in these tents than in their trailers. Even settled-down Travellers had them in their yards for sitting in and entertaining visitors. With this second home, men had somewhere they could gather, leaving the trailer to the women.

Cottage Tent from Martock

Previously, if a man came home from work and found two or three women visitors talking to his wife, the women would get up and leave, as is the custom. After all, the man wants his 'tea' and Travellers consider it bad manners to watch a family eat, unless they have been invited to share a meal. Barry Cockcroft, a Yorkshire Television Producer and Director, was making a film of a Traveller family with a horse-drawn waggon, and having arranged to film the wife cooking a meal, was nonplussed when the family got up from the fire before eating it. He was not to know that Travellers are sensitive about meals. An old-fashioned family eating bacon outside would eat it on white bread, they would not have the plates and cutlery that trailer-Travellers would have, and they knew that many Romanies would see the film. They would be ashamed at such an audience.

If some men come to visit a Travelling man, after making them tea, his wife would slip out and go up into another couple's trailer, however inconvenient. In such circumstances, tents, providing a second room, proved very useful.

Tent designs altered. Tent-covers were made of plastic material in all colours and patterns, stripes or flowers. The heavy wood frames were replaced by lightweight metal. These had to be covered at the joins, or they rubbed holes in the covers. Some tents were cheaper with cotton duck, untreated, which let the rain in. The peaked top gave way to a flat roof and the tent lost its charm. Metal frames were not liked, but they were light. Plastic tents were made by A. Bull and Co Ltd of Guildford, Surrey, among others. Travellers who had discovered these to be non-waterproof were told they could have their money back. We had one and the first storm ruined everything within.

An example of Tent Material – flamboyant and colourful

Small tow-vans or converted horse-boxes then became very fashionable. They were fitted out as kitchens, the work being done by expert kitchen-fitters. These were less trouble than erecting a cottage-tent.

Another tradition from the waggon days was the guard dog. At one time, at stopping-places and large gatherings such as Races and Fairs, the air reverberated to the barks of dozens of guard dogs as the race-horses were exercised and vendors of all kinds, including newspaper sellers, unaware how few readers they would find, made their way into the trailer field and moved among the sleeping Travellers shouting their wares. Lurchers crossed with collies or Alsatians doubled as guards for most Travellers, though some favoured 'nippy' Jack Russells or border terriers tethered by the trailer as a 'ward.' Alsatians and Alsatiancrosses have always been regarded as the best guards, mainly because of the fear that most people have of them. In the confined spaces of the Racetracks, families cannot space themselves as may wish with regard to neighbours' trailers and vehicles etc, as they can in other encampments. Fairs and Races are considered to be different, like the proverbial British on holiday abroad, people and children behave differently – one reason why they find it so exhausting. This confined space causes problems for those with fierce guards. It is not always possible to put some object at every 'corner,' which is actually a circle, of the reach of the dog's chain to avoid people walking into this danger area. The dog's area is soon visible after a few hours by the circle of trodden earth. Notices appear – BEWARE DOG.

Trailer dogs or pets were once in fashion and every trailer had its Yorkie, Maltese or Chihuahua, the smaller the more prized. These minute 'bits of fur' could be seen running loose among the traffic where ever trailers rested; amazingly many did survive to reach old age! Each lurcher, guard-dog or ward has its own kennel known as a 'dog-box,' made to the correct size and often painted to match the turnout. Some Travellers instructed carpenters to make twin dog-boxes, a double kennel side by side. I have lost count of how many I have made, using tongued and grooved six-inch board or marine ply for lightness. I make a wire door for closing when the dog is on a journey. Other kennel makers do not recognise this need. Several times we have been lucky enough to save a dog from being hanged, when in the excitement of arrival at a stopping place it had jumped over the side of the lorry, with the chain being too short to reach the ground. I once stood holding the weight of an Alsatian in such a predicament until two men walked by and lifted it back up. Once, when *en route*, the un-chained guard dog on the lorry ahead of us was barked at by a dog in a garden. It lost its balance and fell off as we stopped at traffic lights. It flew over a garden gate, so we all started up and turned left, then left again at the end of the road. To our astonishment the dog reappeared, jumping over another garden gate, and ran alongside the trailer, which had to stop for a slow moving milk float. The dog jumped on to the drawbar and back on to the lorry, with the owners still unaware of the event! Lorry drawbars are made to order and are often wide and long, making a useful step which is covered in chequer plate. The corners are often cut off and rounded, for a leg knocked against a sharp edge would be painful. It also improves the appearance.

Since the days of Landrovers, of which we had several in keeping with other Travellers of that era, Dominic has always had a heavy iron plate with several double holes drilled at intervals for adjusting the height of the ball-hitch, ensuring that a trailer could be towed level.

There are few things more ludicrous than a trailer on tow, tipped down or up at the hitch. Trailers are built upon different chassis, with different types of brakes or brake-release systems for backing. Many are not at all practical and would only work on a level surface, so in an emergency on a down-hill slope it would be impossible to reverse! The best system was also the simplest; a small flat curved iron bar was fixed by a hinge at the side of the trailer bar, and this stopped the bar from being pushed backward in its casing, which otherwise would automatically put on the brake, thereby preventing reversing. This little bar was manually pushed over the round piece of the drawbar. It was such a good idea that Dominic had a smith make one, heavy enough to stay in place without being hinged, for which there would be no fitting on most trailers. Thereafter he hooked this device over the drawbar for all chassis with bad or impossible braking systems. We once came across a heavy trailer in difficulties, trying to get into a gateway on a downward slope, so Dominic jumped out of our cab taking his device, which was kept there for safe-keeping. By using this, the driver managed to shunt to and fro and finally gain access.

Whippet and Dog-box

I once, before we had even unhitched, sold a lurcher and his dog-box which I had made, at the field outside Cambridge where we are now forced to stop for the Cambridge Fair. At this Travellers' mid-summer Fair we used to stop in the town right alongside the river in a nice setting and where we all felt part of the Fair. Unfortunately, like every other Fair I can think of, the Travellers have now been moved out of the public gaze to a lone field far outside the town. Such sites are often dreary and hilly with, as at Cambridge, a narrow dust track with a narrow metal bridge at the end set at right angles to the track so that a simple forward approach is impossible. The twenty-five foot trailers had a job to get in at all. I don't think the officials were laughing at this hazard, they, like most people, just do not give such practical matters a thought. Travellers, being resilient, are used to surmounting difficulties – mainly by ignoring them! Therefore no-one complained at being charged £32 per trailer and £1 for the motor, for the privilege of being ostracised from the Fair proper and risking their homes on an entry designed for foot traffic. It is just as well that the Fair is not the main reason for the gathering, but the Council is not to know that. One gets the feeling that officialdom annually puts more and more difficulties in the way of the Travellers, in the fond hope that they will eventually decide not to come. In your dreams Mr Jobsworth Killjoys!

Travellers' Field – Cambridge Fair

At Doncaster Races we were crowded into football grounds with high mesh fences and where all gates but one were locked. In the case of fire with the probability of Calor Gas exploding, everyone would have been trapped. It must have given the person who had us all shut in this prison-camp great satisfaction. In nineteen-eighty you had to pay the Council twenty-five pounds for this week of pleasure. Fortunately, I always have my carpentry tools with me, also spanners and bolt-cutters. I worked out that by cutting one lower and one upper strand of the mesh fence, the perpendicular wire would corkscrew undone and push back, so that in the event of fire we could pull into the next football field!

Trailer steps, not the low metal type sold for tourers in caravan shops, are specially made designs of stout construction. Some, with two steps of semi-circular shape, are covered with Formica, matching that used in the trailer, the tops covered with alloy non-slip bars. There are two ornate handles, one on each side. As the top half of a trailer 'stable-door' is left open, one can see the Formica pattern inside. As old trailers were part-exchanged many, sadly, lost their matching steps. Since new steps can cost fifty pounds the fashion for stainless steel covered steps has emerged and is likely to stay. Some steps had a lid and formed a very useful box. One of the last ones I made was white Formica to match the white Formica inside the trailer. I would find the steel more difficult to cut. They look nice but like all the steel trim, need constant washing and polishing. Washing a trailer, not forgetting the roof, usually takes the best part of a day. When it is done it looks lovely, but only for two to three days. After that the once shiny surface becomes covered in acid rain, dirt fall-out from aircraft, neighbours' chimney smoke, or the sticky substances from trees such as maples or limes. Some trailer makers cut costs by not filling in the spaces behind the steel trim properly so dirt gets into the gaps behind, oozing out in the next rain or heavy dew. (I once scraped off a pound in weight of filler from around seams and roof-lights.) Makers, new to the scene, had not realised that roofs are kept clean and thought the bad finish did not matter. Despite the high price, step-makers usually sell-out at fairs because steps have a hard life. A carpenter could be sure of a good return if he were to make good, reasonably priced, fancy steps. These travel on the lorry, not in the trailer, as the base gets muddy, even if put on carpet. I recall a local journalist once talking to a woman about being moved on. As he was leaving he pointed to some tins of diesel, drums of oil, and a generator, and said brightly, "I suppose you have to put all that inside when you move." I hope all I have said earlier about palaces-on-wheels will have dispelled such an idea!

 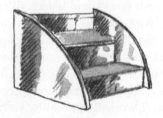

Trailer Steps

Another obligatory piece of outside equipment is the stainless-steel washbowl and stand. Travellers' Specials have no sinks, wash-basins or toilets. The latter in particular are considered unhygienic. Before the cottage and square-frame tents made useful washrooms, women and children washed in the trailer and it was usual to see a chrome bowl of soapy water balanced on a towel on a seat around the children's bedtime. Trying to take a stand-up bath without a shower, with a kettle of hot water to one side and a churn of cold on the other, standing in a baby's bath on a newspaper on a carpet is not easy! Trailers are carpeted all through; few things are disliked more about a *gaujo* trailer than the change to 'practical' floor-covering at the kitchen end. I only put down a small foot-towel since drying and storing towels is so time-consuming. Print on newspaper comes off when wet and sheets of plastic refuse to dry in under a month of Sundays. The outside bowl is used by the men who strip to the waist and wash at the back end of the trailer.

A great deal is made about Romanies having many bowls, one for each purpose. It would never *occur* to me to wash socks and underclothes in the same bowl, or to wash clothes in the bowl used to wash dishes. This does not pertain to 'Gypsy rites' but to good common sense.

Water Bowls and Carriers

Water jacks, cans or carriers are not shaped like the narrow-boat cans, but have a lift-off lid that fits in very deeply, a long angled spout, side pouring and top carrying handles. These are not made of tin, but of stainless-steel. The earlier similarly shaped cans were of copper with bass bands and handles. Later, they were 'chromed-up,' sometimes with brass bands, a reminder of the earlier ones. Then, as now, they are always sold in pairs, as carrying a balanced weight is easier. These cans are of some importance and are displayed either on the all-round kitchen surfaces or outside on a low table above the ground, mud and dogs. They must be kept at least half full or they may blow over. It is one of the most familiar sites to see men with a pair of water-carriers going to and from the standpipe on trailer Parks or at fairs. Never to stop near a water-pipe has always been my hope, as, like the village well, there is an hourly traffic of men with water-carriers, women with buckets to wash-down the trailer, children with kettles sent to get a 'fresh cup of tea,' and boys driving up to wash down the vehicles. Wherever there is a tap a sea of mud develops, and passing traffic sends it splattering up the trailer walls and all over the outside mats. Stopping near a gateway has similar problems. You may think there would be plenty of choice in a green field, but if you are travelling with another family and you all pull into a field together you cannot detach yourself and zoom across to a far corner, however enticing. This is considered bad manners. The implication is that you do not like the company of the family you have arrived with. There is a great sensitivity about such things. If you are with four or five other families and they head for a hedge where there are already two trailers and seven is all the hedge can take, you may have to go along the lower hedge, which might be of overhanging trees. Or the last space may be down a muddy slope, or where cattle have been fed, and it will be a job to get up out again. It is not much liked to be positioned in the centre, one is on view from all sides, without shelter or privacy; but of course as a stopping place fills up the luckless ones have no alternative. There are times when there is no choice but to stop by the dreaded tap!

Just one or two trailers have a much better chance of getting into the fast-vanishing farm fields whose fame or location is universally known. Irish trailer-dwellers have been coming over here for years; they join up into large bands that travel together. Their solution to the problem of stopping places is to take 'French-leave.' These large numbers, sometimes upwards of a hundred trailers, considerably more than the small knots of English Travellers, just take down fences, cut padlocks, or remove sections of fence from Council land, or even private land. They also stop in Car Parks, on greens by small factories, or on any spaces on industrial estates. There being so many of them, they probably feel secure. This often makes the local house-dwellers apoplectic with fury; they 'phone the Council and Police and often the Press, who trot out the old banner headline 'Gypsy Invasion.' I wish just one reporter, instead of sitting on the opposite side of the road safely in his car taking telescopic photos, would get out, investigate and then report the truth that these huge bands of Travellers are actually Irish, and not English. It really does matter, as their ways and habits are different. He might have discovered an interesting story of Travellers who deal in new-for-old suites of furniture, making an allowance on the old and taking it away to dump it.......wherever they happen to be! This is the real story and not as unjust as bad reporting.

Local Travellers are often shown on front-page photos, or, once the Council has obtained an order, see vehicles arrive to tow away trailers, with headlines, 'Gypsies refuse to leave,' and, 'Twenty Council lorries needed to take away rubbish.' Yes, but not from any local Romanies, but from the Irish, who do not stay anywhere very long and travel vast distances. When they first arrived in mainland Britain they had scrap yard tourers, some with no windows or doors. When they leave they almost invariably have expensive new trailers.

Another lucrative trade for them is laying tarmac. Those who do notice the Irish accents are inhibited by the Race Relations Act, and do not say to the Press, "They were Irish." But this does not stop the use of the word 'Gypsy' being used! Show a Traveller a photo of what to any ordinary person would be an encampment of trailers, and he would immediately be able to spot that they were Irish trailers. The eye of a Traveller is tuned to details lost on house dwellers. Fashions of the trailers, how they are parked, the outside goods and chattels, and the motor vehicles, are all as easily read as a trail is by an Indian scout. We have often been on a stopping place when Irish Trailer-Dwellers have pulled on at one end. There is no love lost between Irish and English Travellers, as the former do not abide by the unspoken rules of the English Travellers. When Travellers stop together, anyone can go out and leave their trailer door unlocked or even wide open, and on their return all their outside things and inside possessions will be just as they left them. Romanies are proud of this old-fashioned long-standing *trust*. But from bad experiences, when Irish trailers pull-on, other trailers soon leave.

Stainless-steel churns, the size of cream and milk churns are taken on the lorry to fetch large quantities of water. Stainless-steel dustbins and buckets, together with bowls and water carriers come from a few specialist suppliers, one such being in Tooting. Should someone be going in the vicinity of any of these, they can be asked by friends to bring back some of the special ware. The stainless-steel man visits

Fairs and Races, arriving in style in a large Ford Go-between lorry (so called because it was between the J-type 30cwt and the 2 ton 'Tip-cab'), on the bed of which is a wheel-less wooden 'Gypsy Caravan.' The lorry is brightly painted to match. On the rest of the lorry bed he displays his wares. He also tows a horsebox containing more stock. Another line he has is of miniature replicas of these traveller-style water-carriers, churns and coal-boxes, for ornamentation, but at far from trinket prices! These are favoured as mantelshelf ornaments by settled down Travellers, as well as by trailer-dwellers.

A superbly crafted model of a Buccaneer trailer made by Albert Scamp of Kent and given to Kenneth Mayhew

Miniature horse-drawn waggons are sometimes made by Travellers, some, unfortunately, on plastic wheels, but others are made entirely of wood and in the right proportions. These can be seen in trailer windows. I dislike seeing hideous china ornaments in shops being sold as 'Gypsy Caravans,' with incorrect proportions or details – a mockery of the real thing. What a lost opportunity for a good craftsman to work with a china firm to produce a beautifully made waggon, to scale.

During the heydays of the recent past, Travellers, sharing in the general affluence, bought large trailers, big motors, and masses of equipment that filled the lorry beds to capacity. Square-frame tents made it possible for such luxuries as washing machines. There were extra solid-fuel fires, large Calor Gas fires which had their own cylinder, huge baby-carriages, full-sized cots, reproduction Colebrookdale cast-iron garden furniture and the same in lightweight aluminium, folding garden tables, fringed garden umbrellas (I had a pink flowered one with a pink fringe!), grass parasols, lobster-pot play-pens, two or more outside carpets and car-rugs. Trailer-brooms gave way to vacuum cleaners, and clothes were pressed with huge steam irons.

Meals were cooked outside in summer in electric cook-pots. Every electric socket in a trailer was in use. If two families had to share one electric output socket on a trailer park, each putting in money. Should a family be out when the power went off, they had to be asked to put more in on their return, but mistrust caused bad feeling; sharing was not a good idea!

Generators, from small portables models to those that we called 'Big Bertha' which chugged away all day and into the night until the last TV programme closed down, were the 'in-thing.' Large colour TV sets replaced the small black and white portables, which even waggon-Travellers enjoyed. Many had a colour portable in the kitchen, tent or tow-van; the children had their own set. What a life of luxury it was – the only fly in the ointment being the ever-present difficulty of finding a stopping place on which to enjoy it!

Once Travellers decide to move, they are ready in a short time, everything being thrown up on to the towing vehicle willy-nilly, with few exceptions. Under these circumstances equipment does not just collect honourable scars, but can be broken, and then there is a new kind of rubbish. It is not well known, but is a true fact, that when Travellers move from a stopping place, local householders take the opportunity to get rid of their rubbish where the trailers had been. They motor out after dark and dump unwanted items such as double bed mattresses, settees, old TV sets and refrigerators. These could be found on stops long before Travellers even had such items. Journalists reporting on "what gypsies have left" never notice the items that would never fit into a trailer! I am not suggesting that *all* the rubbish is dumped by householders, but a surprising amount is.

I once caught two boys in uniforms from a neighbouring expensive school, both well-spoken. One had a large sack into which he was putting 'rabbit food' whenever a car passed, but in fact they were pulling up newly planted Council shrubs. They had been doing this all week, working their way close enough for me to see what they were up to. By dint of getting between them and their loaded bicycles I was able to confront them. I was told that the father had said that the gypsies would be blamed as "everyone knows they burn trees." "Tell your father," I said, "that the trees need to be *dead* first." At the same place, the Council was not only convinced that Travellers had stolen the shrubs, but that they had also taken several hundreds of yards of chestnut-paling. Every now and then during daylight hours a Police car would come in, when the men were out, and cruise around. Had they had the sense to come after dark they would have seen an old Irish Dosser, who worked for a Traveller, with his evening fire outside the old motor caravan in which he lived. He it was who burned several rails a night, in full view. A police car passed along a near-by road unheeding.

It is not a bad thing that possessions, like bicycles and motorbikes, get broken so soon. A family only has to pull on with a small boy who has a bicycle, resplendent with all accoutrements including plastic discs in the wheel spokes and streamers from handle-bars, for discarded bikes to be unearthed from under tarpaulins or behind tar drums, to have punctures mended. Soon a noisy throng with hooters horns and bells is whizzing up and down, or round and round according to space, scattering livestock, and followed by barking erstwhile dog playmates. This is of but little nuisance to those not engaged in something needing concentration. Coffee drinking morning jabberers, heads bobbing in trailer windows, remain oblivious even when collisions occur and screams rend the air. Only a mother can tell the anguished scream from the screams of delight. Motorbikes are machines of dread. Not necessarily powerful or large, but extremely noisy. Once one child has one, they all want one. Some are made to wear helmets, but most do not, and girls ride as well as boys. Travellers are good drivers it being an art that comes naturally to both girls and boys. Very few need to take the test twice, failures being of the oral test since this needs help from one who can read. The motorbike riders take small passengers, slipping and sliding on the mud. Mothers say the noise gives them "a terrible headache." When on a stopping place where there are only young children, I scan the vehicles of new arrivals for signs of these expensive 'toys.' If they run out of petrol before the fathers come home there is a little peace!

The fashion for carrying transistor radios has gone. Few radios are seen outside now, but such stations as one hears in small shops – disc jockeys' and housewives' stations – can be heard coming from the car radios when the motors return. This powerful source of entertainment with strong signal receivers and stereo speakers, benefits not only the vehicle owner who turns it on and opens the doors, but also those at the very end of the site! Most trailers have huge cassette-radio recorders with cassettes of Country and Western or recordings of Travellers singing, bought at Fairground stalls. Radios with rival stations engage in a continual crossfire through open windows and doors, until the children turn on their own television stations and programmes. The whole scene is a world away from peace and quiet and a *free* life. The nearest I came to being able to block out unwanted noise in order to listen to Vivaldi – which enters a kind of relaxed conscious area of my mind yet enables me to concentrate on creating – was when I bought a car-radio from a Rolls Royce radio fitter who put up two speakers at each end of a divider in a trailer. Running on its own battery, it battled bravely with disc-jockeys and generators!

Whereas pop music has a tremendous uniform beat, so that a song at the far end of a stopping place can only be heard as loud throbs and bangs, classical music, because of its expressiveness and quiet periods needs to be turned up. Then suddenly one's ear-drums are nearly shattered by a loud crescendo! It all seems a long way from the romance of the wooden waggons in a green country lane with horses grazing quietly and the linnets and greenfinches singing, which we once knew as sufficient entertainment.

Chapter Seven

Interiors and 'Bits and Pieces'

With but a few variations, the layout of the inside of a waggon followed an age-old pattern stemming from certain fixtures dictated by practicality. Taking the fire-stove for example: in order for the tall chimney to miss the overhanging trees, it was placed on the offside. The bed, in order to be out of the way, was placed at the back, running from side to side. In a waggon or Open Lot built on the narrow bed of a trolley or dray, a shelf was built out over the back wheels. This shelf ran outside on all but Showmen's waggons, to provide the necessary width. Between the bed and stove there was a seat, and on the forward side of the stove there was a cupboard. On the opposite or near-side wall – to the right as you look in through the door – next the bed was a chest of drawers, then another small seat and a corner glass-fronted cupboard.

The bed could pull out as a double, or be shut away from view behind sliding doors. You could just sit up in it without hitting your head on the roof. The area underneath the bed formed a children's bed the sliding doors of which were usually kept closed during the day. Additionally, some waggons had a pull-out table. Around the stove chimney was a small cupboard designed for airing clothes.

The fire-stove evolved from an open grate, in very early waggons, to the Colchester – at first placed in the corner which caused the waggon to be wrongly balanced. The Colchester was eventually followed by an open grate stove which had a side-oven. This in turn was superseded by the Hostess Stove, made by Smith and Wellstood of Bonnybridge in Scotland, the famous firm who created the universal 'Queenie' Stove, a small Victorian waggon-stove once used in sailing-ships. This came in sizes of fourteen inches, sixteen inches and eighteen inches. It is still available and in use today. There is a very decorative piece of cast-iron, which rests on top of the two cooking-plates. An elongated hot-water boiler could be placed over these plates. The decorative top is of a quite breath-taking filigree-like design. It is a long time since I have seen one of the water-kettles. The little fire-stove can be opened at the front with the two doors slid back. A fluted, semi-circular ember-catcher can be reversed to close the lower grating, and with this and the top doors closed, one or two chunky pieces of wood will burn very slowly.

The beauty of these free-standing stoves with their graceful Queen Anne legs – hence the name 'Queenie' – was that the iron, when it became hot, heated the room as well; a fact rediscovered with the import of Swedish wood-burners.

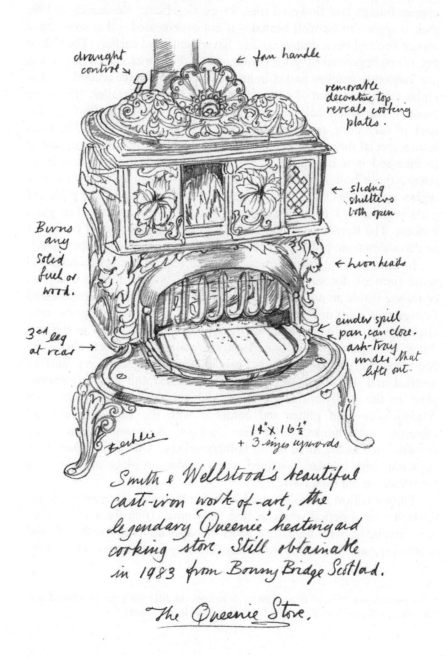

draught control →

← fan handle

removable decorative top reveals cooking plates.

← sliding shutters both open

Burns any solid fuel or wood.

← lion heads

3rd leg at rear →

cinder spill pan, can close. ash-tray under that lifts out.

14" x 16½" + 3 sizes upwards

Smith & Wellstood's beautiful cast-iron work-of-art, the legendary 'Queenie' heating and cooking stove. Still obtainable in 1983 from Bonny Bridge Scotland.

The Queenie Stove.

Originally purchased for ten shillings, the 'Queenie' at its smallest size would now probably cost eighty pounds.* Waggon stoves came in various sizes and degrees of ornamentation, which spread to the surrounding stove-box (fire-place), hearth and mantle with brass and copper fittings and flowered tiles for exotic effect. Romanies so love their waggons to be well heated – if not *over*-heated – that some have caught fire and been destroyed, as I have mentioned earlier. The risk of fire is not improved by poor maintenance. Fire bricks in trailer stoves are frequently cracked and chimneys burned out. I have recently had to replace the glass-front of a large fire-stove in my own trailer. These are made in one and a half inch sections, but the entire iron frame at the back of each door, retaining the glass, has to be unscrewed. The bolts have a special thread and cannot be replaced. The heat causes the metal to fuse and it is beyond even the powers of 'UB40,' as I call it, to release these bolts. If they are drilled out, the thread prevents easy replacement. This small iron frame is essential to keep all the pieces of glass together. I recall sitting in a trailer which had the fire glass broken. The Romany woman owner told me that her mother could not be dissuaded from poking the fire, after a lifetime of poking open fires!

In the best waggons, then as now, the lockers and cupboards had some form of decoration, panels, scrolls or bows. I wish everyone could see inside an authentic waggon with all the original furniture and fittings – so very different from the interiors of many 'waggons' now *posing* as 'Gypsy Caravans,' yet bearing no relation at all to the real thing. Compare the elaborately carved and gilded screen above the bed-place, carved over-mantle, carved fire-surround, every surface scrolled and decorated, the roof ribs chamfered and gilded, coloured glass in the mollycroft roof-lights, and cut-glass at the ends – an Aladdin's cave of glitter and colour – with the very different sad travesties with bunks, Calor Gas cookers, sinks and cheap nylon curtains such as are hired out to holidaymakers. One firm makes them *en masse* with tubular V-shaped wheel-holders in place of axles, and the wheels in old motor-tyres!

The transition to trailers, as I have explained in Chapter 5, passed through a grim period when, at first, only *gaujo* (non-Romany) trailers were available, with their bare walls of paper-covered hardboard, and containing only that which was cheap and easy for the makers but of no

*This passage was written three decades or so ago. In 2011 the price of a brand new 'Queenie,' still cast from the original Victorian moulds, is £380.00.

real appeal to the Traveller – or the discerning holidaymaker for that matter. But as soon as coachbuilders emerged who would obligingly make living-trailers to order for Travellers, as in the waggon days, trailer interiors became of equally elaborate splendour.

Unfortunately, large ornate foreign fire-stoves had not yet been discovered (now imported and available) so large plain square, usually brown, stoves, intended to heat several radiators and a hot-water system in a house, were used. Each of these was more obstinate than the last for lighting or keeping going, and with design faults. There was no place to boil water or keep food hot, let alone to cook. Despite those inappropriate stoves, fire-places regained their position as focal points for the family. They featured surrounds of stainless steel or coloured mirror-glass, rounded over-mantles of steel or cut-glass, mirrors of cut or etched flower-baskets and grapes and small airing-cupboards. The mantle-shelves had 'fiddle-rails' around them. This kept ornaments safely in place. Indeed, these rails were often added to the edges of all horizontal surfaces.

Anything in a coachbuilder's workshop which caught the eye of a Traveller was used to make the interiors as full of objects as possible, regardless of the total weight and expense. Huge circular ceiling lights, as many as could be crammed in, had a dazzling effect when they were switched on and reflected in the many mirrors. Strip-lights were put at the back of all the glass-fronted roof-lockers to show off the china. Bevelled, spoon-edged, mirrors with cut glass and etched designs, were fitted from floor to ceiling on wardrobe doors, the fastenings concealed with cut-glass flowers in various colours and with diamond-cut centres. In these already fantastic glittering palaces-on-wheels, 'bits and pieces' filled the cupboards. It was a time of visual splendour, the like of which we shall probably never see again. 'Bits and pieces' were not haphazardly and charmingly displayed as bric-a-brac in some thatched cottage might be, or the self-consciously 'good quality' antique collections in up-market houses, mainly single pieces of valuable china. Rather, Travellers' china is always displayed in pairs. Collections are all china, or all glass, or all of silverware.

From before the affluent years, many young Romany couples set up home in a new trailer given to them by their parents, fitted out with wedding presents. Many Travellers still have, as I have, the very first ornament they ever bought, which acquires a sentimental value. The china to which I keep referring is not 'using-china,' or kitchen-china, although the latter in some trailers and settled-down Travellers' chalets is often Crown Derby. Aynsley, Minton and Hammersley are also used every day. These are these are manufacturers of bone china, not the names of the actual designs. Not any pattern of Crown Derby will do;

the pattern collected is the very rich, blue terracotta and gold known as the 'Imari' or 'Cigar' pattern. During a brief period of refined taste, the white and gold pattern was the fashion. More recently collected, equally rich-looking but less refined and more flash in taste is the Burtondale, made in Burton-on-Trent. This pattern can be ordered through certain shops. It has far more gold than most other patterns, with red and a certain amount of black. Another china, Abbeydale, of the antique 'Chrysanthemum' pattern, with black, terracotta and gold, less expensive than Crown Derby, is bought by some Travellers. The favourite Royal Worcester and Aynsley designs are a contrast to the famed Crown Derby. These designs, on tinted creamy grounds, are of luscious fruit – nuts, peaches, grapes and pears – a subject matter that must appeal to Romanies. I have some Royal Worcester, Aynsley and Minton all-gold Exhibition plates. One has a miniature of fruit painted in the centre, embossed with 24 carat gold which takes several weeks to execute. I could have sold these many times.....and have been tempted to *do* so as I find it nerve-wracking packing up and unpacking such expensive pieces each time we move!

The famous Crown Derby

Handpainted Worcester and half-handpainted Aynsley bowls, urns.

Crown Derby, Royal Worcester and Aynsley

While plates, which are easy to pack, form the basis of a collection, there are also urns, tall classical vases with side handles and lids bearing gold finial, salad bowls of three sizes, goblets, various oval or rectangular dishes, ornate tea-pots and jugs, cups and saucers – available in all the aforementioned patterns. These form very carefully-arranged displays on sideboards, front window shelves, mantle-shelves, kitchen work-surfaces (on which no self-respecting Romany wife would leave any domestic object), and of course in the many mirror backed glass-fronted cabinets and roof-lockers. These are never used to hold any other possessions. The china is usually purchased in pairs of urns, vases or goblets, so that these can flank a bowl.

Buying a different make of trailer, or a larger size new home, means a visit to the china shop to buy more ornaments to fill the gaps. Travellers do of course buy from each other, sometimes selling a whole collection of a hundred pieces or more of blue or red glass, should they have *chopped*-in (exchanged) a trailer to which these were colour matched, but are not suit the new. Antique china is not favoured for its age. People have made the mistake of thinking that Romany Crown Derby is second-hand or antique; it is not. A visit to the factory at Worcester, for example, is not an infrequent event for Travellers as they have a long established connection with the factory.

I recall once being in the china department of a well-known and very expensive store. This department appeared to be reserved for the most elegant and snooty of their staff, who hope never to come into contact with customers buying Tupperware. A tartan skirted, shawled and outstandingly Romany woman and her equally colourful 'rinkletted' (with ringlets) daughter were being looked up and down with frowning disapproval by the tall Manageress and her two colleagues. She approached the Romanies and said, "Perhaps, Moddom, you are looking for the Kitchen Department?" But they ignored her and made for the shop's most costly china display. The other two assistants smirked. It was quite rewarding to see their faces as the Romany woman bought the most expensive item in the cabinet, a huge tureen, which they had to pack under her stern eyes.

At one time, a leftover fashion from waggon days was for silver bowls, candlesticks and rose-bowls, though these were not as highly prized as huge punch bowls embossed with flowers and fruit. The constant cleaning led to their eventual demise. Waggons had been lit by oil-lamps. The very best of these was the 'Angel-lamp,' which was in fact a cherub finial on an elaborate bracket with a bowl-shaped holder for the base of a glass, often ruby-glass. It was an oil lamp with two wicks, a good sized chimney and an etched round shade. The beauty of this lamp was that it was also practical – the bracket swung in a semi-circle, so that the lamp could be brought out into the centre of the waggon by night and put away in the daytime. The glass bowls were excellent as one could see at once when the oil was low and needed topping up. It amuses me to see an oil-lamp being lit on Western films. The wick is turned up to maximum height and the flames shoot up the chimney, which would very quickly have sooted up and cracked. The correct way is to start with the wick low and only when it is alight, and burning steadily, should it be carefully and slowly turned up. The wick should always be cleaned with care so as not to unravel the weave; it can be trimmed with scissors. A nice steady bright flame is what gives a good light. Soot was prevented from damaging the ceiling by means of a circular 'hat' with pointed edges, hung by a D-ring. Around the early 1900's lamps were made of brass with a patterned fluted globe. Later waggons had the same design but they were nickel-plated. Although above the lamp-place a vent took off the fumes and soot through the roof, the disc acted as a reflector, if kept polished! There is a present day version of that early lamp, also in cut glass, fitted for electricity. This is a table-lamp in the shape of a vase or urn and has a mushroom-shaped shade, also of cut glass, and a replica of the little cherub in gilt. There is a ring of gilded metal around the edge, which holds pear-shaped crystal drops. The lamp stands on a gilded plinth with antique style clawed feet. It is twenty-one inches high and twelve inches across. These lamps are for sale on the 'Glassman's Stall' at Epsom on Show-Out Sunday. It gives a nice suffused light sufficient to see to eat by, and good if watching television.

The expectation of visitors requires that all the trailer lights be turned on, along with the now universal awning or porch light to illuminate the steps. Sometimes twin lights are left on all night, and some later trailers have even had lights fitted to the usually very dark underneath! With all these outside lights switched on a stopping place is well lit up. Trailer Parks have their own powerful lights, like streetlights, and if there is one of these near a trailer window it penetrates any blind or curtain. I cannot say I care much for the very high wattage bulbs, like a supermarket all night long, although Romanies tend to like them and feel safer under their glare. The lights are usually left on in a trailer when the occupants go out.

Stainless-steel water-cans (a pair of course), bread-bin, bowls, coal-scuttle, companion set, mirror glass photo-frames (replacing the silver ones), china, saucepan sets on stands, Minton tea-set, 'using' china, electric kettle, vacuum cleaner, iron, hair-dryer, baby's cot, cushion-sets, rugs, TV and radio-cassettes are a few of the things a wife has to pack for each journey.......and clean or dust every day! During the time of 'possession-mania' there were even *more* chattels, not forgetting the outside things. Moving began to lack the essence of the 'free' life, and families were literally bogged down by possessions. I quite believe that some were 'accidentally' broken on purpose by rough handling; things that men became tired of lifting up and down.

Because over-loaded electrical installations can fail, I keep and still find use for my silver candlesticks. Originally these were wall fittings which used to go above the waggon bed. I have put this same pair up and taken them down countless times. When a main fuse goes, it is nice to have the trailer lit up in seconds while everyone else is fumbling around in the dark. We have 12-volt battery lights as well as the mains electric lights. The old Calor Gas lights were never any good; mantles and globes were always falling off, and it was difficult to replace with the correct matching pattern. They were fitted in *the* most useless positions, often only inches from a ceiling, soon sooting over the whole area or blistering the wood, even when the lamps were properly adjusted. I have had several new trailers in which the gas system leaked, usually behind the floor-fixed oven where one cannot reach the pipe, or in the wall! Horror upon horror!

Vase and Potpourri

Chapter Eight

'Iron Horses'

Earlier I referred to the high-powered motor lorries (the old spelling was lurry), which one sees on the motorways, sprayed to the firm's own colours, sign-written and lined-out at great expense, notwithstanding the resultant devaluation of a lettered van or lorry when it comes to part exchanging. This tradition for a tradesman's vehicle to reflect or enhance the owner's reputation in the face of today's recession and depression, is, I think, much to be admired. It never fails to give me great pleasure to see this expression of imagination and individuality among other stereotyped traffic. Showmen's vehicles, lorries and ex-buses, usually had to be repainted, as being more mechanically minded than Travellers, and having longer experience with motors, they keep their vehicles longer. Repainting, lettering and lining out, as with Circus People, was done in the winter when they were 'resting' in true Show-business manner in their winter quarters. As soon as Travellers owned motors, these were usually second-hand and often needed painting. There was no need to spray-paint, since these old vehicles had more than one 'denge' (dent) and a long history of inner surgery.

It was soon realised that if the *gaujo* trailers had little aesthetic value, the cab and body of a lorry afforded the artistic sign-writer or coach-painter a large canvas. I wish that some museums had had the foresight to buy and preserve one or two of these early lorries, not old enough to be vintage, but in years to come they would have been historic evidence of Romany struggles. I can but hope that some wealthy retired Romanies will do just that with some of the best examples. I suspect that they would then take these to Fairs, Steam Rallies etc.*

After the waggon-horse, the 'iron horse' became almost part of the family in the same way as had been the horse. Travellers often had deals just for the sake of it, and if they had a lorry 'going well,' might *chop* (swap) it away for no other reason. At a time when few could afford a new vehicle, they struggled with the strangeness of the faster, in all ways, motorised world. Many were *chopped* away countless times, so one lost count of the numbers of owners. Logbooks had pages

---

*Since this was written, this is now happening, and many splendid examples of favourite lorries, glittering with chrome, are brought out to be seen and admired.

and pages of stamped information, like a World-traveller's Passport. So the erstwhile 'iron horse' could, and often would, be followed on its various stages of ownership, and greeted at future meetings with some nostalgia if not affection. Not only was one's own vehicle noted, but should a Traveller drive up to a group, it would not have been unusual for someone to remark, "Got Royston's old lorry, then?" Like the majority of horses, each 'iron horse' would have its faults; it was a question of which had the least! A nicety of horse-dealing days was, after the deal was done, to tell the new owner of any small faults it would be to his advantage to know. A leaking radiator might need an immediate spot of Radweld.

Bedford J-type

An 'Iron Horse'

I can remember carving out, with nothing but a small-toothed dowling saw and a Cobbler's rasp, a piece of wood to put along the back of the tail-board, in order to make a 1946 Austin lorry a bit more decorative. I have just added a similar shaped board, with scrolls, painted horses heads, and horseshoes, to slot on the ladder-stays so thoughtfully provided by the makers of our present pick-up truck. Early lorries favoured the colours of waggons, the famous red-maroon lined out in a straw colour, grass-green lined-out in red, or blue lined-out in yellow were the basic colour schemes. These should be recorded, since many early photos are in black and white. Many vehicles had double lining-out, in wide and fine lines of different colours. The lining-out followed the lines of the cab; the long bonnets afforded plenty of space. Where the lines met at the corners they were scalloped or crossed into elliptic shapes or even more elaborate cross-over designs. The wooden body was usually painted, the oak polished body came later with newer vehicles, and here the lining-out followed the rectangular shapes between the ribs which were often lined-out as well, emulating the carved waggon ribs.

Waggon doors had always been a focal feature and carved with significant motifs: a horse looking over a gate, a standing horse, a horse rampant, birds, fruit or flowers. The early waggons had one-panel lower doors, then two-panel, a small panel at the top and a large one below. Then the lower panel was divided down the centre, unless the horse rampant was used, which needed a full panel. The edges of the frames around these panels were butterfly chamfered. Elaborate lining-out, with fluid lines and crossing-lines with corners of small relief carvings, made the whole very rococo indeed. So it was that the garter or belt that had long been the accepted design for coach doors and trade lorry doors, was used by Travellers on their lorry doors, as a frame for either a horse's head, or horse-shoe, or the owner's initials. At one time it was so much the fashion that no lorry of a traveller of any self-respect was without the 'buckle-belts.' I once painted one for a scrap yard owner with a jay (the bird) flying in the direction that the lorry was travelling. I took a photo of Dominic sitting in the cab, in the field where the yard owner allowed us to stop. He drove the lorry in for me to paint in more peaceful surroundings than the yard. It was a novelty for us to sit on the high seats, having not the faintest idea that one day we would own such a vehicle as we moved forward with the majority of Romanies forsaking horses for mechanical horsepower.

It is interesting, I find, how Travellers take an idea and turn it to their own use and advantage. For example, lorries are supplied with a ladder-rack just behind the cab; the makers under the impression that no lorry driver is without his ladder. This consists of two upright stanchions and a crossbar close to the top, the projecting stanchion tops prevent a Builder's ladder from falling off. The whole design is very basic and ugly.

On the back of horse-drawn waggons there was a rack or cratch, consisting of a frame with a centre support-bar, the end being bowed, all the frame-wood being carved to match the waggon. Bars or rods of round iron were slotted through the frame at intervals. The frame was fixed to the cross member by two hinges. Two chains fastened to two hooks on the end of the frame. This arrangement enabled the rack to be adjusted into as many positions as there were links in the chain. It had a waterproof cover and was used to hold all manner of equipment. Its original purpose was thought to be a hayrack. It could hold almost anything, including a supply of dry morning sticks in wet weather.

Imagine, if you can, this rack having been removed and now standing upright with the bow at the top: this is exactly what Travellers would have had made, and what some still do have made, and which in all its glory, replaces the ugly utilitarian Builder's ladder-rack. A friend of ours has recently had a splendid rack made by a waggon-builder and restorer of waggons, Peter Ingram, in his yard. The rack had gold leaf on the chamfers and was carved with fiddle-ends.

New lorries, which can be bought as chassis and cab, can be taken to a Coachworks to be fitted with a Traveller's Special body. These are craftsman made, sometimes a little shorter than the standard body, either panelled in tongued and grooved boarding set in a frame of sumner or runner top-rail and ribs. Sometimes a double height body is ordered, the top section hinging downwards. Polished oak, varnished ash or red cedar were appreciated for their effect. This was not hidden by paint but improved and preserved by ship's varnish; still better than any polyurethane. Lorries without a coach-built body were preferred with the famous Hawson body, which was of a good design with improved stanchion fixings for the drop sides and tailgate.

With all the decoration and special bodies and racks, you might think the lorry fashion had gone the limit, but various additions and embellishments, reflecting the ornamentation on the harness, were often added. Having an eye for symmetry, two number plates were, and still are, used, one each side at the back, and two reversing lights, also an essential step-drawbar. There were large, often coach-size chromed mirrors, originally wing-mirrors but which moved up to the hinged-edge of the door, chromed horn atop the roof, chromed grill across the radiator, chrome bumpers and huge 'cow-catcher' bars, not forgetting the bonnet mascot, usually a horse. When horse and jockey mascots were available in car accessory shops, they replaced the more difficult to come by horse rampant mascot. I once bought a brass horse from an antique shop and had it chromed. I'd like a pound for every bonnet I've drilled, levelled with rubber cut from an old tyre on which to place a horse mascot.

The cab interiors were not neglected. Seats had all manner of extra covers, flower holders – vintage cut-glass, fixed to the window jam held a small amount of water for a posy, the latter now replaced with plastic roses. Window swinging-mascots became and still are a fashion, lucky boots in particular, or occasionally dice.

No vehicle is complete without its radio-cassette player. Now it is C.B. Radio, the drivers talking to each other as often as possible. Nicknames are often given to people and things, vehicles being no exception: 'Show-knees,' 'Brazen-faced,' 'Three-penny bit,' 'Frog-fronted,' 'Tip-Cab' and 'Mouth-organ-fronted' etc are a few that spring to mind. These are the names of models, not individual vehicles. One vehicle gave a nick-name to its owner – a car-breaker's lorry with Hi-Ab lifting gear – he was known as 'Hi-Ab John.'

Waggon horses were bred by Travellers, and the advantages of this were manifold. Running alongside a mare when she was tied on the back, if not in the shafts, or when she was pulling the waggon, was the best road-training. Loose among many people, children and dogs on a stop, ridden by toddlers, crawled under by babies, they became quiet and reliable. A half-feathered cob of good colour and shape with a nice action was preferred to a too-heavy horse of the type used on farms. Ponies with a good colour, palomino, piebald, chestnut or black were bred for the two-wheel carts. During the period when their horses were being bred, each family had more than one, so that the loss of a shoe, or a waggon-horse in-foal, or a bad hill, when two doubled-up or a 'sider,' a novice hitched on alongside for hilly journeys, allowed them to overcome any set backs. Many Travellers still breed horses, especially the spotted and coloured ponies, always saleable. Some now take horses with them in horseboxes. Epsom Downs would not be the same without the horses 'on the top.'

Some more 'Iron Horses'

Chapter Nine

The 'Gypsy Problem'

There has been, and probably always will be, heated argument as to what a Gypsy *is*. According to the Government's new legislation, *anyone* who has 'no fixed abode,' who moves about in a mobile-dwelling, is a 'Gypsy,' – so now we know the official view. The sweeping statement that all who are dark-haired with dark skin, are Gypsies and all who have fair hair and fair skin, are not, deserves but scant attention. Few races can claim purity of blood. Obviously Romanies have intermarried with other races over the many years they have wandered over the United Kingdom. One unusual instance I know of is a coal-black child of a travelling girl and a black man. Brought up with family support, she is now an adult Traveller and has married a fair-haired, fair-skinned Traveller. Having known the mother from before she married, it is interesting to note that the off-spring have lost a great deal of their father's racial features, and are now what Romanies call 'Real Black Gypsies' in colouration. I wonder what future scholars will make of any future black throwbacks. It is not a subject that Travellers delve into deeply, but they do of course recognise any who stand out by reason of that elusive 'olive' skin, suffused with brown colouration, once seen never forgotten. In a crowd of fifty Romanies, all dark skinned, you may find three or four of this olive hue, and instinct rather than scientific fact, impossible to obtain, tells one that that was the skin colouration of the original 'Egyptians' who reached these shores. It is a colour quite different from that associated with the 'dark Gypsy.' So few have it as to make it remarkable, and when encountered it is described as 'real ole black Gypsy,' 'ole black blood,' or 'real ole Romany' by Travellers. That is not to suggest that everyone else is a half-breed, as some writers would like to assert, steeped in romantic ideals of 'stage gypsies,' but as with some Jewish people for example, the colouring and features of their very beginnings can be seen in comparatively few. There used to be a Jewish Academy of some sort near to one of our stopping places, as several times we saw small groups of be-skullcapped boys in the charge of a young man, undoubtedly an Orthodox Jew. It was interesting to note that if all but one third were deprived of their side-ringlets and skullcaps they could be of any race, but the rest had classic colouring and features and could not have been anything else. My point being, that for them to be in that situation, they were obviously from orthodox families and bloodlines, yet, like Romanies, the race features were not shared by all.

Christmas under the Holm Oak

An interesting point I might make here is that Travellers are rather confused themselves on this issue, having no written history for refererence. It has not been made any easier by *gaujo* writers, professional and otherwise, who like things to be neat and tidy, trying to card-index degrees of what they regard as 'Gypsy,' under titles which have in all instances been given to the Travelling people by *gaujes* in anything but a complimentary spirit: such as Romany, Gypsy, Didicoi, Tinkers, Mumpers, Hedge-mumpers and a few more. The first two combined, 'Romany-Gypsy,' to make doubly sure, is used by Travellers when referring to themselves; 'Hedge-mumpers' when they refer to the lowest end of the social scale; 'Tinkers' when referring to those Scottish Travellers who remain north of the border; 'Pikies' or 'Tinkers' when referring to Irish Travellers, or more generally these are called 'Irishmans' (mans,108

not men). The word *didikai* became changed by non-Travellers to 'didicoi' and abbreviated to 'did' – similar to, and equally insulting as, the Jewish 'yid.' In some television serials, scriptwriters have picked up prison slang and all too often refer to Travellers as the ugly meaning and no better sounding 'didicois.' Actors pronounce the coi as 'coy,' possibly unaware of or indifferent to the disgust of Traveller viewers. There is also the regular misuse of the word *dinilo*, meaning half-witted, or fool, which scriptwriters sometimes call 'didlo.'

Occasionally the first or second generation from a Traveller who has married and settled down with a *gaujo*, comes back on the *drom* (road), marrying back into Travellers. No matter how dark of colouring, Travellers will always refer to a resulting child as, 'not a proper Traveller,' yet one can see the Romany features, or colouring, or sometimes none of these, but they have the manner of speech and Romany ways. I only refer to one instance but know of many. Travellers do not call such persons by any of the foregoing belittling names that *gaujes* use, and apart from the aforementioned, 'not a proper Traveller,' might say, "His mother (or father) was not a Traveller," and leave it at that.

It should be borne in mind that it is only in comparatively recent times that the population has become more settled. Once, many people other than Travellers moved about; those seeking work at Hiring-Fairs, if unsuited would move on to the next. Workers in brick-making set up temporary dwellings and when the building was finished moved on to the next site of work. Teasel-gatherers, withy-cutters, coppice-cutters, carpenters, thatchers, stonemasons, farm-workers, tinkers (tin and pot menders, peddlers), caddy men, brush and broom makers, bodgers (chair-leg turners) and chapmen to mention but a few of the constantly roving population under the heading of 'itinerants.' Henry Mayhew (of Mayhew's London, 1851) mentions travelling-butchers, and the caddyman whose arrival was a welcome event for the remote farm or the cottage-bound, who could not just pop round to the corner shop or catch a bus to the local market for the small items most people take for granted today. A legacy of the days when these wandering and often frightening strangers, sometimes, thieves, and cut-throats, who came and went, is the great respectability put upon a name, and even more upon an address. Without a name or an address, one must be a person of 'low-degree.' *Ab initio*, Travellers must have found that the spread of their fierce reputation and the large numbers in which they travelled, a safety measure against the robbers and brigands waiting in ambush for drovers and their like returning from market with their takings. It was unwise to travel the roads alone or in small numbers. The persecution instigated by Laws, lingers on in attitudes. Since our new multi-racial Britain, the following quotes seem even more outrageous and should be set down as a record of these difficult times for those trying to make a living on the roads.

I see from a note I made in 1961: a headline in the Daily Mail read, "Colonel wants Gypsies put in camps." Another press quote reads "Herd Britain's Gypsies into Compulsory Sites." Angry because Travellers stopped on land at the bottom of his garden, a reader wrote, "Britain must do something; I have written to the Council about a plan for the *regimentation* of Gypsies throughout Britain." I have also made a note of another quote: "They are a dirty race," and, "Militarise them under *army supervision*." Strong stuff. A North Baddesley (Southampton) Residents' Association suggested, a six-point scheme, part of which would be to allocate one family to each Parish. Allocate! Can one imagine what the wife of the 'lucky' Traveller 'allocated' to one parish would do after she had sold pegs to every house, or needed to be with her daughter, in another Parish, during the birth of her first child? Travellers have a horror of loneliness – one family on its own imprisoned in a Parish would be just that. One Council proposed "A *Rehabilitation Centre*." The mind boggles at what Travellers would have been forced to learn. Luckily the residents successfully fought this idea. There was a proposal that all other Hampshire Sites (which meant *anywhere* Travellers were stopping) should be *"Cleared immediately*, and *all gypsies gathered together at Stockbridge*." A member for South West Herts was quoted in the press as referring to Travellers as 'Didicoi' and defined the word as "Followers or successors originally of the troops of Alexander the Great," and, "these people," he said, "are not Gypsies, they are not *true* Romanies."

The foregoing may make strange reading in these more enlightened times of recognised 'rights' of racial minorities. In the 1960s, Norman Dodds M.P. tried to see that some justice was done. According to him, three other M.P.s of his Parliamentary era were descended from Gypsies; other people too. Again a Daily Mail headline: "No Gypsies. Free Site plan is dropped by Trust. Villagers won battle against Gypsy camp at Welham Green, Herts," and the Barbara Cartland-Onslow Romany Fund said they would withdraw their application.

Like the old joke of helping the old lady across the road when she does not want to go, Travellers have had to tolerate the undignified and inhuman position of being mere chessmen on a board. Does it never occur to these bureaucratic 'chess players,' that Travellers are people? At the time of the foregoing quotes, holiday caravanners were allowed to go anywhere and stop as long as they wanted, in or on the New Forest among other places, whereas nearby Verwood declared, "Verwood will not tolerate Gypsies." Another Press headline reads, "Night swoop on Gypsies." Stop for a moment and think how you would feel, asleep with your children tucked up in bed, then, suddenly, headlights, dogs barking and police cars; police banging on the doors and windows, even on the sides of the trailers, and being told to hitch-on in the dark when nothing is packed for travelling. The devilishly wicked mind that could think of that ploy as being an excellent one must be a mind empty of thoughts regarding the necessary preparation both inside and out, before a move. Sleep well, whoever you were! Romany women are on the whole modest, including being properly dressed, and they do *not* open the door half-clad, and certainly never with nothing on at all, as in some instances of *gauji* women encountered by Travelling men when out calling! The very women, no doubt, who would look down on Gypsies.

I recall, once we were staying on a small piece of land near a little tributary of a river which had flooded the year before. One night, when all were asleep, a police car zoomed in, siren blaring. The residents had said that the river was rising and we would be flooded. The fact that the land had just been sold for building may or may not have had anything to do with it. The air was rent with the screams of frightened women and children. Few possessed torches and only one worked. Terrified animals had to be got up and into boxes. Horror and panic as one trailer got stuck in the only way out. China was smashed as people hitched-on in panic. I remember it well. To add to our misery it was pouring with rain; we slipped and slid in the mud trying to locate things, undoing Calor Gas bottles, trying to get the trailers turned round (which is one reason why one instinctively likes to face the direction in which one has to leave) – it was utter chaos. People were plastered with mud as they tried to help the stricken trailer; the entry was too narrow to get another vehicle past to assist by towing. And after a miserable night and following day, the river never did flood. We all had our doubts as to whether it was a genuine emergency.

"Night-swoop" on Travellers became a fun-game for bored patrol-cars; they would drive into encampments, sirens blaring, circle round until lights came on, then, roaring with mirth, drive off. The public was indifferent or unaware. I think that Britain's immigrant population now term such behaviour as 'harassment,' and have access to various sympathetic bodies, and can even complain to the police. Britain's own ethnic group had no supporters. We have encountered fair-minded decent members of the police force as well as those who are a disgrace to the uniform and all it stands for. One nice old-fashioned Bobby used to lean his bike against the hedge and sit down by our fire, one of my tame bantams on his knee; it is sad to reflect that his like will never be again. Perhaps he did not make many arrests but there was very little malicious damage in his area. Many Station Sergeants, however, believed that the easiest way to avoid any trouble, was to move-on any waggons or trailers from their 'patch.' They did not need any reason or excuse. Let the next station deal with the Gypsies – a technique, it seems, which is used in many government Departments. The Travellers would move on, but a horse can only go so many miles pulling a heavy load, walking at four miles an hour. Motor vehicles must have fuel in the tanks, and garages don't materialise to order. Having just set up an encampment for the second time in one day, along comes the local *gavver* (policeman) nice or nasty. "Sorry, my Super has told me to shift you lot; you'll have to move or you'll pulled off," or, "You've got an hour to get off, then the tractor will come and pull you off." This could happen three or four times a day during the period of the worst persecution, until waggon horses and people would be exhausted, especially any following foals, when some decent *gavver* might let them stop overnight. Can you wonder that normally docile Travellers, seeing their families thus treated, and being driven out of their own country, objected and tried to make a stand? I have a heavy book of press cuttings reporting depressing incidents. By 'own country' I do not mean the British Isles, but a particular part of the country, which 'belongs' to a family by reason of birth or long time association. All Travellers *belong* somewhere, like most other people. This fact is not liked (if known) by romantics who see the Gypsy life as having no limits in length of journeying, and expect Travellers to travel from Land's End to John O'Groats, with no regional accents. They are due for a rude awakening!

I believe it is generally thought that Romanies roam at will. This is what books and films infer. Few people that I have discussed this with have any idea that Travellers are mainly parochial and have lifelong associations with certain areas where their families are buried, and have regional accents. This is not the *gaujes'* idea of what a Gypsy should be. That is their problem!

The structure of the Traveller's family life, the wide circle of friends and immediate family, is of paramount importance to the continuance of tradition, and depends upon a network of friends and relatives. Should a move be made, their whereabouts is noted, even if it is not known exactly where the family is, the *area* is known, and all the 'stops' in that area are known – in an emergency it is just a question of going round them all. But now it is more and more difficult as so many of the age-old and traditional 'stops' have been obliterated. The lifeblood of a less resourceful people would have been squeezed out.

This quiet deadly erosion of the way of life of Britain's nomadic people increased from the early 1950s, by the 1980s 'stops' on heath and common-land, roadsides etc, indeed any well known 'Gypsy Site,' were fenced off, ditched, banked-up, or made inaccessible by poles set in the ground at short intervals. Some Councils used dead tree trunks, bricks, rubble anything they could lay their hands on, once such methods became universal. These unsightly ploys were worse than any rubbish left by Travellers . Before the days of the Council verge-cutters, rubbish was hidden by bushes and wild flowers until it rotted away.

Parliament was being urged to legislate, to make new laws, not just issue guidelines or policy as hitherto. Many Residents' Associations, as well as police and influential landowners, pressed for this sterner stance. So at last the Caravan Sites Act 1968 was passed. As is usual with laws, it is the small clauses one should be wary of, and this was no exception. Councils were obliged to provide Gypsy Sites. They did not want to do so, as money and time was wasted battling with one objection after another, to each proposed site. Meanwhile, until all these sites were built, Travellers were allowed to stop in the area if their name was down for a place on the proposed site. With so many old stopping-places fenced off, greater numbers congregated on the few stops still available. This led to Travellers becoming more noticeable than before. They were forced to stop in very exposed places, alongside main A-roads with lit-up road signs and all-night traffic; to go outside the trailer was to be deafened by motors. Not their choice, but there was no alternative.

To add to this miserable time in history, huge numbers of Irish Travellers, learning from relatives how well they were doing on the 'black-stuff' (tar macadam), brought over anything on wheels that would tow without collapsing. Gangs of them descended upon the outskirts of towns. They took down fences and gates to Council and private property, pulling in with flair and wild abandon that secretly gained admiration, yet frightened the Native Travellers who had never declared such open war on authority. Eventually newspapers sent reporters to various scenes. Television cameras followed. The usual pattern of misreporting with news-flashes of 'Gypsy Invasion,' the old tatty trailers with broken doors, no windows, parked higgledy-piggledy, as the Irish do, with much household rubbish strewn about. No mention of Irish, of course, the reporters keeping to their cars. Headlines such as, "Council spends taxpayers' money on large-scale towing-off operation." The public could not be expected to know that these were not local Travellers. Had the reporters been more professional what a story they could have unearthed! This invasion went on for over ten years with only local Councils and police aware of it, as they bore the brunt of hundreds of Irish Travellers stopping together. They moved with speed from one end of the country to the other, which is why, once they left an area, interest in them faded; unlike Romanies who have regional associations and expect to return in due course.

Circular 49/68
(Ministry of Housing and Local Government)

Circular 42/68
(Welsh Office)

Joint Circular from the

Ministry of Housing and Local Government
Whitehall, London S.W.1

Welsh Office
Cathays Park, Cardiff

Sir,   *23rd August 1968*

Caravan Sites Act 1968

1. We are directed by the Minister of Housing and Local Government and the Secretary of State for Wales to say that the above Act received the Royal Assent on 26th July, 1968, and except for Part II comes into force on 26th August, 1968. Part II will come into force on a date to be appointed by Ministerial Order.

Part I—Provisions for Protection of Residential Occupiers

2. The provisions of Part I cover any licence or contract under which a person is entitled to station a caravan on a protected site and occupy it as his residence, or under which a person is entitled to occupy as his residence a caravan stationed on any protected site. Such a licence or contract is referred to as a "residential contract" and the person so entitled as "the occupier". A residential contract may thus be a contract which relates only to the right to station a caravan on a pitch, or it may relate both to a caravan and a pitch. A protected site is defined as a site in respect of which a site licence is required under Part I of the Caravan Sites and Control of Development Act, 1960, or would be so required but for paragraph 11 of Schedule I to that Act. Part I thus covers sites run by local authorities. Part I does not apply to land in respect of which the relevant planning permission or site licence is expressed to be granted for holiday use only, or is otherwise so expressed or subject to such conditions that there are times of the year when no caravan may be stationed on the land for human habitation.

Part of the Caravan Sites Act

Chapter Ten

The Solution?

There have always been some 'Irishmans' over here; some long-established families are well known, and respected, they are known to Romanies and accepted, some are related to the newcomers, but one is not one's cousin's keeper! Once Councils had provided sites, Travellers who came into the area and attempted to pull onto on land which had been their traditional stopping place for generations, could be obliged to leave by means of the Council obtaining a Designation Order. Thus a family might go into an area to visit friends or attend a wedding, only to find the Official Site full and be forced to leave. There was no Human Rights Bill in those days. Each time I use the word 'move' I would be grateful if you would pause and journey in your imagination beyond the word. To come to a full-stop *at* the word, cuts out all the implications. Move? Move to where? Not back where they came from. Any space available on an Official Site or a 'stop,' is immediately taken, there being more Travellers than there are places available. It is no joke, literally to race others to a stop, to round a bend and see a turnout ahead of you, and instead of the old feeling of delight, a feeling of depression descends in case they should turn right at the crossroads indicating that they are going to the place you yourself have in mind. They will, of course, get to the only space left. How sad it is to be forced to pass the famous Hog's Back traditional Romany stop, on the way to Epsom. Here the waggons and trailers used to line up along this enormous green stretch atop the World, amid the pre-race excitement. Since 1974 there has been an ugly line of poles, with great bars of wood at car roof height across all entrances to picnic areas. The Hog's Back is so vast there is more than enough room for cars, family picnics *and* Travellers' trailers.

To us, this exclusion means an extra stretch added to the journey to the Races; no handy one-night stop before reaching the Downs. I was dumbstruck the other day, when a friend who I supposed I had told a good deal about the Travelling life and its problems, and who is moving because of an unpleasant neighbour, said, "It's alright for you – you never have to be with people you dislike, you can just move." As with lots of problems, dithering does not lead to the best decisions. My own view is that it is mainly a question of communication and understanding, with the more difficult Travellers' requirements coming later. The expensive Official Sites, designed, I was told, by an architect somewhere in central government, and for which the design plans are universal, could surely have consulted Romanies destined to have to live in them? In the same disastrous way that friendly families from back-street neighbourhoods were scraped up and put into tower-blocks (many later blown up) because that is what others decided they needed, or *ought* to need. The facilities that other people decided Romanies needed, they did not and do not need. What the *gaujo* decided was essential, Romanies were happy to do without. That which Romanies do regard as essential, the Site Planners expect them to do without!

I recognise that a number of humans living on one place permanently without toilets, flush or chemical, is not ideal, but what has not been discovered is Travellers' attitudes to this delicate problem. Once, while stopping on an age-old stop which was designated for an Official Site at some later date, we were awakened early one morning by a vehicle driving in, the guard dogs going mad, and screams coming from a trailer as if we were all being murdered in our beds. I have referred previously to the square-frame tents: several trailers including us, had them at this time and in one or two belonging to those who stayed occasionally on land owned by other Romanies, were Elsans (Chemical toilets). Apparently a new and enthusiastic Health Visitor had thought that our "night-earth buckets" – as she referred to the Elsans to everyone's mystification – ought to be regularly emptied by the Council. Thus it was that, before anyone was up or dressed, a very smelly sewage lorry, which had open buckets swinging on hooks for emptying the effluent from Elsan to tanker, drove in. Two men jumped out, and possibly being used to non-Travellers caravan sites, they donned gloves and walked straight into the tents! The noise from the dogs awakened the first woman who saw a man walking into, or coming out of, her tent, and caused the screaming. It is traditional for men and women to have separate toilet arrangements, and thus, for a man, not only to go into a woman's tent but to empty a bucket in full view was humiliating to say the least. From the health point of view men moving aside the canvas doors, handling one object after another was unwise. All the women objected strongly. Luckily our fierce Alsatian kept them away from our tent. The next week I was ready for them and bribed the man not to enter the tent, being contractors they were not averse to this and each week thereafter the lorry just circled round and collected the 'protection' money. Little things mean a lot; it is all a question of not *assuming* anything where Romanies are concerned.

I referred earlier to the different strata of Romany. At Fairs or Races, it being a holiday, in principle, all members of the hierarchy stop together, but in actual practice, families and friends try to find one another. The consequence of this is an unconscious dividing in some measure. A glance at the field will enable the newly arriving trailer-driver to decide in which direction to point his vehicle so as to end up in the company he desires, or feels at home or comfortable with. While it may be an idealist's dream for everyone to be equal, just as some people are happy to be led, while others are only happy when leading, so it is that some people know their place, but, contrary to the ideas of the champions of the underdog, actually want to stay there! Equal opportunities will never ensure an equal society. So it is with Romanies. This fact has not been taken into account at all, therefore to the Council and Ratepayers' puzzlement, some sites in certain areas where there are only a few of one particular kind of Traveller and not enough to fill the site, remain half-empty, or did until a Council had the bright idea of filling the plots with homeless people in old caravans!

No way are the 'flash' or top Travellers going to stop on such places. They are not going to be 'scraped up' by a Government, uninterested in, or ignorant of, Travellers' needs, with incompetent handling of the 'Gypsy Problem,' as it has been called for at least fifteen years. They have not got where they are without the initiative and resourcefulness needed to survive against the most daunting odds. Those not able to own their own land and obtain Planning Permission for trailers, become one of those who stop on another Traveller's land. They still travel in summer but over winter on these Trailer Parks as they are called. Even here they are not free from officialdom. Only recently a yard running smoothly, each family friends of one-another with no problems regarding non-Traveller neighbours, was completely upset by a Planning Officer who happened to be visiting a neighbouring property. Seeing the trailers, he noticed that they were not lined up in a regular pattern. Someone somewhere, with nothing better to do, had ordered that trailers on a Trailer Park should be placed in a certain order. As I said earlier, Travellers prefer their trailer doors a certain way round, and as it is impossible to get a drawbar into a corner facing inwards (since the motor has to go in first and be able to unhitch and get out, and twin-axle trailers cannot be turned by hand), there are only a certain number of permutations possible.

In ordinary circumstances Travellers would have laughed at just another example of *gaujo* ignorance of the practical common-sense of their ways, but as the property owner had always had good relations with the Authorities (who could cancel his Licence) he had to ask all the Travellers to rearrange their trailers which meant packing up their belongings – a small matter the Planning Officer had overlooked. It being winter they had not expected to move, and all the china was up ready for Christmas visitors. Clothes lines, electric cables, tents, outside paraphernalia, all had to be untangled and moved in a small space at the same time. After a chaotic day, three trailers ended up facing in different directions from hitherto, for which all the others had had to move. Planning Permission had been given for the trailers to be in the owner's lorry yard and not in his large green field where there was plenty of space and freedom for the children to play, safe from vehicles coming into and out of the yard. An application for a licence for the field was rejected, in case the trailers could be *seen* by anyone coming up the owner's private road, yet only Traveller's ever came up there! He still had to use it as a lorry park for his business. After the shuffle round of trailers to please the Planning Officer (wanting every trailer facing the same way!!!), those nearest the lorry backing points were worried about their small children. One family decided to leave despite the difficulty of getting into another Trailer Park at this late date before Christmas. These were not Council Site Travellers. Into the vacant space came a family with five spoiled and unruly children. Within a week the children's quarrels had spread to the parents, as it is not done to reprimand other people's children. If only the Planning Officer could have seen the disaster he had caused. All was unhappiness, where all had been contentment.

I think it was once generally agreed that there is a need for what are called Transit-Camps, or Transit-Sites, for Travellers passing through an area, or who need to visit for a funeral or wedding. These would have none of the dreadful fixtures and fittings – concrete slabs, tarmac plots, seven feet high wire-mesh fences – just a field with a rubbish collection.

Regarding rubbish-skips which are left on some stops, it is not that Travellers do not put their rubbish into them, as one person thought seeing refuse lying all about on the ground, but rather the local dogs that tear open bags and boxes. Bags left outside shops which are being refurbished have no food in them and so have no attraction for dogs. Stray dogs will pull rubbish from dustbins when a family is out. Cunningly, dogs on Fairgrounds and at Race meeting go a long way from their own trailers to pillage. It's impossible to catch them or the owners. It is disheartening to spend hours clearing up outside a trailer for wind to blow it back from somewhere else, usually from a dog-ripped bag a little way off. This is one reason to keep a guard dog, to protect your own rubbish! We live in an age of killer diseases, drugs, war, atomic waste, famine, floods and drought; yet a 'job's worth' man disrupts happy family life to enforce what he see as several trailers untidily not facing the same way.

Regarding trailer dogs, a friendly dog is useless. As soon as new arrivals pull-on, they let their dogs down from their lorries or vans and the first thing they do is a tour of inspection to see if there is a trailer without a guard, and anything to plunder, or one with a bitch good for visiting! A friendly dog will bring all the others to your door to see if there are any loose dogs to go hunting with. The state of one's outside carpet can be imagined if a pack of dogs are playing on it. Dogs are one reason why the water churns and water-carriers are kept off the ground on low tables. One cannot protect tent corners from leg-cocking, and they have to be washed. Tents are fast going out of fashion. Transit-sites mean that a Council has to find a plot of land, as there will always be the type of Traveller who needs, and who is relatively resigned to, life on an official organised site; even though they often become dispirited and lethargy sets in. The very same-way facing of the trailers, uncharacteristic uniformity, crowded space and tall fencing has an adverse effect. It is the *gaujes'* idea of how Travellers ought to want to live. Alcoholism was a problem on the Native Indian Reservations – considering the condition of some Council Sites, I think Travellers behave well under such depressing circumstances.

Other classes of Traveller hope to avoid this style of life, to which they could so easily be doomed, by providing their own accommodation as they have always done. As you might expect this is not done *gaujes'* style. They buy a likely house or a bungalow – often several families, all related, will buy houses in a row. Sometimes there are many houses in a street owned by Romanies. All will have a tourer-trailer in the garden in which they go away to Fairs or Races. The Travellers I was referring to at the beginning of this paragraph, are those who buy small plots of land from a Traveller who has bought a large piece of land in order to divide it up into small plots. In 1981 a Council closed down a scrap-yard: the reason given was that it was unsightly. The Traveller who owned it, his livelihood taken away, divided it in half and sold it. Since then it has been subdivided until there is no more division possible. Each plot is fenced with lap-fencing, provided with oak gates gravelled over, tarmac drives made down the centre, and lawns and flower beds landscaped. On each plot the owner has put a chalet, usually delivered in two sections and bolted together. As these are on wheels, although too long to be legally towed, they have to be moved on a transporter. Once settled on the plot the wheels are then hidden by decorative bricks. This was once a 'show' village and Travellers drove miles to see it. They were speechless, but not for long, unfortunately, for it all went 'pear-shaped.' What could have been an example for more happy families, was doomed because the owner, who had not yet arrived in person to take up residence, had allowed the other owners of plots to pull on, and had also allowed us to pull onto his own plot until his chalet arrived. The Council was outraged at this *fait accompli*. One Official marched up to a Traveller who was putting up a dividing fence. "You are not allowed to put that up; take it down at once." "But it is *my* land," the Traveller argued. The fence was only three feet high to keep dogs and children off his plot. The Official went away and debated what to do. At last the Authorities thought of a solution to squash such enterprise and to send those who were not wanted on the roads, *back* to the roads. We had travelled with several of these families endeavouring to take their lives and those of their children into their own hands, trying to find their own solution to the 'Gypsy Problem,' and who, without help had so far managed it their way. What the Authorities thought up, was far better than the Planning Officer's insistence on regimented trailers, they thought of the seldom used, much dreaded COMPULSORY PURCHASE ORDER – as one Romany put it, "They've put a 'pulsery compurchase' order on us all." I doubt whether the reader will ever return home to find that he or she is forced to sell their home and land to the Council – everything you have ever worked for, all your efforts and dreams, gone. When you have weathered many a storm sent by an old enemy, you take it calmly, which is what they did.

Some families got together and bought Legal Advice, engaging a Barrister to speak on their behalf at a public hearing. The Order has not yet been executed but hangs over the would-be Travellers' settlement like the sword of Damocles. The idea, let alone the act, of ploughing up the prepared plots is horrific. At the Enquiry Meeting the Planners said that the land was 'unfit' for the Travellers to settle on. Asked what the land had been used for previously, one replied that it was 'beautiful.' Pressed for more detail he admitted it had been used for *glasshouses*. We all have our own idea of beauty! The Planners had been upset both by the number of families and by the speed of the landscaping. They argued that a small number of families using the land as smallholdings would be acceptable. Quite a change of occupation for Romanies, pig keeping. Who would decide the lucky families? Some long-settled Travellers on land attached to the nearby village, had been granted permission for three chalets, if they then registered as a smallholding, and kept a few ponies and hens. Near to them was a Showman's Winter Quarters: they had no problems stopping there in their trailers. It is not as if the Travellers' settlement was an eyesore in a suburban area, there being existing trailers and chalets. The latest news is that a private builder has offered a hundred thousand pounds per acre, an offer few could refuse. The Planners will have won another battle and the Travellers will have to go back on the roads searching elsewhere for the elusive, and rarely given, Planning

Permission.

On Travellers' settlements the chalets are hard to distinguish from housing with fixed foundations, and are nearly as expensive. How many of the Travellers on such places manage to elude the dreaded Council Sites, is by the expediency of each buyer of a large plot, dividing it into three and selling each small plot for the original sum. Things have a habit of escalating with tremendous speed. The first landowner might boast to friends, and they see a chance that may not come again. He is sometimes persuaded to sell off half. Close relatives then ask to buy from the *second* purchasers, and there can be jealousy and ill-feeling if they are refused. An observer might point out that those who came last had smaller plots yet paid the same prices. Beggars can't be choosers! – it is accepted as the luck of the deal. Had it all been done at non-Traveller speed, involving 'searches,' etc, there might be time to reflect. But again, with the ways of a minority conflicting with the ideas of Authorities and Bureaucrats, no one wants to get involved with the latter, there being all too many bitter memories.

Soon any settlement would be running smoothly, with water-pipes, electricity, telephones, flush toilets, nursery-bought trees and shrubs looking immediately established. living-trailers are put up for sale, and tourers bought. Lawns are laid and flower-beds planted. Brick walls are built with oak or wrought iron gates to each plot, and drives are constructed. The way in which it is done, with the speed and the panache of people often unable to read and write, must be admired. But still there is their old enemy, the Authorities, and, as has come to be expected, it is not long before the Planners descend to end the dreams – frequently succeeding.

One cannot fail to notice how many Council Sites or so-called 'Gypsy Sites' are placed by sewage farms, old rubbish tips, pig farms, or indeed *anywhere* no-one else would want to live. But of course they are good enough for Travellers! Councils usually arrive at such unsavoury locations via costly and time consuming debates and Public Meetings. Citizens who are normally well-behaved go berserk at the mention of a proposed Site in their area. Private house owners objected to a proposed Site on a traditional Travellers' stopping place near Leatherhead, by the River Mole. The land was over a mile away from the houses and totally invisible to any private dwellings. It was land which had had been taken away from Travellers when the road had been widened and a new and incredibly ugly bridge had been built to replace the old one. In place of the age-old Travellers 'stop,' the Council built a Car Park which was hard to find, the access being under a one-car wide railway bridge. No tourist would be likely to stumble upon it, so a Car Park it remained – with no cars! Occasionally an angler might fish from the bank in lone splendour. It was a car park so large it could well have served a Town! Once it attracted an invasion of dozens of Irish Travellers who needed a large space for so many trailers in a convoy. A few local Romanies moved on, knowing the ways of the Irish who never stay for long. They tried to keep it tidy, but the rubbish left after the invasion, was of course, blamed on *them*. There was an incredible amount. Supermarket bags full of 'sewage' had been thrown down on the newly cleared bank in the mistaken belief that they would land in the river, which they failed to do.

I have intimate knowledge of what I am writing about, having witnessed the whole unhappy event at first hand. The local Travellers spent days clearing up the scattered rubbish and putting it in a Council skip. It was a thankless task. They had hopes that the Council, seeing the failure of the car park, might relent and give the Travellers back their old stopping place. This story had a happy ending, although with an unhappy twist. It *did* become an official Site. We were allocated an unfenced plot, but did not want to stay there once it became a Council Site. An elderly Traveller couple came in one day and said how much they would like to retire there, as the wife was not at all well. We said that they could have our place and in fact could have our trailer as we intended selling it and buying another. They only had a small tourer being at a low ebb in life. We felt sorry for them, old with no family and nowhere to go. They were overjoyed. We moved out of our trailer and they, having paid us for it, moved in. Just as we were about to depart, a Council Official arrived and said we had no right to offer them our place as they had not been through the 'standard procedure.' We argued that the old woman was not well and they had nowhere to go. But the mighty hand of callous officialdom descended. They were told they would not be allowed to stay. It was quite unbelievable. We all had to back-pedal; we had to return their money and they had to take their possessions out of their new home. She was heart broken, and we were none too pleased. We at least had another trailer to live in. I think they had provisionally sold their tourer, but I never heard what happened to them. Who cared? – certainly not 'officialdom.'

In 1974 The Surrey Comet reported how the Epsom Downs Conservators had been refused police co-operation when they proposed that their officials and workmen would tow-off Travellers' trailers that were parked illegally (arriving too *early* for the Race Day or staying too long *afterwards*). The Police said that the Council could then be cited for a breach of the peace, or causing an obstruction of the highway. Good for the Police! For such towing-off, the most inappropriate vehicles are used, such as Council tractors which do not, as a rule, have the correct towing attachments. Travellers have returned home to find frightened children in trailers left lopsided on a main road, china smashed, goods ruined, and everything much damaged. Teenagers, who cannot stand up to such action by Councils, are sometimes left in charge of children during the day. One can have nothing but contempt for anyone who has so little regard for someone else's property, let alone the Law, for wilful damage; or even for the feelings of the men whose job it is to move a home so roughly. This lacks the ethics of a civilised society. 'Towing-off' is dastardly in thought and deed.

Returning to Official Sites; one of the first considerations of Travellers when looking for a 'stop' is its situation. Is it off a main highway? Is the lane or approach road wide enough for trailers to pass an oncoming cattle-truck? Are there any passing places? If the stop is on private land (with permission) is the gateway wide enough? A ten feet wide gate is not much use for an eight feet wide trailer! Too many Official Sites fail in these considerations. There is a very narrow one-car wide lane into the Denham Site; a quagmire of mud at Norwich; to reach the one at Wythall, trailers must go through a ford. At Footscray in Kent the site is too narrow to turn trailers round, so they have to be reversed in, or, if driven in, then reversed out. There is, however, a Site in Buckinghamshire where there is a decent distance between the trailers, which are allowed to face *any* direction, and storage space for outside things behind the individual washrooms – an improved design.

As Romanies are being forced to change their way of life, so it follows they will have to change their way of making a living. When an area has been thoroughly 'called over,' Travellers on sites find they are often forced to seek Social Security as the only source of survival. Those who for years have accused Travellers of not paying taxes, never take into account that until the Caravan Sites Act, even with all the difficulties of fast-vanishing stopping places, Social Security was not sought by Travellers. Neither do Romanies put their old people into 'homes' at ratepayers' expense. Britain's problem families cost millions of pounds a year. This proud race of people, who have inspired some of our great poets and artists, people who are self-reliant, are not asking the irate ratepayer for anything. Had they been allowed to continue to travel, and to rest on their traditional stopping places, mainly on common-land, old bomb-sites and unused waste land, they would go about their business as always, mysteriously to the *gaujes*, changing with the times, and surviving against all odds. Aborigines regard land as part of their heritage, culture and religious tradition. What the static *gaujes* cannot appreciate is, that in the transient way of life, *land* is all important. It is only the interfering in the long established way of life that has caused or is causing the genocide of a race as we know it. The plight of the Travellers has interested a few champions, but after the Caravan Sites Act, they probably think that there is now no problem at all. Councils secretly own many thousands of acres of land all over Britain. Much of this is in the White zone or non-green belt areas of unused land which could well be used for Travellers to stop on, and with no neighbours to object. But Councils are allowed to hang onto land without any enquiry by citizens who practice the national characteristic of 'It's rude to be inquisitive,' or to ask questions. That, and not Travellers trying in their own way to comply with Government policy, is a mistake. Questions *should* be asked. Why are Councils allowed to own large tracts of land? It should all be sold, and the money used to lessen property rates.

Twin-axle Astral

Chapter Eleven

Travellers

Temperamentally, Traveller's veer towards the Latin. They are emotional; quickly roused; quick to anger, to laugh, to cry; flamboyant; devil-may-care; optimistic; ostentatious. They share the sins of us all; greed, covetousness, backbiting, gossiping. They are no better and no worse than others in a competitive 'every-man-for-himself' society, and a 'cut-throat' business world. One tends to wonder whether the old adage *honour among thieves* is true, with so many super-grasses in our time, yet professional villains have their own strong moral code. They dislike perpetrators of certain kinds of crimes; they have contempt for 'bent coppers.' The world of the criminal is a one with its own codes and language, but has little interest, except professionally, of course, in any other: It is 'them' and 'us.' And so it is also in the closed world of the Romanies.....and about as easy to enter as that of the Mafia. The polite conversations that go on in the presence of a non-Traveller visitor, or someone anxious to be friends with Travellers, is as different as chalk is to cheese, from the real conversation that ensues after the visitor has gone!

No-one can change their nature. Quick-to-flare tempers can and do lead to terrible consequences. Injustices, slights, or bad-deals, rankle. Travellers do not forgive and forget. Bad blood feuds often linger for many generations. One rarely hears of a 'wild Englishman,' but 'wild Irish,' and 'wild Scots,' are often found in history. Today Travellers from Ireland and Scotland are known among Travellers as 'wild,' and more unruly in every way; less easily intimidated by Authorities. Yet compared to the average *gaujo*, Travellers from South of the Border are thought to be 'wild.' They suffer a lifetime of persecution, for not accepting every law unquestioningly, and for craving the freedom of the roads and of open spaces. This freedom, and their temperament, cannot and should not be stamped out. I am not overlooking the settled-down, seemingly respectable and conforming Traveller; although the true nature of this fiercely proud Gypsy, his respectability only skin-deep, can rise to the surface in fraught situations!

It is surely this very wildness, this untameable quality, this admirable flamboyance, which has attracted poets, artists and writers and even some non-Travellers. From these ranks people emerge of such strong character as to outshine the rest. Such a person commands great respect. He has that quality which actors who reach the top of their profession have. No one in Hollywood would deny that all the 'greats' had it, namely charisma. An entry by someone with this aura, can cause a roomful of people to fall silent and stare. It plays about the heads of those blessed with, and those lacking physical beauty. It is a gift which money cannot buy – intangible. Although Travellers are, like everyone else, all different, they nevertheless share certain characteristics; mode of speech, manner of forming conversations, being in general agreement on, what in other societies would be an area of contention, a moral code. They practice none of the mumbo jumbo accredited to them by some writers. Academics concerned with deep *Romani*, seem ignorant of the far more important unusual speech patterns.

It is odd how narrator and cameraman in a natural history film will impassively talk and film during the death throes of some hapless animal, making no attempt to rescue it (and ruin a film), the argument being, "that's nature." Surely it is also 'just nature' when some other larger animal arrives on the scene and scares off the predator, man! Why should not this animal interfere? Yet as soon as this same animal prowls among Travellers, he cannot forebear to interfere! He acts the role of a missionary rather than observer. George Borrow confined himself to truthful reporting, and this truth of his early encounters in the *Wind on the Heath* and *Lavengro* speak to us across the years. Would that all who dabble, wrote with his quill, instead of perpetuating second-hand myths, that cause Romanies to despair of ever being truthfully represented.

Travellers are very sensitive to any slight or rudeness resulting from prejudice and have an unerring instinct for a person's hidden dislike or false smile. It is a fact that one becomes sensitive to certain words. We have been encamped on the roadside and people have passed afoot, on horseback or in vehicles who have been talking, we have been unable to make out any words, yet the words 'Gypsy,' 'Dids,' or 'caravan' have been clearly audible! I am not quoting cases of shouted abuse which is *all* too audible and clearly understood. On one occasion a silly woman remarked to me in all seriousness, "I suppose you snatch turnips from the fields as you pass by."

The outdoor life has, of course, never been a preserver of looks. Like women in countries with hot climates, Travelling women blossom and fade early. The legendary 'Old Gypsy woman at the door' who looks like a grandmother carrying her daughter's baby, is actually the mother, and is nowhere near the age she appears. As the Travelling life has become more motorised, however, and less time is spent by the wood fire, women's appearance has improved. The fact that women became 'aged' enough to qualify as matriarchal figures long before they were old as judged by their year of birth (this was often not recorded), led to the myths of the great ages that some great-great-grandmothers were supposed to have attained. In actual fact, it is noticeable to an inside observer how relatively few old people there are. The number of deaths which occur among those in the prime of life is depressing. Really old Travellers are few and far between.

Drying winds, scorching-fire, un-shaded sunshine, soap and water with no moisturiser are no recipe for lasting beauty. Speeded up childhood and early marriage ensure that adult life lasts as long as possible, and this means the 'best' years are not lost.

Some larger than life Traveller characters have become 'Legends in our Time,' stories of their achievements being remembered and passed on verbally, as were stories of old. Many have earned nicknames, although this does not automatically signify charisma, since quite a number of nicknames are from childhood days. One from recent years is Concorde – the unfortunate Traveller having a long proboscis-like nose reminiscent of the drooping nose of the famous aeroplane. Then there is Nose-and-a-Half, Bug-eyes, Bugs, Tip-cart, Flaxy-haired Boy, Half-eared Henry, Nan-nan, Mouth-and-Trousers, Hi-Ab John, Winkie, Flat-Face, Peg-Leg, Needles, Jay-Bird, Tolly, Hacky, Boney – no doubt a derivative of Bonaparte – and so the list goes on.

These 'Living Legends' are familiar faces, appearing at most Travellers' functions. Some have their 'own' stopping place, like a reserved chair in a gentleman's club, and no one else would dream of pulling their trailer into these. To be in the inner circle of a Travellers' drinking-school, including one of the well known figures, is tantamount to dining at the Captain's table. It is a man's world. I recall one of the Assistants of some Gypsy Liaison Officer appointed by Councils as a mediator between them and Travellers. Naturally few had ever before encountered a Traveller! Having had some experience in Social Work this girl swung into an encampment with the dangerous qualification of very little knowledge. She walked straight up to a group of men, and to their and the women's shock and astonishment attempted to engage them in bright conversation. During her official visits, on the way to and from the trailers, she would innocently stop to talk to groups of men, all embarrassed. She did not make much headway in her job and did not last long. The next Assistant had had to do with settled-down Travellers and knew better than to behave in such a 'brazen' manner – 'brazen,' 'forward,' or 'flash,' in the old fashioned way of the "flash gals" in the old Romany song. Flash women are avoided by men and disliked by women. A producer of a television film about Travellers, once needed a man to visit a Fair. He made the grave mistake of sending a car to collect the Traveller, driven by a continuity-girl. Although the family was on its own, the wife suffered this occurrence as an humiliation from which she never recovered. His filming relationship went down hill. Travellers are very sensitive about such etiquette and easily offended.

To my mind, one of the nicest things about this old world attitude is that Romanies do not kiss and cuddle in public. It was noticeable at a Showman's Ball we attended at which there were some Romanies who were related, how the behaviour of young people differed in this respect to a Traveller's Ball. The traditional way of 'running off' together, eloping, is still carried out, but to comply with the now usual Church wedding, the couple return for this. As the essence of the running away was secrecy, courting was carried on by a kind of fan-language, eye flutterings without alerting parents. It always amused me that in the film *Golden Earrings*, a couple acted a scene of courtship bang in the middle of a crowded encampment, surrounded by Gypsies who were supposed to be none the wiser! Crowded conditions dictate discretion. Great significance has always been put upon that which to other people would arouse no comment. Hence the careful way in which women act in mixed company. Landladies and barmaids used to a free joking semi-flirting relationship with male customers, arouse disdain and dislike. One evening each week it is usual to 'take the women out,' to whatever local pub is accepting the custom of Travellers – they tend to take over the Pub, mainly the lounge. Gradually, however, these ways are becoming watered down by the 'progress of time' and the influence that television has on Travelling women, erstwhile modest, now exposed to the ways non-Traveller women behave. During the full-frontal nude film era, women were genuinely shocked. It only confirmed how they thought non-Travellers behaved. During these evening outings, the women sit together at a table, the men stand or sit at the bar. The only difference for them, from any other night, is that every so often one of the men will come over and ask the women to name what drink they want, usually asking his wife to ask the other women, unless he himself knows them well. According to the kind of Traveller, and the number present, the women will have a 'pot' on the table and everyone will put in a note. This is used to pay for each round, each taking a turn to fetch the drinks; a nightmare to remember twenty-four drinks! Bacardi and coke, Babycham and whisky, or some other potent 'short' are popular drinks, but never beer, although some older women may prefer a Guinness. Being able to write I am often asked to write a list. Two women go up together to check on the

117

drinks, change.....and the barmaid!

Evenings end with songs from the ladies' table. Many a nondescript middle-aged mother comes into her own with a voice and delivery as professional as any Country and Western singer. Good singers are known and they are never allowed to go home without performing. I know of no violin players although there are some in Scotland and I expect Ireland. (In Scotland kilted bagpipe players entertain tourists on lay-bys and at beauty-spots, before returning to their Trailers!)

There are some good 'cordeen' players (accordion and melodeon). One of the very best I ever heard, 'Scotch Tom,' could take up an old instrument and silence would fall all about him at his magical playing of an endless flow reels and Strathspays. That so many old and delightful tunes could remain in the memory of someone who could not read note of music was unbelievable. Whenever we had a melodeon tuned to the same key, we would spend many a happy hour – or three or four – playing our instruments, matching tune for tune. I had no advantage as I cannot read music either and had not long learned the melodeon. Being an optimist he preferred all joyful tunes, but I tried to get him to play the more mournful poignant laments, or *coronachs* as he correctly called dirges but which I find hauntingly beautiful. I have repaired old instruments for him although I don't know much about them – simple repairs such as mending bellows. We first encountered him at Epsom when we stopped 'in the Bushes,' across the road from the grandstand. The family, with married sons, formed a circle, much like Prairie Schooners awaiting an attack by Indians. The position was too near the main road, and all the dust and dirt from passing vehicles landed on everything. However, there was a good view of 'the scene.' His family numbered among our closest friends; in a life of such insecurity it is comforting to know there are people who one could call upon and rely upon to show the old true meaning of friendship in times of trouble. One good thing which persecution has forged is the tendency of families and close relations by marriage to band together in their struggle against the unfeeling, uncaring, unfair Laws.

I heard Richard Adams, author of *Watership Down*, and former President of the RSPCA, talking on the radio, and one of the things he said pertaining to the experiments on animals, could well fit the Travellers' situation. If I can be forgiven for taking it out of context, he said "Laws are usually made, that people want." He also said, words to the effect, that if people were better educated as to the facts, bad laws could be changed.

118

The Gambling Ring

'Muggy, King of the Ring' was another very memorable character. The ring being one of gambling, set up every year at Epsom Races. It was managed in an orderly manner by Travellers exclusively for Travellers. Inside the ring the archaic game of pitch and toss was played. Two men are inside the ring and the players line the four rope sides. Two coins, identical old pennies, are tossed high up in the air, twisting and turning and coming to rest as close together as possible. Both must be either heads up or tails up. The players bet against the 'Ring Master.' Wads of notes are to be seen under the toes of their boots, the money-holder taking and replacing the notes as needs be. There are lots of 'side-bets' going on non-stop at the same time! Women do not take part in this man's game, but one year our trailer was parked in a good position for me to have a clear view. Then, the minimum bet was a five pound note, but bets in hundreds of pounds are not uncommon, some Romanies walking away with several thousand pounds! In true Gambler tradition, homes, in this case trailers, have been won and lost! "Sorry dear, can you take our things out; I've lost the trailer." Muggy had great 'spinning' skill and was renowned for his luck as well as his addiction to the sport, frequently leaving the Downs, several thousand pounds better off, in a cloud of envy from his fellow gamblers. Muggy was a great personality, universally known. I write of him in the past tense, as sadly, while on his own without his two sons, one of whom was a professional boxer, he was murdered in cold blood.

The funeral of such a well known figure caused hundreds of Travellers to converge and become part of the cortège, which was so long that when we ourselves were in part of this procession driving up the hill from Epsom town to the Downs, the front of the cortège was passing us coming down! The procession had wound round the grandstand as it was his family's wish that he be taken round the Downs and racecourse with which he and his family had such long associations. When they came to the place where the 'Ring' was usually set up, the cortège halted and his sons took his two pennies and spun them into the air, only a few yards from where Muggy had been stopping such a short while before, when he had been pointed out as the lucky man who had bought the 'Show-Trailer.' This same, brand new Exhibition trailer was then, of course, for sale. When we went to see his family some time after the funeral, we were shown inside. It was a very tempting bargain, but quite apart from the very sad association, wherever it went, it would be pointed out as "Muggy's trailer." The family would have used the money to try to obtain justice for his killing. It would seem like taking advantage of another's misfortune. Muggy was buried in the Cemetery on the Downs where many Travellers are laid to rest. Travelling people have been born, and some have died at Epsom during race week. There is now an official Site near Epsom but the less said about that the better. I was flattered to be asked to compose a poem, an 'Epitaph for Muggy,' which is engraved upon the huge tombstone, carved with horses and dogs which I drew on the card I made for them to keep in remembrance.

Romany floral tributes are always the largest possible. The immediate family often ordering life-sized reproductions, in appropriately coloured flowers, of the deceased's lurchers, or greyhounds, horses or ponies, or horses and jockeys, waggons and horses, even lorries and trailers. Written messages could be two feet high. Hearts, bottles and glasses, overflowing white-frothed beer mugs, and yards and yards of wreathes and baskets of flowers can be seen. For the traditional Romany funeral, the deceased lies in state. This used to be in a tent, in which his widow and children sat at head and feet, while mourners passed in and out. In the past, anyone hearing of this from the undertakers could be forgiven for thinking that a Gypsy King had died.

Of the funerals I have attended, which, on principle, like weddings, were only those of families I personally liked and knew well, this lying-in-state is always observed. Once when a really large coffin was too big to go through the trailer door, the problem was solved by breaking a hole through the wall! A splendid decision – an example of people getting their priorities right in the face of death. At one time the traditional practice was to burn the waggon of the deceased. This contributed not a little to there being so few examples of fine old wooden waggons left. In 1976, the 'Gypsy Caravan' of Matilda Smith was burned at Sandford in Oxfordshire. When waggon-builders had turned to motor bodybuilding, and waggons became hard to come by, fewer families did this, but they would sell the waggon and buy another. I have seen many a photograph of such an event that has caught some writer's attention and imagination and it is, of course, invariably a 'Gypsy Queen' being mourned.   Age, being an achievement in itself, has always been revered. Ageing Travellers looking far older than they actually are, and therefore not suffering from senility and still able to converse with wits as sharp as ever, command respect. They are called 'Auntie' or 'Uncle.' All families have one, since it is not the habit of Travellers to slough off any responsibility to the elderly who can no longer earn. Like many a revered stern Aunt in non-Traveller families who used to 'hold court' such matriarchal figures fostered the myth of there being a tribal Queen. I have known really splendid elderly women of waggon times who would pictorially fit everyone's idea of this. An enquirer at the burning of a waggon, asking if it had belonged to a Gypsy Queen, would of course, to honour the dead, be answered in the affirmative.

The son of another well-known Epsom personality was murdered outside his trailer which was parked on a lay-by. His father offered a £10,000 pound reward for information, and again the funeral was a large one with hundreds of floral tributes. The father was not one of those Travellers who go about incognito. That so few *gaujes* recognise Travellers could account for the often heard question, "Where have all the gypsies gone?" Proud of being a Romany, he had his vehicles painted and lined out in the old style. When making the funeral arrangements, he arranged for his son to be carried to the graveyard on his own lorry. It was covered in a green cloth and wreathes hung from the rack. Floral tributes were placed on the casket, with representations of dogs and horse-drawn vehicles, made of flowers, placed around it. This is a family which is trying to find an alternative to life on an official site, and so have bought their own land. After the funeral the family could not bear to be in the chalet where their son had lain-in-state, so they sold it, and bought another in a matter of days.

I shall not forget the procession to the church, because of the terrible, ignorant behaviour of non-Traveller car drivers. Just in case it was assumed that he had had his son taken to the church on a lorry because he could not afford a hearse, the empty hearse followed the lorry, along with twenty large limousines with the family, plus hundreds of vehicles with 'followers.' I don't think anyone seeing all this proceeding at a snail's pace, behind the decorated lorry could have mistaken it for anything but a cortège. Yet, to our horror, traffic overtook and cut in, joining the mourners – a tatty old 'banger' amidst the line of splendid limousines! At one point there was an old car with jocular messages painted on it, and at another a butcher's van. Then came a housewife with a car full of children eating ice-creams, leaning out of the windows and yelling. It was distressing for the family for these ignorant non-Travellers to intrude their vehicles into the cortège, even between the family limousines and the actual hearse. It made a mockery of what is a very serious 'showing respect' for the dead in the traditional Romany way. One car cut in so sharply that the following limousine had to brake suddenly and could not avoid crashing into it. The car which had caused the accident sped away, leaving the mourners shocked, shaken and bloodstained. We and another vehicle directly behind, finally succeeded, where horns and gestures had failed, in squeezing out the old 'banger' and its laughing driver. We forced him onto a roundabout where he sat among the flowers, no longer laughing. I wondered where the Police were. They were, in fact, at the cemetery, along with plainclothes detectives, so they must have known of the cortège and could have escorted it. One police car would have made all the difference. Only *one* driver, of a vintage car, showed any manners at all, and courteously gave way, when it was his road — a gesture from a past age of good manners. There was more than an ethical reason for 'foreign' traffic not joining the mourners since, when the traffic stopped at red lights, and many mourners were halted, with various vehicles already split up, the line of funeral cars got so separated by more and more 'foreign' cars, and further and further from the hearse, that it appeared to new cars on the scene as if the separated cars had no common purpose, and even fewer showed any deference at all. It was halfway through the service before some of the mourners, thus delayed, arrived. Some people had come hundreds of miles to 'follow,' only to be prevented, and then to miss half the service. Non-Travellers were shown in a very poor light. Since this funeral, another large 'following,' headed by a horse-drawn hearse, accompanied by police, had no such trouble.

After the funeral the mourners returned to the settlement for refreshment. Later that day the nearly new Travellers' Special motor-lorry was set alight following the old tradition of waggon burning. I wonder how many of the 'pig-ignorant,' as Travellers call them, car-drivers, owning a nearly new vehicle, could have brought themselves to burn it? The next day the remaining iron chassis was cut up and destroyed. This incident will join the unwritten word-of-mouth stories told and retold at Fairs and Travellers' gatherings – as I said earlier, a people of flamboyance and extravagant ideas, with nature to match. Actions such as this must be expected. There is a strong vein of non-realism, of fantasy, a theatrical flavour running through a life of unrest, where *something* is happening all the time.

Travellers' news is seldom World news. One might hear above the racket of conversations, "Come quick; Billy's felled down and broke his leg;" and, "Oh my poor dear blessed Lord, his leg is broke in two." Knowing full well of the Travellers' practice of exaggeration for dramatic impact, those hearing such cries will expect Billy to walk into the room with a mere bruise! News being greeted with age-old reservation leads to the need for, and practice of, melodrama. So it is that gestures really do have to be flamboyant, to qualify for amazement value.

A well-known Romany ordered a wedding cake for his daughter; nothing much unusual about that, except that this one was ten feet high with forty tiers! It took nearly a week to mix and bake. Containing 72 lbs of flour, 54 lbs of margarine, 54 lbs of sugar 279 lbs of fruit, 28 lbs of orange peal, 56 lbs of marzipan, and 72 lbs of icing sugar. It cost a mere thousand pounds. The confectioner hoped the Guinness Book of Records would recognise it as the world's largest wedding cake. We attended the reception of a recent wedding, which was notable for the interest it caused in Windsor. Collecting Dominic's suit from, the tailors, we became aware of streams of ladies who stood out from the well-dressed ladies of Windsor, for each was clad in restrained pastel colours, and almost without exception every young woman was dressed in a replica of Princess Diana's 'going away' outfit, with jaunty ostrich feathered hats. This fashion parade made its way to the church, opposite which was a large crowd of bystanders, far more than normally stop to watch a church wedding or even the changing of the guard. On the church steps the guests assembled and went in. Seven or eight Rolls Royce cars were lined up. I heard someone ask why they had hired so many. We knew they all belonged to a very wealthy Romany family. When they emerged and posed for photographs, the crowd gasped, as, instead of the little band of bridesmaids, there was a Matron-of-Honour and the *Groom* had seven Best Men. ,The groom was in pastel blue 'topper and tails' while his attendants were all in white 'topper and tails,' which, one presumes, could not have been hired. The crowd murmured, "Show-business."

Another story of determination and enterprise that has gone down in Traveller's history is that of Uriah Burton (known as "Big Uie"). Uie Burton was famous as a fighting-man for several decades, invariably unbeaten in bouts of either bare-knuckle or 'rough and tumble' combat. Indeed, during the '60's I witnessed his battle with the South-country fighter Tommy Roberts ('The Perfect Man') on Epsom Downs when, rather ignominiously, the contest was ended by Uie Burton throwing his opponent across the bonnet of a nearby Traveller-owned Jaguar car, whereupon he was 'given best.' But I digress. Before Uie's respected father passed away he expressed a wish that he should be buried on a Welsh mountain, Wales being the country of his birth, and the land he loved. His son not only agreed to this but decided to erect a monument to his father's beloved memory. Thus he obtained permission from the owner of *Moel-y-Golfa*, the highest of the Brendon Hills, to construct this memorial. It comprised three granite blocks, brought up from Cornwall. They were reputed to weigh twelve and a half, ten and a half, and five tonnes respectively. Twenty-eight tonnes to be borne up a mountain! Offers of help came from friends and businessmen, one of whom loaned an eight-wheeler low-loader lorry for the transportation.

When the time came to commence the task, human nature being what it is, many volunteer 'helpers' had faded away. Uie is quoted as saying: "I am a gypsy and proud of it, and my word is my bond." He was insistent that those who had promised assistance should honour their word. So it was that when vehicles were sent to collect these 'helpers,' from as far apart as Scotland, Wales and Ireland, the less enthusiastic among them were, by means of handcuffs, persuaded to fulfil their promises! He provided this assorted crew with food and accommodation, and although many of them had never before engaged in any form of manual labour, nonetheless not one of them complained to the police of their treatment. The great monument is still there now, to be seen atop the mountain; a tribute to the indomitable spirit of Romanies, and the age-old tradition of keeping one's word.

Scenes of high drama are often enacted at Race meetings. For example, once there were plain clothes detectives at every Tattersell turntable in an operation to trap a well known villain who was expected to bet on the horses. Then, it is foolhardy to carry a wallet in the back-pocket, unless it is a special 'fool's wallet,' attached by an invisible chain and empty of course. Once, when most of the Travellers had gone to the rails or the Grandstand, to watch the main race, I was watching proceedings, outside, on our portable TV set – I often did this, preferring not to join the crowds around the Beer-Tent as I could then keep an eye on the trailers and animals – and I had a strange experience. I was watching only a few yards from one of the cameras making the actual film. I noticed three well-dressed respectable looking people, a man and two women, in their fifties or sixties, walking amongst the trailers. One stopped and picked something up. It glittered and instinct told me that it was one of the sovereigns or half-sovereigns that Romanies wear as earrings or on bracelets. Looking so much like the honest citizen who would hand anything in to a Police Station, I was astonished to see the second woman snatch the object from her companion, glance around surreptitiously, and with a swift movement put it in her handbag. One of the women staying at home to look after some small children also saw this, and advanced upon the retreating trio. I locked the door and ran after them. As I arrived, they were vehemently denying having found anything. I added my 'witness' and said a girl had been searching for it earlier. It took the both of us to resort to the 'Gypsy's curse' before the woman weakened, or rather the man did, and grudgingly handed it over. I put the word out that we had found a *half*-sovereign; anyone claiming it would be lying, as it was a Victorian *sovereign*, an 'old' head. Later in the week a Traveller said to me that she had lost a sovereign earring. I asked if the milled edge was worn or not, and if it was in a mount. Coins are devalued by having a hole drilled for a hook. She said it was not holed and showed me the mount in her bag, and her matching earring. The coins were also of the same date, a perfect matching pair. So the coin was returned to its rightful owner.

Other people of note who one expects to see at race meetings and Travellers' fairs are the boxers. Of those among Travellers who have reputations as good bare-fisted fighters, quite a few have turned professional. A famous name that springs to mind, is that of Johnny Frankham, who fought under the name of 'Gypsy Johnny' and was a Southern Counties Welterweight Champion. Great was the anticipation if word was put about that he had issued a challenge. In 1981 there was an arranged fight between two boxers, Stevie Welsh known as 'The Kid,' who came down from the North with his supporters having issued a challenge to Leo Gumbo, known as 'The Bull.' A traditional bare-knuckle fight took place near Cambridge and 'The Kid' returned to Yorkshire, the victor, but it was an unsatisfactory fight as spectators joined in. Hundreds of Travellers had arrived for the event, many in 'Mercs' and 'Rollers.' News of any fight caused by rancour spreads like wildfire. If more than two running figures are sighted, everyone joins in, on one occasion, at a fair, running over *everything* including dog-boxes and vehicles. The crowd ignored every obstacle in its path; they were like lemmings. It was a sight I'll never forget.

Bare-knuckle Fighting

When Travellers fight, they do it as they do everything else, with a speed and gusto, which might amaze anyone unused to it. In Westerns or gangster films, savage fight scenes are arranged by a 'fight supervisor,' and savage blows are accompanied by thuds and groans superimposed on the soundtrack. The blows are feigned of course. As in any wartime battle scene, there is very little reality, injuries are rarely being seen. I think this is a bad policy, the inference being that no one gets hurt after such violence, which could lead to people thinking that savage blows to the head can be delivered to another human being with no ill effect. Having seen such fierce blows at close quarters, I can vouch for a far different and devastating effect. If films are going to show such scenes they ought to show the consequences. Not to do so, is another awful British compromise, or lack of commitment to the truth. This cloud-cuckoo-land mock-up is as insulting as it is dangerous.

Fighting to settle disputes and satisfy honour is traditional amongst Travellers. While size and weight are not considered important, age is a serious consideration. A young man would feel ashamed to fight someone of his father's generation, but if they cannot be persuaded to desist, it will usually end up with the older man's son taking his place. Many a time, however, the older man will take off his jackets and fight, which can result in his being seriously hurt, as defeat is but rarely admitted, such men being as hard and impervious as any street-fighter. This can lead to brothers taking sides and it is then only a short step to a family fight. Women too can fight, but this seems to be becoming, a thing of the past. Matriarchal figures can show elongated earlobes with split ends with earrings set in a top hole of a series of enlarged or 'growed-in' holes; it being necessary to pierce a new hole above that where "evil 'omans" had ripped out an earring. I do not like to see women fighting, although some have great reputations commanding respect. They will attack a man fighting their husband or son, but men do not like to hit back in public, although some are not averse to hitting their *own* wives in private.

It is surprising just what things that can occur within the safety of a crowd – people passed by while a murdered Traveller lay dying in the street; an elderly couple were robbed, whilst stopping on a well-used lay-by almost opposite a busy hospital. Travellers have been shot at whilst beside main roads – including us....twice! Petrol-bombs have been thrown, and, perhaps strangest of all, on Epsom Downs two elderly Travellers, brother and sister, who each had their own trailer and travelled with a large number of Yorkshire terriers, were robbed in broad daylight, whilst encamped in the midst of other Travellers! London villains were suspected but no one was apprehended. Nowadays Travellers are nervous of staying anywhere on their own, and some Trailer Parks have electric gates opened by code number locks! This security issue has caused Travellers to become more conspicuous as they travel in larger numbers; but I wouldn't like to be in the shoes of any villain who was caught. Travellers are used to having to help themselves, so, taking the law into their own hands, as in days of old, would come naturally – for rarely has 'Authority' or 'Officialdom' ever been on a Traveller's side.

Travellers are alike in many respects, but have different lifestyles and vocations so it is only natural that those sharing the same interests, should seek each other's company. Some Travellers have their favourite spot and return to it year after year, others un-hitch their trailers as soon as they see other members of their family. Yet others prefer to have several days isolation before being surrounded as people more arrive. It is not, unfortunately, generally known, that there are several strata of Traveller, apart from their geographical origins, yet Travellers are Travellers and there is unity in diversity!

Chapter Twelve

Foods, Fallacies and 'Gypsyologists'

The Romany people, like any other secretive minority group in society, have long been at the mercy of writers. Some of these writers have been good-hearted romantics and have endowed the Romanies with powers which they simply do not possess, and they describe them as "the *real* Gypsies," dismissing those from one of the lower social groups within the whole Traveller community as 'Diddikois,' or "Poor-class persons who have taken to the roads." This stance was taken by Brian Vesey-Fitzgerald when he first reviewed Dominic Reeve's book *Smoke in the Lanes* claiming that the persons written about were "not Gypsies......just rootless Travellers." A several letter argument in columns of either The Times or The Observer, I forget which, ensued between Dominic Reeve and Brian Vesey-Fitzgerald. Vesey-Fitzgerald *then* wrote in The Birmingham Post and Gazette (4 February 1958), reviewing *Smoke in the Lanes,* "I have now read this book three times and each time with more absorbed interest. Here is personal experience, lived and savoured to the full......a social document of the greatest value." Quite a turn-about!

Up until 1970 or so, however, one feels that all who wrote books about 'The Gypsies' were at least well-intentioned and genuinely moved by the subject. Alas, the social anthropologists and social workers then came upon the scene, the former sometimes spending months with Travellers, annotating their habits and customs, their homes, their relationships and their means of livelihood, all with the sole purpose of obtaining doctorates and setting themselves up as 'Experts.' On one occasion I encountered 'Dr A' on the Downs at Epsom during Derby week. He at once began addressing me in *Romani*, which for sheer pretension took some beating. Three other academics proved themselves to be equally unpalatable. Scholarship without genuine experience is a poor thing, and I hope I do not have the misfortune to meet them again.

Perhaps one of the most extraordinary subjects of myth and exaggeration amongst both writers and the dreaded social anthropologists, is that of food. Indeed, even television is not above contributing odd material. Just the other week, a lady was giving a recipe for 'Gypsy Stew.' She told the viewers, quite seriously, that, "Many are the vegetables that the Gypsies might snatch from the fields as they pass by." The vision of Travellers leaning from the cabs of their lorries attempting to grab the occasional turnip or cabbage from the fields, is one I have yet to witness! With regard to Traveller's food today, this, I fear, mirrors the rest of society. The poorer Travellers exist on what we are told is an unhealthy diet – too often based on over-fatty food, bacon and meat, few fresh vegetables or fruit, but large quantities of white bread and sweet tea. Foods such as sheep's paunch and the legendary meat-pudding are to some degree dying out, except in memory. Convenience foods as advertised on TV are becoming increasingly popular among all strata of Traveller. Nevertheless, as with wealthier non-Travellers, the wealthier Romanies incline towards more expensive foods which are possibly rather more healthy, and more nourishing, especially in regard to fresh meat and fish. Foods prepared for the expected visitors at Race Meetings are home-cooked ham made into sandwiches, fresh salmon, strawberries and cream.

Until a decade or so ago, Travellers, like all people, especially those in country areas, were to some extent reliant on herbal remedies rather than medical science, but nowadays, like everyone else, and especially since motorisation became universal among Romanies at the end of the 1950's, herbal remedies have been largely abandoned in favour of a visit to the Doctor. A jab of penicillin is preferred to a leaf of pennyroyal!

It would seem to me, as one who has lived the Travellers' life, both in 'accommodation' and earning a living, that outside observers cannot see the wood for the trees. They build on the trivia of the lifestyle yet ignore much of its essential motivations, its fashions – in *all* things, and its ability to adapt itself without losing its identity. I remember a few years ago asking a Gypsyologist what his favourite make of living-trailer was. Gazing at me with astonishment he, replied, "I don't really know one from the other." To me, this was as ridiculous as being told by a student of the theatre, that he had heard of Shakespeare, but did not know the names of any of his plays. Just as, in the old days, waggons and horses were the mainstay of the Romany life, so today are the lorries and trailers.

Appertaining to the grant-supported would-be chroniclers of the intimate details of the site-dwelling Travellers, one recently admitted in print that she was unable to make much headway with the men. She had soon discovered that men do not discuss certain subjects with women. This, I would have thought, would make her research incomplete, and effectively null and void. To those of us familiar with the habits of Travellers, which remain the same in this particular, on or off official Council Sites, another great pointer of her non-acceptance by her 'guinea-pigs' was evidenced by the following: she relates that she "befriended the children, who unlike the adults, invaded my

129

caravan at all times." When a stranger is accepted and deemed worthy of respect, the natural good manners of Travellers come into play. Adults *frequently* visit a newcomer's trailer, leaving immediately if the husband returns, whereas children do *not* visit unless accompanied by an adult. It is considered bad manners to send children to spy-out conditions in another trailer. Therefore if a person is *not* accepted as worthy of respect, they are likely to suffer such happenings as she described, unaware of what Travellers call the 'meanation' (meaning). My point being, if a researcher is not accepted, he or she is unable ever to get at the tantalising truth any more than a notebook tout, and there have been plenty of those.

I have never personally claimed to be a Romany, but I think I have been *in* the life long enough to be able to speak with some authority. Yet, having a strong sense of loyalty, wild horses wouldn't drag from me, the Pandora's box of knowledge I have unwittingly gleaned over the years which I consider to belong to the Romanies and to no one else. I don't think I have ever asked a Traveller a thing; it would never occur to me. There is something most insidious in taking advantage of anyone's hospitality, be he King or Commoner.

Worst of all are those who try to hide the fact that they are 'researching,' posing, for example, as Wardens or rent collectors on council Traveller Sites. Such practices rightly arouse disgust in those who believe in freedom for the individual.

'Field-studies' of humans, resulting in documented accounts containing the usual 'interesting' subjects – 'sexuality,' 'pollution taboos,' 'ethnic purity' – leave a nasty taste in the mouth. A warm-blooded people such as Travellers, reduced to sociologists' icy technical terminology, so that a people's lifeblood is published in such chilling terms as, "gender-divisions," "analysis of pollution beliefs" (the pollution to which the mind of the innocent layman may swivel, is *not* meant by the Sociologist!), "cognatic kinship," "political clusters", "nuptial and temporal divisions," and "a group of siblings in the research area." These are just some of the terms of the field-study researcher employed towards Romanies! Chilling is too generous a word by far.

The following report flowed from the pen of one under-cover researcher:

> "Next morning I watched Cathy's parents and siblings leave. (the name is changed) .... the husband is expected to demand from the wife, submission and adaptation. *Gauji* wives are easier to bring into a Gypsy community and less anomalous than *gaujo* husbands .... the *gauji* wives who remain with the Traveller society could more easily be accepted, provided they endured ostracism and initial accusations of

130

pollution. Since fieldwork, three have left their husbands. They could never lose the title of *gauji*. Some were never accepted by the husband's family."

I find this information *very* suspect, since in over twenty-five years with probably three times the number of travelling families she observed, I have never heard of such a number of *gauji* wives, let alone of their leaving! Poppycock say I.

Many are the books which have been written based on references to former works, and on such studies as the one I have quoted from, above. This study contains one hundred and eighty-two quotes and references. This format seems to suit a great number of those who have chosen Gypsies as their subject matter. Of course this ensures that every piece of misinformation that has ever been printed, obtains yet another airing. When it comes to what they term 'Field-studies,' such writers ('deck-chair Travellers') often come to grief. Sadly they are unaware of this. I admit that I am biased and rather scathing, but one would expect a lion-tamer to be scathing about *my* literary efforts should I attempt to write about his profession from a few visits to the circus.

Armchair Gypsies? No – Travellers on holiday!

Travellers, in the best accepted thespian tradition, often speak for effect – not exactly lying, but with the exaggeration of age-old storytelling. The Irish 'gift of the gab' is universally known. With Travellers, their flowery style, being known to *themselves*, is accepted and more importantly, allowances made. Exaggeration is expected; it is all part of the scene. Stories are not written, they are told. A flair for the dramatic statement is an inherited characteristic, added to which, a little wishful thinking does not come amiss. This is all very charming if you are used to it, but ludicrous when taken as *fact* by some scholar, or seriously recorded by some keen researcher ignorant of Travellers' ways. I therefore beg anyone reading this in years to come, to remember that the keen researcher does not seem to recognise that Romanies speak for effect. Unfortunately, the 'notebook visitor' has all too often forgotten to take his or her pinch of salt! Field-studies of lesser primates have to be achieved without the benefit of verbal communication. There could be a grand lesson in that!

Dominic has a great advantage in that he has always been able to move freely among *all* strata of Traveller society. While some large families only circulate among their own class (for want of a better word), this may be entirely misunderstood by Social Anthropologists, with regard to Dominic's reference to 'Flash' Travellers in his book *No Place Like Home*, published in 1960, in which most have enough relatives to make it a very wide social circle. Dominic "knows," as Travellers say, individuals in great numbers from these many walks of Travelling life. At such gatherings as The Derby, where there are representatives from all the different Romanies, any group he happens to be with, are constantly amazed at the number of Travellers he knows and the number who stop to speak to him with whom he can immediately engage in conversation, naming members of their family and passing on news. This is probably something the significance of which, would not be fully appreciated by anyone not in the way-of-life.

It takes a lifetime to know Travellers' names, family-trees and family history, and their ways. Little things easily overlooked by the researcher, mean a lot, such as the Travellers not visiting the researcher's caravan, and Travellers of a different place in the hierarchy not stopping to speak to those considered to be on a lower rung (great store is put upon this). It is not who you know, but who chooses to know *you*, that counts. Anyone can go to the Derby dressed as a Traveller, armed with books on Travellers, plus being able to speak *Romani*, but all this would not get them very far. Those Travellers they approach would 'melt away.' A Gypsyologist complained of this, with a puzzled frown. I can but repeat, it who *knows* you, that is all-important.

What grieves me about the 'academic' approach is that, in years to come, both in the U.K. and abroad, all the 'twaddle' written will be taken seriously. Future students have little promise of ever reading a conclusive report, not least because the upper echelons of Traveller society are now in such an independent and unassailable position as to avoid forever any close proximity with social anthropologists or even social workers, and certainly never suffer the indignity of having one thrust among them disguised as a warden. This leaves those involved in field-studies unable to discover, for example, why first cousins marry, or whether Romanies believe that a shadow can pollute food, or why Romany children are excluded from discussions (by teachers) on sex and reproduction – all, apparently, considered questions of vital importance by Social Workers.

Keeping the Yog burning while Mother is busy

Chapter Thirteen.

Sartorial Elegance

From the cradle to the grave Travellers share an overwhelming interest in their wearing apparel. There is a strong desire to be considered 'smart.' Men and women, when talking of a Travelling woman in a complimentary way, say, "She's a very smart woman." This is the image which most desire to achieve. I say most, because when speaking of Romanies, one can safely say, that what *one* does, they *all* do; but of course there are the few exceptions, the odd ones out, as in every society. Members of the Royal Family have long been taken as safe guides to refined or respectable styles to adopt for grand occasions such as weddings or christenings. For less important functions, television personalities, and actresses in films, all play an influential part. There is no leader of fashion to follow, but with incredible coincidence certain fashions appear together, and those who do not possess this instinctive flair, make all possible haste to obtain the necessary clothes or accessories to follow suit.

Almost as soon as a baby can sit up, it seems to show that it has inherited this preoccupation with appearances. If this comes as a shock or news to you and you think nostalgically of those romantically clad Romany flower-sellers of the past, I can assure you that the old-time waggon Travellers were every bit as particular. Many had to wear second-hand clothes and 'cast-offs,' clothes given at the door for 'rags.' Even so fashion was observed, rather more subtle because of available shapes – long skirts and small waists – but every attempt was made to follow and wear the current styles. Some details would not have been known to artists and writers who described or portrayed 'Gypsy women.'

New babies receive countless 'layettes.' Few visitors would arrive with only one item to offer for the baby's wardrobe. Thereafter the constant attention and changing of clothes becomes etched on the child's mind. I have seen toddlers rush out to look at a new arrival of their own age, and, whereas a little *gauji* girl might inspect the other's doll, the Romany child minutely inspects her contemporary's clothes! Listening to small children playing, one can hear them recite lists of what they have just bought, endless and lengthy descriptions of clothes and shoes, and what, in these childish games, they intend to buy.

*Romany family—
about 1908*

A Traditional Romany Family

A Romany family going to the races around 1908, could have been dressed as follows: Father in a moleskin or fustian suit with a long-sleeved shirt, the sleeves gathered just below the shoulder, with gathers to the back and front yoke. His waistcoat would also have had long sleeves, being originally 'a coat to the waist;' this and his jacket would have had high lapels. He would wear a fob-watch and gold chain with heavy seals. He would wear laced boots and narrow trousers. His wife would wear a pin-tucked blouse and a skirt of Petersham, over which she'd wear her newest and best white linen apron sewn with lappets and laps (folds and frills) with embroidered horseshoe pockets. Under her skirt would be lace-edged petticoats. Her eldest daughter would wear similar clothes but a dark apron. Both would wear the popular Luton Boots with dainty pointed toes. There would be decorative punched leather designs around the toes and heels. The mother would wear a large brimmed hat with ostrich feathers or 'osprey' (egret plume). These fashionable hats can be seen faithfully recorded by that great artist Sir Alfred Munnings in his painting entitled *Gypsy Life*. The models may have been the Gray family, and the races Bungay in Essex.

Munnings owned a horse-drawn caravan in which he travelled to Norfolk. Like other 'Gypsy Gentlemen' he had a groom and he left him, a small boy, in charge of both waggon and model, while he himself deserted the Bohemian life and repaired to an inn at night! And here, it was said, he stabled his horses, which were, of course, his great love. Augustus John, on the other hand, loved the seemingly free life of the Gypsies and embraced it fully along with his large family. After a pause from the Romany way of life, John once again took to the road in his original waggon, together with a second waggon, a cart and some tents. He protested that Gypsies were excluded from the race course on Derby Day.

Augustus John and Dorelia moved to Fordingbridge, where he had two studios in the grounds of Fryern Court. Here he allowed us to stop in our waggons, and later in trailers. During the painting of several portraits of me, he would describe those far off idyllic days at Effingham in Surrey and the Dartmoor encampment where the children ran as free as any Gypsies. He gained the respect of Romanies with his knowledge of deep Welsh *Romani*, and his love of the Travelling people who called him the *Romany Rai*. While he was content with a horse-drawn waggon with traditional features inside and out, those who regarded the caravan as a hobby, and were wealthy enough to have 'vans' built, were never satisfied with the traditional lay-out, and various 'vans' had all manner of features without which these gentlemen felt unable to travel: writing-desk, baths, wash-basins, large cooking-stoves, book-shelves, musical instruments – one included a harmonium. Weight seemed not to be a consideration, and often waggons had double shafts, the owner using two horses to pull them. These waggons were rather like halfway-houses between the comfortable existence in a house and the rougher life of the roads. One very famous horse-drawn caravan called The Wanderer, was to be seen retired in some Museum, I hope well preserved. The owner, Gordon Stables, was a great character and part of the history of horse-drawn waggons.

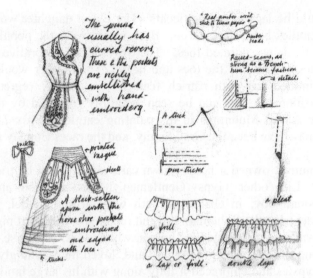

The 'pinna' usually has curved revers. These e the pockets are richly embellished with hand-embroidery.

"Real amber worn stick to tissue paper"
Amber beads

Raised-seams, as strong as a French-hem became fashion detail.

A tuck
pin-tucks

a pleat

pointed basque
Waist

A black-sateen apron with the horse shoe pockets embroidered and edged with lace.
tucks

a frill
a lap or frill
double laps

Typical details of Women Travellers' Clothing

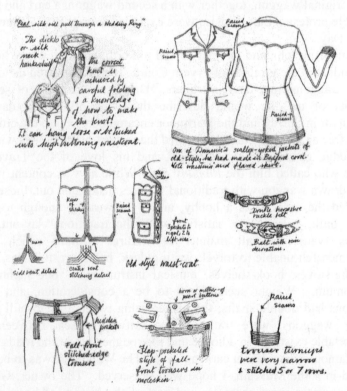

"Real silk will pull through a Wedding Ring"

The dicklo or silk neck-hankerchief the *correct* knot is achieved by careful folding & a knowledge of how to make the knot!
It can hang loose or be tucked into high buttoning waistcoat.

Raised seams

Raised seams

One of Domenic's scallop-yoked jackets of old-style he had made in Bedford cord. Note waistcoat and flared skirt.

Rows of stitchy
Raised seams
step collar
front 3 pockets to right, 2 to left-side.

Side vent detail
Centre vent stitching detail
Old style waist-coat.

Double horseshoe buckle belt
Belt with coin decorations.

horn or mother-of pearl buttons

Raised seams

Fall-front stitched-edge trousers

Flap-pocketed style of fall-front trousers in moleskin.

trouser turnups were very narrow & stitched 5 or 7 rows.

Typical details of Men Travellers' Clothing

Back to our fictitious Romany Family, off to the fair. The small boy would wear a suit cut on the lines of a Norfolk jacket. The small girl would wear a frilled pinafore over a full skirted dress. The baby of whatever sex would be clad in a long lace dress. Mother and daughter might wear a fissue, pinned by a broach. These early days have left a legacy of men's and women's fashions which can still be found to-day both among the old-fashioned Travellers and the sartorially elegant 'flash.' I refer, among other things, to the 'suit-of-clothes' known as 'Traveller-style.' This is detailed in the following illustrations which I drew originally for the journal of the Gypsy Law Society.

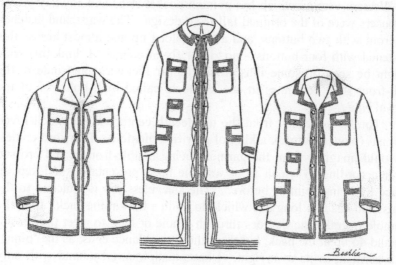

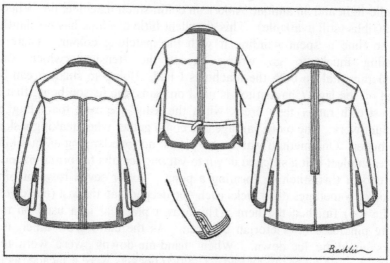

Traveller-style Suit – Front and Back

Moleskin and Melton were once used, also the real old type of corduroy that bargemen's trousers were once made of, like moleskin (which is *not* the fur of the animals) so thick that it 'stood up when the wearer sat down,' and also, though rarely, a very rough tweed known as 'Owd-Dog.' Those who have these suits tailored today, tend to have them less 'boxy,' less like the short American jacket, but long like a hacking-jacket, to thumb-nail length, with two vents. Also, not all the original details are incorporated, such as the five rows of stitching round the lapels, cuffs and hem, or the rows of snake stitching down the front which strengthened where the buttonholes were. There is a kind of Western version which has pointed pocket-flaps and cowboy yokes. Trousers were of the original fall-front design. The waistband fastened in front with two buttons, and a flap folded up and almost across this fastened with four buttons – no zip or fly of course. I think this style might be seen on some illustrations of Mr Pickwick, and indeed, the fall-front style continues in use in the so-called 'bell bottoms' of the Royal Navy.

The ladies legacy from the nineteenth century is the much loved 'pinna' (pinned-before), a kind of glorified pinafore. The word comes, I would imagine, from the garment being double-fronted and crossed over according to which front was the most presentable, and kept in place by being 'pinned before.' The sleeveless top is attached to the waist and has two long ties which do up in a bow at the back. Like the humble overall, one tie goes through a hole or loop to meet the second tie and do up at the back, but there the resemblance ends, as the 'pinna' is a garment in its own right. I have made many by hand with only candle-light and an antique American chain-stitch machine, the Wilcox and Gibbs (still available). This excellent little machine has no shuttle, so no time is spent winding it with the matching colour. There is nothing much to go wrong except the 'tension' which was temperamental on both the machines I had. Being so small it can be used on the lap. Chain-stitch is used on jeans, the reason being that it will stretch rather than break when the jeans are used for riding or manual work. The more yardage one could gather when making a skirt the better. One method was to use pleats, not overlapping as in a kilt, but each pleat being stitched down to varying lengths to form a pattern, the end of this stitching forming a point. Six or seven rows of pin-tucks, or sometimes deep tucks each one deeper than the last (narrowest at the top) finished the hem. This was a practical idea used on the white pinafores of Victorian children. As the child grew taller, the tucks could be let down. When 'hand-me-downs' were worn the garment could be easily altered. The two pockets were a façade, as in poachers' pockets, the surface shaped like a horse-shoe and entered by

139

a perpendicular slit. Behind these embroidered pockets, were the real practical pockets reaching to the hem.

When 'calling' a Romany woman would have her wares carefully laid out in the *kipsi* (calling-basket) which had hoops of willow all round the edge with a gap for her arm.* When given baby clothes or other objects by a householder, to avoid mixing these, they were put down into the long 'pinna' pockets. Once the wares were sold, food was bought and took the place of clothes-pegs or bunches of cow-slips or violets. Such is human nature, that should a lot of baby-clothes be on view, a kind housewife might feel that any further gifts of any kind from her would be 'coals to Newcastle.'

On these 'pinnas,' the collar revers were embroidered with flowers to match those around the pockets, and edged with narrow lace. The machine-made lace which Travellers sold was thought to be hand-made. Who were they to disillusion a customer silly enough to imagine the woman had time to go out working, bring up a family, cooking on an open fire in all weathers, living in the 'mud and water,' yet still had time to make lace! In Victorian times it was usual for tradesmen's wives, hawkers, street-sellers, laundry-women, fishwives, and servants to wear an apron in the street. It is rare now-a-days to see a woman wearing an apron out of doors, unless she is a market-trader or street stall-holder. Travellers are somewhat puzzled by the habit of *gauji* women who remove an apron before answering the door.

The colour for pinnas for everyday wear was black, with white reserved for Sunday, and best wear. After World War Two, there was a never ending supply of black-out material much of this was the type known as 'satinised-cotton,' or 'sateen.' It was excellent for 'pinnas' and readily available, thus many curtains took on a new life. Even today there are Travellers who prefer the old-style of dress, and, defying all fashion frivolities, staunchly stride out in a black pinna over a bright tartan wool skirt with a red flannel petticoat. These petticoats were made of a material called 'Doctors red-flannel.' At one time I used to purchase this from a small drapers shop in Salisbury. This proved to be the very best means of insulation against the extreme cold and damp – long skirts had their advantages. Attics where maids had to sleep, most without coal fires, and the outdoor life of the Romany women were two inclement environments, damp, windy, draughty and cold. How they must have blessed the good doctor whoever he was.

* The photograph on page 32 shows a *kipsi* in the foreground. The gap in the scalloping, to allow for the carrier's arm, can be seen in the bottom right-hand corner.

140

It is noticeable that some of the younger travelling women have taken to wearing trousers as the most comfortable and practical daytime wear. Short frilly skirts are useless and long full skirts a hindrance. In the old days clothes were not washed as frequently as they are today. However, underskirts and aprons were kept clean. Black, while practical, is difficult to wash. It takes several rinses to dissolve soap, which, if not entirely removed, shows up as an unsightly grey stain. A trailer is easily 'steamed-up' by boiling anything on a gas-stove, and even washing-bowls cause condensation on the many mirrors. Single-glazed windows poured with condensation overnight. To remove this one had carefully to hold the Nottingham-lace curtains away from the glass to avoid their being soaked.

Welsh Travellers retuning from Calling

I made this sketch of some Welsh Travellers which demonstrates the old style of dress. The pinafore one of the small girls is wearing recently had a fashion revival when Laura Ashley resurrected the 'romantic look' and many of her designs incorporated frills, lace and pin-tucks, also full ankle-length skirts. It was a pleasure the see small girls transformed into Alice-in-Wonderland visual delights – a style calling for long hair and ribbons. The cruel practice of shearing small girls' beautiful hair is not favoured among Travellers. I cannot see the need for this unlovely habit. If Travellers without running hot-water, warm towels and a bathroom, can, as they do, keep a girl's hair clean, this cannot be used as an excuse. I remember one Romany father weeping when his grown-up daughter cut her hair. There are so many ways that long hair can be dressed, whereas with a 'pudding-basin' cut, girls look, to me, like clones.

Wealthy Travellers' babies wear hand-made clothes. These can be ordered in colours to match a brother's or sister's outfit. As soon as a baby girl can toddle, she has 'party' dresses. These too are often made to order. The addresses of those who used to be called 'the little sewing-woman' are jealously guarded by a family, as such useful and skilful craftswomen are hard to find. If there is only one year between infants they can be dressed alike, either in the same style but contrasting colours or different styles but identical colours. Frilled petticoats help the party dresses to stand out so that the wearer resembles a Christmas tree fairy or a ballet dancer from Swan Lake! This has become a 'classic' style, so well liked that there are always some children somewhere dressed in these 'party-frocks.'

It is every small boy's ambition to dress like his father. Boys have very little babyhood, being made into small men as soon as possible, so one sees very few 'Just William' knees and wrinkled socks. Long trousers are worn from an early age, and these little men expect to have new suits made for occasions such as weddings, birthdays or fairs. They are most particular as to style and colour of suits and also the shirt and tie. The famous Luton boot has been replaced by the next best thing, the jodhpur boot. It is the elegant shape of this boot, together with its horsey association which is responsible for its prolonged popularity. Such boots can be found in all colours and of all qualities. The elasticated sides make them easy to put on, and so ideal for being ready quickly for a sudden emergency. A man without his boots on is at a disadvantage. It is only recently that young boys have begun to buy 'sports' shoes for non-social occasions. It will not be long, alas, before the jodhpur boot is a thing of the past, except, of course, for the armchair Gypsies trying to dress like Romanies.

Around 1969, the fashion-conscious Traveller, by which I mean those who follow Travellers' fashions, had given up his 'three-piece suit' for the 'country look' or 'gentleman look.' Check hacking jackets with two vents and horn buttons were worn above plain coloured trousers. Check or plaid trousers were worn with a Harris tweed or a Donegal tweed jacket. Some gave up jackets altogether and wore thick expensive cardigans, with double edging (double-knit). These kept their shape well. Sometime later the suede-fronted and the leather-

fronted cardigan became popular. These were expensive; but no-one
wore an *ordinary* cardigan! The older man, perhaps loathe to part with
his long familiar image, narrow trousered flap-pocketed suit, solved the
problem by wearing waistcoats in plain bright colours with fox-head
buttons. This flash of red, green, or yellow carefully echoed by tie and
snap-brimmed hat, achieved the casual look, while maintaining the suit,
so long a symbol of prosperity. The suit was, of course, not off-the-
peg, but tailor-made with rich satin lining, often patterned brocade to
the jacket, trousers being half-lined. Revers were hand-stitched, and all
the cuff button-holes really opened!

The Country Gentleman Look

Although Romanies are Traveller-fashion conscious, I think those who most slavishly follow every trend, are girls from seven to seventeen, growing up so quickly – a situation shared in some measure by Circus and Show-business families. A mother of seventeen children, who I know well, cannot have had many, if any, years when she was not 'calling,' walking many miles a day, in what ladies in less strenuous ways of life call 'an interesting condition.' I feel sorry for any eldest girl who, if she is followed by two or three siblings, is expected to be a 'little mother' and has to share work and responsibility at an age when non-Traveller girls are *acting* the part with dolls! Travellers tend to have smaller families today, women revolting against a life of drudgery with little pleasure. Smaller families help to keep the parents young, and there is more space for everyone.

The life of the waggon Traveller was very hard, out in all weathers, sitting hunched up only feet from a blazing outdoor fire, face burning and back freezing. It was worse inside a bender tent with thick smoke rising slowly all around. When in a waggon with a fire-stove, it was necessary to go in and out in all weathers to get fuel or food, clambering up the wooden steps in gale-force winds, hanging onto the grab-handles. Whilst house-dwellers have a cloakroom or hall in which to hang outdoor clothes, a waggons or trailers have nowhere for wet garments. A habit lingering from these times is noticeable when Travellers visit one another; they use a towel thrown around the shoulders or head, which can be folded up and put on the lap. I recall some *gaujo* people, visiting me on one occasion, entering the trailer bundled up in hats, scarves and thick coats. Once inside they realised there was nowhere to put their outer garments. I found it amusing, if annoying, as it was but three yards to their car! Throwing masses of clothes on the floor soon turns a trailer into the kind of home neither I nor Travellers want to live in.

We suffer some pains to avoid it becoming the kind of holiday caravan non-Travellers assume we live in. To which end we suffer inconvenience and privation. Nowadays, in self defence, I greet non-Travellers thus; if the visitors have stopped their car some distance from the carpeted outside platform with rugs on, and there is mud between the car door and the platform, I suggest that they drive closer to avoid the mud. Maybe one of them does not hear or understand. I once had to watch helplessly as a well educated, and I thought intelligent, lady walked the whole length of the trailer, some 23 feet, in mud. Upon reaching the cleanest rug opposite the door and below the carpeted steps, she scraped and wiped her dirty boots with mud-clogged heels, on this rug, smiling at me all the while.

In 1970 small girls indulged in the craze for hot-pants. *Gauji* children could be seen wearing these, and little else, in the streets. But in order for such a revealing garment to be acceptable to a Romany family, the thigh-high pants were worn with coloured tights or knee-length stockings. Only very small girls wore the stockings. The pants with bib-front or crossover braces were worn with frilly feminine blouses.

Note: Black shoes with silver heels.

During the craze for 'hot-pants' the sporty and bare-legged look was neatly overcome by wearing coloured tights and *frilly blouses.*

Hot-pants

During this period, hair was worn as a large flat bun on top of the head with a ribbon around the bun. In 1971 girls of around ten years old had in their wardrobe both ankle-length, high-waisted dresses and the new craze, 'pyjama-suits.' Clothes leaned towards the tailored look of stark plain colours, edged by contrasting colours. Tall suede or leather boots in white were worn with skirt to the knee and long jackets that almost reached the skirt hem. A well dressed girl had to have all three styles, not knowing before hand which her contemporaries would wear resulted in quaintly contrasting fashions. Sisters would dress alike. The bun on the head had the addition of 'rinklets' (ringlets) at the side of the face or at the back.

Due to girls keeping their childhood long hair, women can indulge in many elaborate styles. By helping each other they can achieve incredibly professional coiffures. Any hint of grey is banished by dye or colorant. The most care-worn grandmother is at pains to do the best

145

she can, and retain as far as possible any good features she had as a girl. Not for a Romany woman the depressing slide down the path of the frizzy-perm leading to masses of older women of clone-like appearance! One hopes that the new generation, having enjoyed a more colourful and individual first fifty years, will not be brainwashed into thinking there is any merit in identical greyness or the awful habit of giving up altogether and cutting off the gift of lovely hair, looking like bristle-brushes after some cruel medieval punishment given to fallen-women!

Hair Styles

I have great admiration and respect for the older Romany women who have had a long hard fight and still make every effort in trying circumstances to look well-groomed, so that when they meet each other there remains some truth in the greeting, "You haven't changed a bit," or, "You looks just the same." It has long been a source of puzzlement to me that some housewives appear before their husbands in the morning with curlers in their hair, and no make-up on their faces. This unlovely vision is also seen by the rest of the family and any tradesmen that call. I do not have a snobbish objection to the curlers themselves, but to the ghastly effect of a woman's great asset, her hair, being thus disfigured. The bald heads, possibly with knobbles, of women cry out for privacy, or at least a scarf.

Whist on the subject of hair I will mention something about trailer windows; they are set at sitting height. Only a few trailer interiors

146

include a dressing-table. This is really a 'mock' dressing-table as it is set against a wall, never in a window, and incorporates a chest-of-drawers which prevents anyone from actually sitting down in front of it. Hair, therefore, has to be brushed standing in front of one of the two full length wardrobe mirrors which face the doors. The piano-hinges are put on the outside edges of the fire-place unit which includes the two wardrobes, and the doors open outwards, preventing what would otherwise have been a convenient double-mirror in which to view one's back. Putting another two mirrors on the inside of the doors would mean too much weight, hence the use of piano-hinges.

About 1972 it became noticeable that the 'flash' wives or the 'cream' of Romanies, were appearing in garments trimmed with mink; hats, collars, muff-bags, etc. Those who did not have these expensive luxuries, wore mink broaches in the shape of flowers or animals. As time went by the quantity of mink increased until bevies of mink-strewn ladies appeared, and everyone owned a tippet. Capes were considered too old-fashioned and only for *gauji* ladies in evening-dress, so the next step was a short mink jacket, in the still much favoured cream colour. With so many wearing mink coats, taking no heed of the weather, those who could not afford mink, bought cream coloured musquash, worked like mink. This fur from the underside of the rat, is very delicate and does not wear as well as mink. Luckily none knew which animal it came from, as there is an age-old horror of 'bang-tails' (rats). Teenagers were given fun-furs of dyed chinchilla, which furriers realised sounds more exotic than rabbit. At a Travellers' party one New Year's Eve, I counted eight mink coats and two jackets. Even small girls could be seen at the Autumn Stow Horse-Fair wearing fur coats down to their ankles, the hems dragging in the mud.

You may wonder if there is a 'best-dressed' Romany in this society. There is: she out-shines all others at social functions, wearing the most expensive ensemble. Over the years she has caused comment by the weight and number of her pieces of gold and diamond jewellery, perhaps wearing bracelets with numbers of the largest gold coins. Such coins are considered so valuable that just one worn on a gold chain round the neck is a considerable asset. The criterion is not the good taste as recognised in other societies. During the mink era, slim young women in well tailored suits, with mink coats, stopping to talk as they met in some shopping arcade, caused comment, as from such expensively clad and scented apparitions, with crocodile shoes and handbags, their deep Romany voices issued forth. I recall once in Cheltenham, in a very exclusive shop – there are quite a few there – the suitably subdued counter staff were serving several customers amid the hushed tones encouraged by the management in such refined establishments, this one being the very model of the upper-class type of emporium. Through a door at the end of the shop came a small group of Romany women intent upon purchasing goods for a coming social event. These beautifully dressed ladies drew the attention of all eyes, the moment their voices, foreign to that environment, reverberated down the whole length of the shop. Assistants and shoppers became transfixed, as if struck by the wicked fairy in the Sleeping Beauty. I recall the amusement I felt then, at the look of incredulity on their faces. Magnificently unaware that they had caused any sensation, the Travellers departed upstairs to cast their spell on Lingerie. In true English manner, service was resumed with no comment, with only the youngest of the Staff swivelling her eyes towards the stairs as if it must have all been a dream.

1973 saw a fashion for suede and leather. Patchwork jerkins of coloured suede, matching shoulder-bags worn with trousers, which the younger Travelling women rather daringly began to wear, first in and about the trailer, and then, as the men became used to seeing them, shopping in 'going-out' clothes, sometimes trouser-suits. Think of the active life, in and out of the trailer, up and down steps all the time, taking out fire-ash, bringing in fuel, emptying the teapot, taking out the washing to hang up, bringing in the baby, put out to get fresh air, folding and putting out the outside tables, climbing the ladder to wash the trailer, washing the tent, bending down to pick up toys – the space underneath the floor is a veritable wind-tunnel. Awning makers are aware of this and a special canvas-strip is supplied to fix along the bottom of the trailer. Even in summer, to sit beside a trailer is to sit in a wind-tunnel. Packing to move, and unpacking again, along with all the foregoing tasks, is far easier to do wearing trousers. This suitability of trousers was soon universally learned and I am no longer taken aback to see women in this less romantic mode of dress.

It is sometimes hard to come to terms with change, more especially if one is a romantic, or an idealist. We have often winced to see a *gaujo* couple on holiday with a hired horse and waggon, the latter painted in what is fondly hoped to be Gypsy-style, with non-traditional patterns like narrow-boat painting, which is quite different and inappropriate. To a casual observer, both being brightly coloured, they may appear similar. The waggon is often accompanied by a woman wearing an ankle-length skirt, which, without the petticoats, draggles on the ground and shows the sun through it, something no self-respecting Traveller woman (who she is aping) would allow. Above this may be a short-sleeved T-shirt, or a duffle jacket or a puffa-jacket. The man will wear jeans and a polo-neck jumper or anorak, all of which looks pretty 'naff.' Romanies do not have the sole right to horse-drawn vehicles or to go wandering on the roads. If other people wish to do this they can, but their sad and failed attempts to copy traditional Romany design and decoration for their waggons presents a sad spectacle indeed, as do the non-Romany clothes which they wear. Few things are worse than a travesty of a thing of beauty. A dredger can never be a cutter, which is not to say that it has to be a bad dredger, when it is not masquerading as a cutter!

It rarely occurs to these pseudo-gypsies that they should not expect to be received with open arms by the Travelling community. It seems to them to be a foregone conclusion that Romanies will be flattered by their preference for the travelling way-of-life. In the days when it was a novelty for the 'gentry' to go 'a-gypsying,' or travel for short periods in a specially built waggon, then Romanies who recognised 'quality' when they saw them, travelling with a groom and valet, were of course flattered. Writers and artists did this but with authentic Romany waggons. Wrongly dressed folk with hen-houses on wheels can never hope to gain any respect or even interest. The best way to obtain Travellers' respect is to have a good horse-drawn waggon painted in the correct colours and well lined-out by a craftsman, a good waggon-horse, not a hired riding-school pony, a good harness, and if possible be earning a living on the roads, even if it is only by selling paintings door to door. Making a living on the road is the key to the whole matter, the keystone to the bridge, the most important thing of all. With this comes the only chance of forging a true bond. There is too great a rift between those who play at travelling, and genuine Travellers for the gap to be closed.

During the year of the coloured leather, little girls wore skirts cut on a circle, the dress bodice had puff-sleeves or long sleeves with cuffs also cut on a circle. Another favoured design was a dress with matching trousers, for this a 'border' print was used. In making it up, the border print was kept at the hem and the trouser bottoms. The rather ugly fashion of platform soles invaded all manner of footwear, a hazard to young and old alike on uneven ground. Often wet grass caused the leather covering to peel off the wooden heels, yet everyone wore them, children included. 'Handkerchief-points' were everywhere, on sleeves and at hems. I usually make my own clothes, but I recall once buying a black satin skirt which fitted tightly at the hips and fish-tailed out into points at the hem. I liked that!

During 1973 children discovered the unadorned tailored look, with clear uncluttered lines. 'Laps' and flounces were *out*. Unromantic smart little dresses with knee-length, A-line skirts, in plain colours with rounded white collars that would not disgrace a Quaker, were worn with white button-strap shoes and white socks. The sketch of Welsh Travellers returning from calling, shows their disregard for fashion and preference for the 'old-fashioned' style of dress. The uninformed observer might well think that this was a family in the low income bracket, hence the overall effect of 'raggedy-rush,' people no strangers to poverty. In fact these women, and many like them, are the family breadwinners, hard working, going out early to catch a bus into town, while the men stay at home – a custom among the Welsh Travellers, and one of the ways in which they differ or differed from Travellers from England, Scotland and Ireland. These colourful and traditional costumes are no hindrance to their hawking of white heather, lace and charms, combined with fortune-telling when the opportunity arises; in fact they are a distinct advantage, enabling a large family to own the most expensive trailers with lavish furnishings and ornaments. Often, these are the glittering monsters you pass on the roadside, these people preferring the free open spaces to any fenced site. Not only do they preserve the traditional dress, but many of the lovely old names, ousted by flash-Travellers in favour of those heard on television.

It is lovely to see their splendid homes with sparkling cut-glass mirrors, stopped on the roadside with the family sitting around the outside fire. This scene signifies, nine times out of ten, that the family is Welsh, but many have never been back to the 'land of their fathers.' The riches of the South pass not into the gateways of Wales. I speak from personal experience of calling in both areas. To return would mean a drop in earnings. They use a great many *Romani* words in every day talk. I have heard other Travellers say of them, "They are a breed apart,' and they are not far wrong. We both like Welsh Travellers and once they accept you, you have friends for life. It is interesting to note that despite travelling outside Wales for many years they remain a group to themselves; but then so do the Irish. A friend of mine from a Midland travelling family who married into them, enough years ago now to have ten children, told me she still felt like an outsider. Not that anyone was unkind to her, but she had that 'alien' feeling, common to all when in company with those who are 'not the same' as oneself. They share the general Welsh characteristic of hospitality and politeness and are some of the nicest people one would wish to meet.

The younger generation of Welsh Travellers are extremely fashion conscious. I recall three brothers who had the most vivid and loud check suits I had ever seen made for them. To see the three suits together was an unforgettable sight. In the mid-seventies young men wore huge two-inch check, square not diagonal, knitted woollen pullovers. If jumpers were of the same large check, then the ribbing at neck and cuffs were plain.

It is rare to see a Welsh Traveller girl with short hair. Since many have dark luxurious 'rat-tails,' it would be a wanton act to shear them off. Recently, I noticed that most Welsh *gauji* girls had had a mass shearing. By 1982 it was rare to see long hair – such a pity; it was like entering a land of pudding-basin clones.

At Race Meetings, the children are expelled from the trailers one by one in the mornings, as each reaches the final stage of dress. 'Little Mothers' – elder daughters, as I described earlier – can be seen rushing about, trying to keep their 'brood' from scattering and getting their new clothes dirty before they complete the walk across to the cheapjack stalls. They are at a disadvantage themselves, in long flowing dresses and wide-brimmed hats. The young ones have caught the aura of excitement and are wild and unruly, and like most children 'play-up' at the most inconvenient time.

In 1975, navy-blue was still in evidence. It had hung-on as a colour strongly associated with 'smartness,' often worn with cream. Shoes were of the new pearl-effect leather, high heeled with a small platforms. Women favoured 'off-the-face' hats like the Queen Mother often wore and they carried huge pearlised handbags. Rather formalised flower-prints returned in small quantities, mostly just on bodices of long dresses of plain material. These often had a flounce on the hem. Long hair was un-platted and ringlets returned with the more feminine look which slowly crept back.

Small boys wore suits and even straw hats, small-brimmed, like their fathers. There was an outbreak of patriotic red, white, and blue so the Travellers' field resembled a gathering of ardent nationalists! White clad children with red or blue dress-edging roamed about as if just mislaid by their 'Nanny.' Romany children are not schooled to call their grandmother 'Nanny' in the ridiculous attempt to make people think that the family has a genuine nanny. It may have once worked, but people are wise to it now. White hats were worn with the brim turned up, and long ribbons hanging down the back. It was one of the years that I particularly remember the attractive Romany girl twins. Both parents were strikingly good-looking, so it was not surprising that the twins, always together and dressed identically, gained a great deal of attention. Very few could tell them apart, as you'll see by my sketches of them (made in different years, of course).

The Twins

In 1976 the 'Romantic' look had again taken a firm hold and ankle length skirts were back. Elegance had returned for that year's teenagers. Two girls 'out-did' all the others by parading with their lace parasols which matched their lace trimmed dresses and hats. Each girl rustled by in stiff petticoats as if she had entered a competition for the fullest skirt. Young and old women gave up hats for tall 'hair-dos' decorated with fancy slides, combs and pins holding sprays of flowers. Little boys wore check trousers. Men appeared in check shirts with bright coloured or embroidered braces, and jackets being 'out,' these showed to advantage.

Travellers have always been flower-sellers so it was no great step to sell strawberries. During the Epsom Derby of 1977 two *gaujo* strawberry sellers appeared and unknowingly sold strawberries to Travellers who when not on holiday, sold punnets themselves! It is not unknown for Travellers selling white heather to encounter other Travellers, dressed in a less old fashioned style, and attempt to sell to their own kind! Such mistakes are easily brushed off, since they often tell stories against themselves, recounting happenings that would cause *gaujes* to blush at the memory, but they neither blush, nor feel any shame.

1977 was a rather dull year for fashion and I cannot say there was one specific fad or fancy, unless, for men, it was the braces! But in 1978 men blossomed out in bright flowered shirts. Not the large flowered Tropical Island designs – prints synonymous with holidaymakers – but bunches of flowers or all-over flower designs in lavender or pink and other colours besides. Boys wore cowboy boots (real ones, imported), cowboy hats, and also straw hats blocked in the Stetson shape. Boots with the Cuban heels are not, as the cowboy said, made for walking. Girls also bought these boots, the decorative coloured stitching on the uppers and legs, together with the stitching on the old-style clothes, rang a bell of appeal, as did Western shirts with yokes and pockets. Colour was everywhere and it was good to see.

There was another lull in inspiration in 1979, an assorted year in terms of dress only memorable for the 'bare-arm' look, not to my mind at all attractive if this is achieved by a unisex T-shirt or vest, or indeed if the wearer's arms are not their best feature. Travellers do not go about at Fairs in sun-tops or shorts despite being a sun-loving people. To their credit such clothes are considered only for the beach. Having said that, it is possible someone may have gone to Appleby in that era and seen a girl dressed thus, but there were – and are – many non-Travellers at the well known Gypsy Fair, with trailers and even waggons to live in whilst there. So a girl dressed like this going into a waggon or trailer is not conclusive. One can see a few *gaujo* summer day-trippers shopping in swim-wear, too thick-skinned to be embarrassed or notice other shoppers' and the shop assistants' cool looks. This is in bad taste. In Bath I overheard a customer say, "I pity anyone who has to go that far to get attention," then the terse rejoinder "Covering up would be her best bet." A Traveller regarded the large expanse of unlovely red blotched flesh bulging from unsupported fabric, and remarked, "And they look down on *us*!" To my mind, quite the worst garment ever to hit the world of 'dress,' is the T-shirt. Its practical properties for children can be appreciated, but only the few neat of form should attempt to wear it. The majority who need underpinned support appear to be wearing a second thick skin which cruelly reveals what old fashioned corsets were designed to hide. At one time it caught on among the younger set with romantic flowing flowered skirts inappropriately teamed up with these awful tops. Any attempt at a pretty or attractive outfit was ruined by this incongruous pairing. A few older women wore them but only round-about the trailer, mainly because T-shirts need no complicated laundering. Young men discarded suits and leather jackets and wore bright coloured vests – the British not American interpretation of the word – in red, blue, yellow, and violet, with black piping. Those who 'fancied' their own physique continued to wear them long after the fashion had waned. Vests were for daytime wear, and not considered the correct thing for evening, when satin shirts in the same vivid colours were worn with dark trousers.

Velvet was greatly in vogue for both sexes in 1980 – panne, crushed, striped, cut-velvet on satin, cotton-velvet, silk-velvet and stretch-velvet. Flowered-velvet dresses were worn with suede waist-coats or striped velvet skirts with matching waistcoats. It has always been a material much loved by Travellers, the richness and opulent feel being appreciated. Shoes returned to normal soles, but with two inch heels. Handbags were of suede or leather, both the genuine skin and very expensive. Heavy gold coins, 'Krugers,' were hung on gold chains round the neck. Men wore thick gold chains called 'Belchers,' often with some thick gold pendant. These were worn with open-neck shirts over coloured vests. Pastel coloured leather jackets, sometimes cream or biscuit, trimmed with fur down the bodice and cuffs, or fur-trimmed leather jerkins were 'in' for women. Trouser-suits with straight cut legs were worn with wide leather belts and matching shoulder-bags. For evening wear there were alligator or snake-skin shoes and handbags. It was a common sight to see a table top covered with these very expensive bags, left there while the owners danced. Two-toned suede skirts, sewn with alternate panels shaped to flare out at the hem were popular. Some girls had suits of this showy style of contrasting colours, black and white, red and black, brown and cream. These outfits were worn with knee-length boots, often cream or white, always the most impractical colours!

Although some men disguised their greying hair by colouring it themselves, many men quite openly had their hair dyed a different colour. Dark hair became blond locks. Straight hair was permed and heads of thick curls were everywhere. In the main, young Travelling men's hair is worn much longer than *gaujo* men's (with the exception of hippies) and is often curly – it is a pleasure to see. Older men have shorter hair styles in keeping with the respectable image they hope to achieve but not shorn up the back and sides like an army haircut. Personally, I hope that the countrywide practice of cutting off human hair is short-lived. It leaves the face stark and naked, which in ninety-nine cases out of a hundred is not a pleasing sight as unattractive ears and ugly necks are revealed. When this fashion originally came in there was little freedom of choice since any style other than that approved by society was ridiculed. Now that anyone can wear red, green or striped hair of any length without turning heads, there is no excuse for exhibiting near hairless pates. The fashion for down-turned moustaches gave some dark-haired Romany men the look associated with 'Real Gypsies.' It suited them, as did the long sideboards; both improved many a face.

For as long as I can remember some Romany women have always dyed their hair, either because they wish to hold back the years or just because they fancied a change. A woman may have shoulder-length jet-black hair when you 'make two roads of it' (go different ways), but should you meet again a few months later, you might hardly recognise her with curly blond hair. At a party I overheard a woman apologising to another for having talked for half an hour to her under the impression she was her sister. Some *gauji* women who take to the roads to 'go a-gypsying' have plain, scraped-back unflattering hair; they often have a shock when they meet Romany women and realise they have great pride in their appearance and are quite vain, which is 'unnatural' by 'Plain Jane' standards. My own personal view is that it is vain to assume that nature has made one so wonderful that one does not need any improvement to be a delight to the eye.

Chapter Fourteen

Epsom Diary extracts and varied Recollections

Pulling-on to the Downs at Epsom is rather complicated by the fact that there are two separate entrances for Travellers onto the stopping-place. Having taken the left-hand fork, it is difficult to get back, should one wish, to the areas reached by the right-hand fork. Steep slopes meet in a rough edged valley path, fringed by thorn bushes. This makes a barrier, invisible until the last moment; very deceptive for those coming along that path for the first time. Many is the innocent driver who has set off for the distant green hilltop with his trailer, only to find himself at the foot of a very steep incline, and the daunting prospect of climbing back up again. I once watched a lorry and trailer get stuck eight times – not good for the clutch! According to which variety of Traveller arrives first, the following trailers choose either route and area, so the positions are decided to a general degree. For a suburban Yorkshire family to find themselves marooned among, not just next to, some of the rougher London Travellers, could spoil their holiday.

On the other hand, it has been known for some rough and ready Travellers to depart from the Downs altogether, ashamed of their turnout, after a day among the chrome garden loungers, full-sized awnings, and geranium-filled jardinières of 'flash' Travellers, seated outside at matching table and chair sets with their straw parasols! To the uninformed eye, the living trailers may appear a higgledy-piggledy mess, like a disorganised caravan rally, but in fact it is a family's encamped position which is important to Travellers.

While now paying the reasonable amount of £5 (at the time of writing) for being photographed by the Press, it was just a coincidence but our turnout has featured more than once in this respect. We observed that no trailers this year had gone right across to the far track, by the rails, but that there was a line of trailers some way this side. I asked the man on the gate who confirmed my suspicion that a new rule forbad trailers to go beyond a certain limit. A line of mud was visible along the front of these trailers, as it was drizzling, and had been raining for the past week. We had no wish to get stuck in the mud (caused by traffic being forced to go through a small area). Naturally, we supposed that there was some tangible barrier, invisible at this distance, beyond the trailers so we took the right-hand fork and stopped on a recently formed grass-track on the opposite side to some Surrey and Cambridgeshire Romanies we knew. The space to our near and offside was yet to be filled and I waited hopefully for congenial and considerate neighbours. Travellers fear being left alone – not one of a couple, but one family – as this is seen as a terrible misfortune. A family who have misbehaved in some way – for example, a man having run off with another man's wife – can be 'sent to Coventry,' being shunned as a punishment. Living in a society where competition forces success rather than mere survival; their working life is geared to keeping their immediate family afloat at a reasonable level. This fosters a selfish outlook from which close neighbours suffer great and small irritations. As Romanies say themselves, "You knows what Travellers are!"

To the many young people who write to me, filled with romantic notions of 'travelling,' I recommend they should possess a certain amount of insensitivity, nerves of steel, and the self-discipline not to interfere in other people's affairs; for example over such things as, nests of small puppies wandering on their first explorations, hidden in the deep ruts of well-used lorry tracks, or pets, hedgehogs, rabbits, ducks, geese, goats, etc., which have vanished on the first night on the Downs, or perhaps much travelled cats spitting their admirable defiance at hare-catching long-dogs and frisky half-grown pups. Small pup litters are kept on lorry backs for safety, but every so often one jumps up on the top of the cab and seeing lots of loose dogs, catapults itself down to the turf below. Such senseless optimism – a broken leg would be the end of its life. I *have* interfered, but secretly, like rescuing, defeated near-death game birds, one-eyed or one-legged, useless for further fighting so thrown away in a ditch.

Through the nearside trailer window I can see the gambling ring, four corner stanchions and one horizontal row of scaffold poles some four feet from the ground, and the grass covered by a canvas sheet. The Ring Master uses a megaphone, encouraging customers with cries such as, "A tenner he heads 'em," and, "Hurry, hurry." Twin coins, are expertly tossed in the manner I described in Chapter 11. Winnings are handed out, the ringside bets settled.

The horseshoe seat in the trailer affords all-round vision through the front windows, revealing a sea of trailers, lorries, square-framed cottage tents – Travellers' style not campers' – new cars and motor vans, reflecting the now shining sun. A family have just returned to their 'West Morning Star' (a Westmorland Star) in their new 'Merc.' The small son puts on his crash helmet and whizzes off down the slope on his petrol driven miniature motorbike, conscious of the envy of his contemporary neighbours. Mother is unpacking the weekend pro-visions and carrying them from the boot to the carpeted kitchen (all

Travellers' coach-built specials have carpeted kitchens, an all-through carpet being preferable to anything practical in the kitchen!). Oranges roll on the grass between the stainless steel water carriers. A baby with unfocused eyes is placed in a pram of the very latest design, and a lace-edged parasol opened over the baby. The trailer dog, in this case a 'Yorkie,' hair in a red bow, scampers around. Starlings from nearby houses wing swiftly in and out. In safety of early mornings, before many people are up, jackdaws scavenge and then return to the safety of the woods. Sparrows practically live under the trailers, deftly evading the loose dogs.

Our offside windows show an encampment of London, London fringe and Kent Travellers, the older men wearing hats set at jaunty angles, and red or yellow braces clipped wide apart at the back to form a cross. The young men are in casual new clothes that do not always hang well upon them, so that the effect is not quite as smart as they would wish. There is a motley collection of 'iron horses' including Mazdas, Toyotas, a few Land Rovers, and Ford and Bedford trucks. Garden tables and chairs help to give, a holiday atmosphere. There are white flower holders – "Oh, where have last year's 'Queen's House' white plastic urns gone?" The flowers are mostly 'instant garden' nursery bedding plants, sadly wind blown. The nearest London Traveller's trailer is a Portmaster Special I note.

One of Beshlie's home-made Bird Cages,
this one being a 'Crystal Palace'

One year on the way to Epsom I acquired, through Dominic's scrap collecting, an antique wire-work jardinière, mid-Victorian, but badly damaged. I repaired with the same method I use for Victorian 'Crystal Palace' bird cages, in which I used to breed mules (cross-breeds). After applying two coats of white paint I stood the jardinière outside. I had so many admirers I decided to put the trailer plants on the three shelves, but dealing with windburn, aphids, and stray ponies, it made the novelty only just worthwhile! But it caused tremendous interest. This and some antique fencing panels I used to keep babies from wandering too near our large Rottweiler, took the fancy of a passing, newspaper photographer. It was a shock seeing Titus on the front page the following day. The following year's Epsom saw a plague of wire flower-holders, perhaps rather less aesthetic, being plastic, but from then on, many a Traveller's love, of flowers was gratified in this way. But this year seems to herald the end of that particular 'fashion.' Settled-down Travellers prefer urns to other garden ornaments

Rumours that a large party of French Romanies with brand new trailers pulled by large new Mercedes vans, have arrived, are causing mild interest. Only a few can speak English, it was said. Today being Show Out Sunday, we saw them appearing to be much at home, among the milling throng, of Derby visitors and Travellers crushed together on the narrow ash, soot and stone path leading to the Cheapjack stalls. Their black hair and dark skin, complimented by pinstriped suits, diamond tie-pins, gold watches and a general air of well-being, no doubt singled then out to the onlooker as fine examples of the '*real* Romany.'

In reality, the true Romany was, in the main, *less* noticeable, preferring the restrained clothing favoured by the Tailor and Cutter. I say in the main, because of course there are still plenty of those who still have amazingly vulgar check suits made, and also those of an older generation who favour 'old fashioned' dark three piece suits, relieved from looking like 'business' attire by the wearer sporting a coloured *diklo* (silk handkerchief) round the neck, tied with the special Romany knot, black hat, and dangling gold watch-chain. But the overall shared aim is for respectability, as opposed to the 'stage gypsy' appearance that hangers-on to the Travellers' scene wrongly attempt, thus at once singling themselves out for what they are. A Travelling woman confided to me that she had been embarrassed to be seen talking to a hippy, who I knew to be a school mistress, who went to Stow Fair and dressed in what she supposed was 'gypsy dress!"

The cross-channel visitors had erected a huge yellow and white tent of marquee proportions, which could accommodate hundreds of people. It was at first supposed that their friendly intention was to hold

159

a Grand Travellers' Party. This idea was very much looked forward to with great anticipation. Disillusion soon followed, however, when a car with a loudspeaker toured the Travellers' area, inviting us all to a *religious service*, "Gypsies for Christ." It seemed that in conjunction with the British evangelists, they thought that our religious and spiritual needs should be ministered to! Very few attended, and those mostly out of curiosity or bravado. In the gaudy tent there were bright-eyed missionaries, well versed in these proceedings, who led the laughter at the speaker's jokes and the clapped in time to music with a vigour and enthusiasm noticeably lacking from the British Travellers' seats. The admiration and respect for the foreign Travellers, who it had been supposed had worked hard for a holiday over here, who could buy and maintain new vehicles and trailers, and who had come as Party Hosts, rapidly seeped away when it was realised they were just part of a large organisation, and very probably supported by its funds.

The Sunday morning mist heralded a hot sunny day. However, regardless of any kind of weather, the first flush of new dresses appeared in a continual exodus from trailers, their wearers marching in the direction of the Stalls. This is where a Romany fashion parade takes place, but rather like a mannequin sharing a catwalk with a farmer's wife, for, unaware of the occasion the public share the same gritty path. One is lucky to catch more than a glimpse of head and shoulders due to the crowds, but the full-length splendour is seen as groups form to talk on the outskirts of the outdoor market. One or two stalls will be selling special china [such as I referred to in Chapter 7].

This china tends to be very expensive. Many a person from the visiting crowd, seeing the unusual china, rushes up, only to reel back ashen-faced when told the price! Travellers are used to this, however, the value being one of the reasons why it is collected. They never turn a hair at its high price.....but they expect a reduction if buying a considerable number of pieces! There is a very sad tale told of the Traveller man who once bought the centre-piece of the stall's china display. This was a Capo di Monte group of the Last Supper, probably costing over a thousand pounds. As he was carrying it away, he dropped it, and the heads of the Apostles were broken off. Not a good Epsom for that particular Traveller.

Then there is the Lamp-man, who has a large stall covered with the modern version of the old waggon 'Angel' lamp, really a cherub [as described in Chapter 7]. The 'Angel' features on the cut-glass crystal-drop chandelier lamps, and in the form of vases, recently much favoured for placing on each side, or in the centre according to size, of the trailer sideboard. There is an electrical shop in Guildford where one can obtain the bulbs for these lamps. Here, also, there is a shop selling reproduction furniture, antique prints and china, where it is possible to order Burtondale china.

Until recently the ordinary nylon net curtains and material sold for house windows did not interest Travellers, as the heavy hand-finished and mitre-cornered Macramé lace, genuine Nottingham lace curtains, matching tablecloths (not the same as Nottingham lace tablecloths advertised in magazines, which is relatively thin lace), and sideboard mat sets, hung in all the best trailers. After the demise of the roller blind and the advent of the 'Finition' (Venetian) blinds, there appeared in shops, ready made window-sets, in the American style, looped and draped with 'laps' (frills) and ribbon insertions, in all colours and designs. At which time the new end-bedroom trailers, having a trailer-width window at the end, this seemed just the right place for these nets, costing almost as much per window as the old Macramé. The new lighter weight trailers with, end-bedrooms had other new features, such as deeper windows. This helped a great deal towards the new curtains style, since the old heavy lace was bonded onto nylon 'tops,' in such intricate patterns that no way could it be lengthened by re-bonding. Here at Epsom and Cambridge, at Musslebrough, and at other Travellers' fairs, fancy curtain sets were sold. To give some idea of the price of Macramé, a tiny 23 inch by 23 inch piece, enough to put on the face of a cushion would cost £5,* and the satin cushion to sew it on, about £10.** These small cushions, the equivalent of the scatter cushions once favoured by some house-dwellers, are not to be confused with the larger 'window' cushions, for which a matching set is obligatory. £40*** per cushion is a medium price for these. More elaborate cushions, sold in zipped up plastic covers, are rather more expensive.

There is also the boot-man. The age-old fondness for boots as opposed to shoes still remains for men. Although women have long ago given up the Luton boot which was very distinctive with much decoration, men of the older generation remain faithful to the elastic-sided jodhpur boots whose shape and horse connections suited their fancy. Newmarket boots of yellow leather and all shades of brown, have a good chance of being sold. Ladies can buy 'fashion' shoes from a stall, perhaps a pair of 'trailer' shoes or baby shoes for outdoor wear and white lace edged socks. The owner of the bed-linen stall, usually a man, is expected to be an entertaining 'spieler.' Sheets must be flowered or lace-edged, and towels must be expensive 'velvet' texture.

* Equivalent of £15 in 2011   ** Equivalent of £30 .in 2011   ***Equivalent of £120 in 2011

Bedroom sets are usually bought from the 'Cushion woman' [see Chapter 5]. Of the linen stalls, a Traveller once remarked, "You don't see nothing you wants, and they asks 'exrageous' prices!"

There is a blanket vendor who visits the trailers and sells from his car-boot the much liked Welsh blankets and patterned rugs to put down on trailer-seats to cover the upholstery. In time, trailers could have as an extra, zipped thick transparent polythene covers – practical but uncomfortable to sleep on, even with blankets under the sheets.

The rest of the colourful stalls can be described as 'Gimcrack' orientated, all adding greatly to the scene as a whole. What a pity that with so much land available, there could not be more space between the stalls; it would make it a far more enjoyable day if there were room for the throng of people to pass one another other. Many, before reaching the end, give up battling the crowds on the narrow paths. It is, after all, the people's day, so why must the organisers be so mean?

This afternoon, hot and weary women in their 'killing me' shoes, with fractious infants in pushchairs loaded with toys, return to the trailers for tea. It is a day of visitors, when Travellers who, for some reason or another, are not stopped here but have come up for the day, lean heavily upon relatives and friends for hospitality. However welcome, at such times, like any other family, the bonds of relationships can be stretched to the limit. Children 'let loose' after the confines of Official Sites can cause any number of 'bad-heads,' and there is much borrowing of Aspirin and allied remedies! The atmosphere is electric; it is the first 'real' day of the Race Week. The early morning noises have imperceptibly built up to a crescendo of tangled discordant sounds. A sea of noise sweeps up and down, in and out of the trailer-caravans. There is mounting excitement in the air.

Monday, and the skylarks are singing above us. After a riotously late night which amazingly ended peacefully, all is calm. The sky is grey, flags hang limp, hugging the poles. No usual brave or foolhardy horse riders hacking, coaxing their unwilling eye-rolling mounts among the unfamiliar chaos, yapping terriers, leaping guard dogs; they will appear tomorrow, in a rather defiant attitude to us, the 'invaders' of their preserves. "No amount of beastly caravans are going to keep me away," their baleful glances seem to say, as they ignore any polite, "Good mornings." They doggedly keep to the path they normally take. It sorts out the genuine horse-lovers. Litter from departed stallholders and their customers lines the ash path, and Dickensian scavengers hopefully turn over cardboard boxes. Rubber buckets doubtless cut down the noise from horse-city across the road where the livery stables are. The Cheapjacks have 'milked' the crowds and gone.

Fairs are still places where young people can meet and 'make a match.' Kind elder married sisters or aunts often bring a single relative to Epsom. Small girls make temporary friendships, becoming inseparable for the duration of the fair. Young men drive round in their fathers' cars, eyeing the prospects – groups of seemingly indifferent girls who stop to chat on their way for kettles of 'fresh' water to make morning tea. There is much playing of musical horns and tossing of curls. The morning was disturbed by a 23ft trailer being pulled alongside us, only feet from our door despite there being plenty of space available. It was an Irish family who had been with some Welsh Travellers. Scottish and Welsh Travellers fraternise with the Irish, being rather more old-fashioned, or perhaps sharing a feeling of being rather apart from the English. Other Travellers are 'wary.' The reputation of 'Wild Irish' has spread. Their children regard anything left outside as fair spoil. When the Irish stop it is noticeable how little clutter there is outside their trailers, whereas the English have a vast amount of outside possessions. The Irish seem to delight in breaking up and removing fittings from Council Sites. That is not to say that there are no peaceful Irish, there are several families known to us who are accepted by everyone. They have been over here many generations and are not their brothers' keepers. One Traveller mother chained her children's toys to the trailer legs with padlocks! This way-of-life has enough hazards without internal worries. Whenever I go outside a pack of children descend upon me *monging* (begging) for things they do not need, being well fed and clothed. Other Travellers make signals to me from windows, glad not to be in my place. I do the same when it is their turn to be waylaid. The Irish often travel in huge gangs of even up to a hundred trailers. As one family can contain seven or eight fighting men, few if any dare upset the women by complaining about the children, as this could lead to their husbands having to fight the 'fighting-men,' It often appears safer all round to hitch on and leave. Countless are the official sites deserted, to the mystification of Council officials, yet seemingly refilled the same day. Since *gaujes* have not bothered to help Travellers in preventing their stopping places being taken away by the Council digging trenches, Travellers don't feel they would get any help if they complained at their Council Sites being ruined. One Irish family admitted that it amused them to burn the trees – rare enough on any site – and daub the buildings with paint.

Times have changed. Sitting in Rosania's trailer, her grandmother tells me, how, when the first Irish tinkers came on the Downs, a great many English Travellers took up kettle-cranes and cudgels and surrounded the waggons, until they was forced to leave and never come again....until now, that is. One cannot but have a sneaking admiration for a people who come over here, and behave with total disregard for authority or land ownership. Acting out their reputed 'wild ways' as they simply take locked gates off their hinges or cut down fences and pull-on to derelict or unused land, staying until threatened with being pulled-off. They live up to the manner of the first 'wild Gyptians' who terrorised the rustic population. It is not so theoretically interesting for Travellers, who, with the closing of stopping-places, and the opening of sites, are herded into the overcrowded remaining places, sharing with company not of their own choosing. The very essence of the Romany life is the freedom to stop on a verge, green or common, and then leave again for verges new.

All this great multitude here today, has got to find somewhere to go afterwards. Only a small proportion will return to Travellers' villages (settlements in areas, where small plots of land were once sold for people to build their own homes upon, in the good old days before even *gaujes* freedom was taken away), or luxurious, ranch-style miniature Dallas-style houses or chalets. The majority will fill in the summer by going to other Travellers' fairs, be moved on in between, and some end up on Council Sites built where no-one else wants to live, hidden from view by earth banks, like lepers.

Tuesday: several more Irish trailers have pulled-on around us. A characteristic of them, is the way in which they pull-on and encamp. Travellers like to stop by a windshield, hedge or trees, even by bushes, and take the trouble to get the trailers level. This habit is a source of annoyance to those in charge of the Downs. We take one or two levelling-boards, but most level-up on the slopes by digging a shallow trench in front of whichever wheel needs it, then pulling forward into it. The Irish with their tarmac shovels have the right tools, but never bother. Some of their trailers have been seen at such a tilt that one wonders how they manage not to fall out of bed, or even cook. Their trailers 'which ways round' shows in my collection of hundreds of press photos with the incorrect caption 'Gypsies Invade.' "Oh dear, oh dear!" exclaimed my neighbour across the way, "now we can't all go to the races together." Various tales are told of 'happenings' when the 'Irishmans' pull-on; of hen-runs and hens squashed to death, of pups too young to leave a bitch, missing and later found dead. Of vanishing washing, and wash-bowls. The Cambridgeshire Travellers told me they were going to move right across the Downs. We decided to join some Devonshire people who were on the other side, whom we had been with some years ago. They had a chalet and had come up in their holiday tourers.

I did not enjoy this at all, but was between the devil and the deep blue sea. One day of Irish children, reminds me how lucky we are to be so well known that when we stop with Travellers we are of no novelty value to the children. What a job, packing all the china again after such a short while. The dog compound has to be pulled up, and the tent taken down. Being surrounded by 'active' infants and loose dogs spurred us on. We all shifted together, and once over, left the Cambridge family some twenty yards away by their old aunt, and became almost the last trailer across the back, where the man on the gate had told us no one was allowed to go! Such mismanagement causes one to loose faith in officialdom and to disregard future diktats, since this is where we would have come in the first place! One can look down on the whole scene with only the night-driving of youths to worry about.

Our Devonshire neighbours are nice people and reliable company. We got levelled up and unhitched, then sat round the fire of some people we last saw several years ago in the New Forest at Stoney Cross. We remembered to the last detail, every part of the turn-out we each had at the time. This is what Travellers talk about, rather than World Affairs. The Mother of the family was wearing a coral necklace and I was wearing an amber necklace, which led to us getting out our bead-boxes. As we sat there, hands full of semiprecious stones, some with gilt Victorian gilt and diamante settings, a Traveller well known for eccentric behaviour went by to see to his horse. He called out, "Them beads is worth nothing," which caused us to laugh, a relic of the waggon era; to him it was gold, silver or 'rubbish.'

At the rails I picked four horses and cautiously bet on them all, among them was the winner, Troy, but I should have put all my eggs in one basket to get enough return and have had more faith in Troy. One Traveller won over three hundred pounds. After the race we returned for tea. One or two people, non-Travellers, came seeking us out. They were interested in Romanies but do not follow the way-of-life. After the visitors had left, Dominic went off to visit some friends. I was a few yards away from the trailer talking to a woman who was also a few yards from hers, when we heard a noise behind us, and saw coming over the brow of the hill, like Red Indians in a Western Film, a huge crowd of people. Instinctively we both rushed towards the trailers and snatched up our little dogs, unhooked the finches' cages and took them inside. Hardly had I done that, than the crowd was upon us. They were headed in the direction slanting across from us, to our offside. Their direct route was barred by a row of closely parked cars, lorries and vans, belonging to us and the Devonshire Travellers; these had been closely parked in the hopes of preventing the night-time drivers getting through. Arriving at the open space in front of these vehicles with hardly a pause, the whole crowd surged across the tops of the vehicles. A sight I shall never forget. The object of this amazing chase was not that they were fleeing from something but that they had been grabbed by crowd hysteria and were running *to* what they supposed was a 'fight.' Had they been in their right mind and not acting as lemmings, they would have seen that there was a clear way to avoid the vehicles. Our Alsatian had a mesh fence to prevent small toddlers wandering too close. There were wooden slats with outside trailer-mats on, in front of the door and side, also a low table with the two stainless steel water churns on. One man managed to fall over the kennel. While a fat boy of about twelve actually ran into it. Dogs have an instinctive fear of madness in humans; the normally fierce hound cowered under the trailer. But the invasion of his kennel was too much, the dog raced out and bit his leg. The fat boy set up a howl and swearing snatched up my carpet broom with which he began to beat the dog. Wresting the broom from his grasp with difficulty, above the racket of the screaming throng still passing like beings possessed, I shouted that the dog was fenced in and it was the man and boy's fault for breaking down the fence and running *into* to the kennel. A youth stopped and hauled the boy away, and, realising it *was* their fault, he ran off and did not, as I feared, set about the dog. I looked around at the chaos they had left; overturned churns, rucked carpets, broken tent-guy, and buckets all over the place.

As my neighbour emerged to survey her damage, I remarked that the men were never at home when they were needed, at which a rather shamefaced man emerged from one of the other trailers, to inspect the damage to his motor. I had just finished clearing up when I realised that the crowd were on their way back again. This time I was ready and stood in front of the platform and mats, with the broom. I waited in some trepidation in case the fat boy, his father and the youth returned. Without the astonishing speed with which it had all happened, I knew the dog would have given a good account of himself. In this way of life you need a good guard. It is no use to have a sloppy friendly dog wagging its tail at a would be rapist. Sadly, it is not easy to convince those who have never had to face danger from rough people, who get quite upset when they are not allowed to fuss the guard dog. I was glad when there was no sign of the fat boy, for I did not want a vindictive blow struck at the trailer. No doubt hysteria can break out in any crowd. There have been occasions in the news of people trampled to death, running in fear from fire or attackers. I had never before witnessed the speed with which, the mention or rumour of a 'fight' can cause Travellers to converge. Usually it is but a short distance they have to run, and never in such great numbers. I would sooner face a single bull than a deranged crowd.

With the now calm crowd returning came two women we knew who told me that it was 'all over' by the time they got there. They had been 'swept along' and had to run in case they fell and got trampled. Under the veneer of respectability lie primitive urges. Hard times leave a legacy of what some may see as strange behaviour. On occasions I have seen beautifully laid out food for a Wedding or Birthday, placed before well dressed, and obviously not starved, guests, attacked with the speed accredited to starving dogs. Dishes of nuts, put out on a bar by a publican for the occasional peckish drinker and expected to last all evening, can vanish with the speed of light, Travellers grabbing handfuls. The returning Travellers said that they had found themselves in 'a crowd of Irishmans' and some very rough people from trailers that had arrived late and stopped at the foot of the hill. No one we spoke to knew these 'strange' Travellers.

When the Devonshire family returned from the races, they were amazed to hear of the human traffic which had passed over their cars, and scratches and 'denges' (dents) were discovered. I locked up and decided to go and see if I could find Dominic as I knew where the Travellers were whose trailers he was visiting. On nearing the valley which lay near the Start, I perceived a crowd of Travellers who were watching a car. This was being driven along the flat at terrific speed. "It's a woman done mad," I was told. Seeing the car heading straight for us, we scattered. She stopped and reversed. I noticed two small children in the back. The last of the coaches were leaving the Downs along the bottom, taking the back way out. The car continued to be driven erratically from side to side, but at the last moment allowed a coach to overtake. There were one or two trailers on their own at the side of the coach and car-track and the car driver drove straight for them causing three greyhound dogs to rush out from under the trailers barking. She repeated this movement and I had to look away in case one of the dogs did not jump back in time. I then noticed two elderly ladies quite unaware of the drama, attempting to cross this area towards one or two cars parked on the other side of the track, the area used by the demented driver being far wider than the track made by the departing; coaches. The ladies, not realising their danger, walked arm in arm. I noticed a line of policemen coming towards me, probably from the extra police-boxes set up this year, on their way home. The last one was a burley sergeant of the old school. I confidently approached him and indicated the car, now skidding and swerving towards another group of fascinated Travellers. I then pointed at the little old ladies about to embark upon probably their last walk. "Would you stop it?" I asked. He looked me full in the face, and very mean-fully, shook his head. I have rarely been so astonished. This, together with the crowd-hysteria caused me to think I had entered a nightmare. The Sergeant and his troops made their way up the slope and left the scene.

No time to stop, puzzled by his reaction, I ran after the old ladies, and as I did so the car drove again up the slope towards the group I had left. The driver stopped at their feet and reversed, although there was no need to reverse. I reached them and pointed out the car, at which moment three man came down the hill, obviously going in the same direction, to their parked car. I asked them if they would accompany the ladies across, and this they did, once having to stand still and let the mad car-driver go by. I wonder if there were any reports of this, or if the papers were only interested in reporting the 'Gypsy Fight.' I suspect the police sergeant thought that the car driver was a Traveller and had no urge to prevent injury to them, even if two of them were children. What made it rather worse, was the fact that he was the very picture of the old-time police sergeant we hardly ever see. The mad car-driver, I discovered to be one of the visiting crowds of race-goers who had had a quarrel with her husband and was in two minds as to whether to kill herself and the children.

We did not stay the full week, and left in the dusk, a departure time only for emergencies. I felt depressed and tired out after all the packing and unpacking. The culprits of the fight had gone to ground. A few miles from Epsom we came upon a narrow lay-by, there was a large Showman's trailer hitched onto a pantechnicon, both in red-maroon with gold lining-out, obviously stopped for the night. I went up to the trailer and said, "Good evening," so that they might judge us to be no threat to their peaceful night. The arrival of strangers is always a worry to a lone trailer, these days. They were friendly and said we were welcome to stop with them, and to pull up closer, and to ask for anything we needed. I have never known showmen to be other than helpful and friendly.

And so we left the races on the Anniversary Year, vowing not visit it again in a hurry. Several other trailers passed during the evening, also leaving early. 'Toot-toot' they signalled to us in the time honoured way of itinerant traffic on the roads.

The Showman's big generator, and our small one, chugged away until ten o'clock.

On Tuesday 28th May 1979, nearly a hundred miles form the town of Epsom, we were heading for a little used country car-park which had been made on top of a long established gypsy stopping-place. We expected to meet and join again some old Romany friends we had spent Christmas with, before we parted to go to Wales. Alas all we found was long-cold fire ash. Earlier this year we had decided to go only to Cambridge fair, the Travellers' meeting not the funfair, as last year's

Derby had not been as enjoyable as usual. Last year we had arrived with a number of Travellers – travelling with, not just arriving with – all friends, we had of course to stop, as is the custom, where the leading trailer chose. Being a large self-contained family unit, they were not looking for friends or family on the Downs, so they halted at the first available space. This was a flat turn-off from the narrow one-car wide track edged in places by a steep bank that winds across the Downs.

Follow your nose to find

The crunch of broken glass amid vomit.

Scenes of joviality or of squalor, depending how you regard it, in and around a Beer-tent.

A Beer-tent

Being just across this track from the main conglomeration of marquees, beer-tents, the Tote, etc, during the racing we were closely surrounded by cars belonging to the visiting public who are not informed that we have to pay to be there, and therefore prefer our friends to be around us. Water and toilets are provided but we have not asked for these. A notice would be appreciated stating, 'Trailer-caravans ONLY. NOT a public Car Park,' since many acres of the Downs are open to public cars, while we are restricted to a small area, and are sitting ducks for picnic parties of badly behaved children who cannot go out into the country to a fair or a beach without a ball. This is kicked into, under and on top of the living-trailers by fathers and children who don't appear capable of recognising that these are people's homes and not holiday tourers. At such times, the men are at the Races and the women are left to deal with whole bellicose ill-behaved families who would soon assert that they were above or better than Gypsies. This would not be allowed to happen in a non-Traveller caravan park. As one Traveller remarked, "They wouldn't want us to picnic in their garden!"

Another year we had two choices. We could go to Sussex, but the stopping-place there was a field at the end of a very rough farm track. After the past few weeks of heavy rain, when the West Country was badly flooded, we knew that this notoriously heavy soil of sticky clay would be like a 'mud-pond.' Not a happy prospect; no longer owning a four-wheel drive vehicle had its disadvantages. There is no room or place to turn until actually in the field, by which time the dye is cast. Perhaps by the end of the Derby Week, the ground would have dried out, so we changed our plans and decided to go yet again to Epsom. Arriving at the Downs we found a fair number of Travellers already set up and in place. It was officially open, several Metropolitan Police-boxes being in position. Many people often arrive well before Show-Out Sunday, desperate for somewhere to go.

So it was that Derby Week held us once more in its spell. And to end these reminiscences, one more scene so typical of the event – the artist, never short of a customer willing to pay to have his likeness captured for posterity. I hope that some of my sketches and these writings will help capture the 'Romany Road' for posterity.

The Artist.

And that's it!

Conclusion – and 2011 Up-date

It seems a lifetime has passed since I wrote the former pages. My prediction regarding the splendid living-trailers has come true with a number of settled Romanies buying examples of these coach-built 'Travellers Specials,' the value now often far greater than when they were originally built. They are wonderfully restored and sometimes taken to the remaining Travellers' fairs. The attempted closing of the traditional Stow-on-the-Wold horse fair, has fizzled out. The Council, none too pleased, has now made unsightly banks along the nice old lane approach where Stalls and trailers once lined the verges. The Travellers and Stall-holders are now in 'the field.' There is still a massive police presence and the denizens of the little town react, by closing the shops, as if they are being invaded by aliens. Nothing much has changed there! The Fair is still held twice a year, and is attended by Romanies coming from all corners of the United Kingdom to enjoy a day out – which killjoys try to deny them.

Living-trailers are still used by those who have no property of their own, but who do not wish to live on the restricted Council Sites, but travel from one private Trailer-Park to another. These sites are owned *by* Travellers and have their own security in these times of poor policing – except at Fairs of course – having electrically operated gates installed!

Weippaert trailers had a rather brief fashion; probably the novelty of all the things interior-wise that the old style English trailers lacked. The German made Tabberts came in and were much in evidence, and are still to be seen, but the Hobby, also made in Germany, has proved very popular. All these trailers are large enough to be 'homes,' but light enough to be tourers. Transit vans and Transit lorries remain popular. They are also much liked by tradesmen as economical and reliable vehicles. Many Travellers prefer the Japanese 4x4 pickups. Each new edition is altered in some degree; sometimes a really good detail, like the back windows opening, is left out, while several seat positions are put in. The preoccupation with rounded and curved surfaces to give a streamlined look along the dashboard takes away the flat surfaces useful to rest things on. Airbags take away the useful space of a good-sized glove-locker. The present vogue for most vehicles to have the same coloured bumpers as the body, means that there is no longer a really strong metal bumper which has long been a tradition of motor vehicles. The slightest tap by another driver can cause many hundreds of pounds of damage. Everything hinges upon appearance. In cities, the 4x4's, nicknamed 'Chelsea Tractors,' have unleashed hatred among the smaller car drivers who are agitating for these 'gas-guzzlers' to be more heavily taxed. Naturally they give no thought to Farmers and Tradesmen, Stable Owners and Smallholders, all of whom need an open-backed vehicle and, on wet or muddy ground, often require the use of four wheel drive.

Several Romanies interested in motor vehicles have bought examples of the splendid J-Type Bedford lorries of the 1960's and 70's, which looked like American cars, and have restored them. I only hope someone saved ours from the scrap-yard, as they were one of *the* prettiest lorries ever built!

Dominic has added these thoughts:

"For those who have surveyed the Derby scene of later years, there can be little doubt that there has been a decline in numbers attending with trailers and motor vehicles, for the week. I would say that from the mid to late seventies, the greatest numbers and the greatest splendour in living-trailers was to be seen, since the time when Travellers forsook horses for motors.

"At the moment, with so many Travellers settling on private Trailer Parks in chalets or mobile-homes, the fashion is for staying in the chalet all winter, and venturing forth for the summer months in big touring-trailers. Indeed, during the latter years, the number of tourers has outweighed the number of living-trailers at all the Race Meetings and Travellers' Fairs."

Taking up Dominic's last point, if Travellers had been allowed to continue their traditional itinerant life-style, even if restricted to the once-hoped-for transit sites, I think, in view of the times in which we live – constant changes at disconcerting pace – they would stop in one place longer than in days gone by. However, prevented by Law from doing this, and being an adaptable people, bending as the willow to survive, they have devised a new existence, wintering in one place, waiting and waiting for the summer to be free. And since their goods and chattels are now in the chalet, there is no need to take these possessions on the road.

Freed from the almost daily task of cleaning the exterior of a large living-trailer, of packing priceless china, often able to stop undetected on *gaujo* holiday sites, the contemporary Romany woman is at last having that which many people always imagined her to be enjoying – a holiday!

From being a mere extra bedroom and kitchen-trailer, the humble tourer, at one time looked upon with contempt (with a few coach-built exceptions) has now become a member of the family. In the past, while the merest glimpse of a trailer-roof ahead, mobile or stationary, would arouse our excitement and interest, both swiftly fading as no chimney came into view, now we look long and hard for any telltale signs; especially when a *cluster* of tourers are spotted. Times they are a-changing.

Beshlie, 2011

Some Romany Names

Women		Men	
Christian name	*Surname*	*Christian name*	*Surname*
Adaline	Smith	Blackie	Lee
Amanda		Blondie	
Charlotte		Bumper	
Crystal		Bunny	Price
Dilly		Chasey	Gaskin
Dinkey		Chinga	Smith
Emberley		Choky	Lee
Florrie-Lou		Crimea	Price
Freedom		Dancer	
Hope		Deer	Price
Lorna	Lee	Frisco	Lee
Merry	Lee	Hezzy (Hezekiah)	
Pemberline		Kack	Finney
Rellie (Cinderrella)		Kenza	
Rina		La la	
Tabitha	Lee	Monty	
Tomboy		Mushy	
		Naylor	
		Nighty	
		Nin Lee	
		Nipper	
		Opi (Hope)	Price
		Peg-leg	
		Pompey	Lee
		Pretty Boy	
		Puppy	Lee
		Righteous	
		Rocky	
		Scobie	
		Seth	
		Toffee	
		Whacker	Cooper
		Winkey	
		Witawaw	Burton

Other books by Beshlie

Beshlie's Meadowmice and Friends Painting Book
Wedding Album
Grandmother's Album
Snailsleap Lane
Romany Wood
Here Today and Gone Tomorrow
Travellers' Joy

Beshlie's Countryside Books of:
The Coppice-Cutter, Trug-Maker and Besom Maker
The Brickmakers, Farrier and Drystone Dyker
The Harvesters, Milkman and Hop-Pickers
The Bodger, Thatcher and Rag-and-Bone Man

Also illustrations for:
The Mouse House by Joan Carter
Many Moons by Diana Russell-Allen

In Preparation

Romany Road Sketch Book

A companion volume to the present book, printed in full colour in large format. It will be a collectors' 'must!' (Spring 2011)

Wayfarers All

Beshlie's Travelling life with various birds and animals. (Late 2012)

The Painting Lesson

An example of the Artwork for which Beshlie is rightly famed – this is from Romany Wood